PENGUIN CLASSICS

THE DEATH OF KING ARTHUR

The author of *The Death of King Arthur* is unknown. What is certain is that he was not the Welshman, Walter Map, whose name appears at the beginning and at the end of the text. Why the true author dissembled himself behind the identity of Map, who flourished some fifty years before this poem was written, remains obscure. From his sketchy knowledge of Britain, apart from other evidence, it seems safe to assume that the author, whoever he was, was a Frenchman; probably from Champagne, writing around 1230–35.

•

James Cable was born in 1940 and was educated at the Universities of Exeter and Nancy While in France he took a doctor's degree with a thesis on Old French. He was subsequently Lecturer in French at London University, but eventually his interest in the modern world became dominant, and he left teaching to work in the field of computers.

THE DEATH
OF KING ARTHUR

Translated with an
Introduction by
JAMES CABLE

PENGUIN BOOKS

PENGUIN BOOKS

Published by the Penguin Group
Penguin Books Ltd, 27 Wrights Lane, London W8 5TZ, England
Viking Penguin, a division of Penguin Books USA Inc.
375 Hudson Street, New York, New York 10014, USA
Penguin Books Australia Ltd, Ringwood, Victoria, Australia
Penguin Books Canada Ltd, 2801 John Street, Markham, Ontario, Canada L3R 1B4
Penguin Books (NZ) Ltd, 182–190 Wairau Road, Auckland 10, New Zealand

Penguin Books Ltd, Registered Offices: Harmondsworth, Middlesex, England

This translation first published 1971
10

Printed in England by Clays Ltd, St Ives plc
Set in Linotype Pilgrim

For Olly

Contents

Introduction

The Death of King Arthur (*La Mort le Roi Artu*) is one of the outstanding Medieval French Arthurian romances, possibly the finest. In it we find none of the absurd fantasy that fills most French romances of the period; there are no fights against giants or dwarfs, and no maidens are rescued from dragons. The magical and supernatural elements in the traditional story have all been toned down, and the author has given us a romance in which the turning points are dictated by human psychology instead of other-worldly events. The few supernatural elements which remain are retained only to enhance the nobility of the story – for example, the hand which rises from the lake to catch Excalibur, Arthur's sword, at the end of the book.

The author of the work is unknown. The only certainty is that it is not by the man whose name appears at the beginning and the end of the text, the Welshman Walter Map (1140–c. 1210), who was attached to the court of King Henry II of England. We do not know why the true author dissembled himself behind the identity of Map of all people, who is not known to have written anything about King Arthur. We have no means of dating *The Death of King Arthur* exactly; the piecing together of various scraps of information has led scholars to suppose that it was probably written around 1230–35 in France, possibly in Champagne. Map, then, died too soon to have written it, and in any case the real author shows only a sketchy knowledge of England. It is true that he mentions London and its Tower, Winchester, Salisbury Plain, Dover Castle, the River Humber, and Northumberland; and it is also true that the geography of Arthurian romance is always vague. However, any educated Frenchman of the thirteenth century could know as much about England, and moreover the author never gives the impression of mentioning places he has actually seen. He evidently believes that Salisbury Plain is quite close to the sea, because after his last battle there, Arthur arrives at the coast in a very short time. One can also add that an Englishman would have been perfectly aware that the monks of Glastonbury had recently discovered the tombs of Arthur and Guinevere, or so they claimed, and therefore would hardly have placed Arthur's tomb in the Black Chapel, by the sea.

The Death of King Arthur forms the last part of a vast ensemble in prose generally referred to as the Prose Lancelot or the Vulgate Cycle. The cycle originally consisted of three romances: Lancelot, The Quest of the Holy Grail, and the text which is translated here. Although the story is continuous in these three parts, and there are many cross-references to earlier and later episodes, The Death of King Arthur is quite complete in itself.* The style of the three parts is so divergent as to leave no doubt that they are the work of different authors, and yet the presence of a detailed overall plan can be explained only by the theory that Jean Frappier has put forward, that there was an 'architect' who conceived the whole corpus and who handed the last two sections of the work over to different authors after perhaps having written the first himself.

The Lancelot is a huge work of immense complexity. In the only complete modern edition of it, it occupies 1200 large pages. The story goes from Lancelot's birth to the time when all the knights of the Round Table set out on the Grail adventure. The theme of Lancelot's love for Guinevere is introduced early into the story.

The Quest of the Holy Grail relates how the Grail adventure is brought to a conclusion by Lancelot's son Galahad, Perceval and Bors. Lancelot is unworthy to join these three because of his state of sin. The atmosphere in this romance is clearly religious right from the beginning, and the whole of the text is about the Christian faith, about sin and repentance, and the merits of chastity. The religious viewpoint expressed is that of the Cistercian order, which had been founded about a century earlier. At the end of the Quest, Galahad and Perceval

* I have given in an appendix brief notes on the most important of these cross-references to be found in the present text.

die, and Bors alone survives to return to Camelot and recount his adventures.

It is here that *The Death of King Arthur* begins, with admirable simplicity, and no time is wasted by the author in presenting the basic elements of the plot.

This text is not the oldest known version either of the story of Lancelot's adultery with Guinevere, or of that of Arthur's death. Little, of course, is known about the earliest forms of the Arthurian tales; still less about the historical facts of Arthur himself and his world. There are few mentions of Arthur before the famous *History of the Kings of Britain* by Geoffrey of Monmouth (completed in 1135). Geoffrey has given us an almost totally imaginary early history of Britain, and there is practically nothing in what he says about Arthur (whose reign occupies two out of the twelve books) that can be shown to have any basis in fact. Geoffrey relates how during Arthur's absence Mordred seized the throne of Britain and married Guinevere; Lancelot, however, is absent from his text. Mordred's name can be traced further back. In a serious historical document of the ninth or tenth century, the *Annales Cambriae*, we find a couple of references to Arthur that may well rest on historical fact. The second entry, for the year 537, reads: 'The Battle of Camlann, in which Arthur and Medraut fell'. This scrap of information is tantalizing in its brevity; we cannot identify Camlann for sure, neither can we tell whether Arthur and Mordred were fighting on the same side or as opponents.

Geoffrey of Monmouth's sober Latin prose was translated and adapted into French verse by the Jerseyman Wace, whose version, known as the *Roman de Brut* (after Brutus, the legendary founder of Britain) came out in 1155. Like all medieval 'translators', Wace altered and expanded his source as he saw fit, giving greater colour to the story and bringing it closer to the genre of the romance that Chrétien de Troyes was to develop a few years later. Lancelot does not appear in Wace's poem, but Guinevere is said to have committed adultery with Mordred even before Arthur's departure. She later repents, becomes a nun anonymously and is not heard of again.

Lancelot's first appearance in literature is in the romances of

Chrétien de Troyes (fl. about 1160–90). After brief references in Chrétien's first two Arthurian romances, Lancelot has a whole text devoted to him in *Le Chevalier de la Charrette* (c. 1177–81). Here, he rescues Guinevere after she has been led off by Méléagant and imprisoned in the kingdom of Gorre. Before her release, Lancelot comes to her one night, and when she gives him permission he breaks the bars of the window with his bare hands, enters, and spends the night with her. Neither King Arthur's eventual downfall nor Mordred are, however, mentioned in this poem.

It is these earlier texts, and perhaps others which have disappeared without trace, and a mass of oral tradition about King Arthur and his knights concerning which we have little information, that served as the sources of the story related in *The Death of King Arthur*. The author of this romance was totally successful in forming from them a unified and consistent tale which contains practically no irrelevant episodes.

The story falls into three main parts. Right at the beginning of the romance we are told that Lancelot has fallen back into his adultery with Guinevere, despite his conversion and repentance as told in *The Quest of the Holy Grail*. This theme dominates the first third of the book; Agravain's denunciation of the couple and his attempt to catch them together follow on naturally, and it is the failure of Arthur's knights to stop Lancelot escaping which leads to the motivation of the second section, for in unwittingly killing Gawain's brother Gaheriet in the ensuing battle, Lancelot earns Gawain's bitter enmity. Arthur is too weak to resist this hostility and is pushed by Gawain into two wars against Lancelot. The second is the crucial one, because Arthur is persuaded to besiege Lancelot in France and so leaves his kingdom at a moment of weakness, having entrusted Mordred with the regency. It is therefore Gawain's hatred for Lancelot which in the third section provides Mordred with the opportunity to betray Arthur. Thus, we see that Lancelot's adultery leads directly to Gawain's exaggerated enmity; and that this is in turn the direct cause of Arthur's downfall.

Although the theme of the book is certainly the *Götterdäm-*

merung, the eclipse of the Arthurian world, the principal character, and the one whose psychology is drawn in greatest depth, is Lancelot. The whole of *The Death of King Arthur* is in fact a sort of spiritual and psychological biography of Lancelot. In the book, Lancelot gradually climbs from the depths of sin to what is practically a form of sainthood at the end. At first, Lancelot's greatest desire is to reassert his pre-eminence at tournaments, after his absence on the Grail quest, but he seems to be prevented from this by some supernatural hand, that of either God or destiny. For example, when Lancelot is wounded by a huntsman's arrow and prevented from attending the tournament at Camelot, the author seems to say that it was no real accident, because although the arrow missed its target, the stag, 'the shot was not a complete failure'.

After Lancelot had fought for Guinevere against Mador de la Porte, the lovers behave less discreetly than before, and are finally caught together. From this point on, the decline and fall of the Round Table begins, and moves towards a certain conclusion. Lancelot's two earlier wounds can be seen as warnings; if Lancelot had permanently renounced the queen then, he could have returned to his own land and Arthur would not have fallen. However, when the two lovers are finally caught together, nothing can alter the outcome. After Lancelot has escaped and rescued Guinevere from execution, he is quite aware of the serious consequences of having killed Gawain's brother Gaheriet, and of the fact that the beginning of the end of Arthur's world has come. It is at this point that Lancelot and his friends are expelled, in their absence, from the Round Table. It is also from this moment that Lancelot begins his spiritual ascendancy. In the battle which he is forced to undertake against Arthur and Gawain despite his love for them both, Lancelot shows up as a truly Christian knight when he refuses to strike the king, whom Hector wishes to kill. Not only does Lancelot speak sharply to his brother; he even goes so far as to remount the king. This is a moral victory for him, and an act which much impresses Arthur.

When, after two months of siege of the castle of the Joyeuse Garde, the message comes from the Pope ordering Arthur to take Guinevere back, Lancelot tells the queen to return to her husband, and he makes this decision on the basis not of what he wants, but of what honour demands. This honour depends in part on public esteem, as Lancelot admits in the following lines, but at least, for about the first time in the romance, he is not putting his own wishes first. Once again Arthur is highly impressed with Lancelot's act, and seems to doubt again whether any adultery had ever taken place.

The parting of the lovers is described with great nobility, and they are both aware that their separation will probably be permanent. However, Lancelot's gradual moral advance is still nowhere complete, since he is still for example capable of blatantly lying to Arthur; when he hands over Guinevere he still insists he is innocent of any wrong. We can see, though, that Lancelot is becoming more concerned with spiritual questions by the way in which, once he has returned to Gaul, he gives up all his worldly possessions, makes Bors and Lionel kings, and hands over Gaul to Arthur's charge, since he no longer wishes to hold it himself.

Lancelot has one last encounter with Arthur, when Gawain persuades the king to continue the war against him. Lancelot is angry to hear the news, particularly against Gawain; however, the situation will enable him to achieve the highest level of Christian knighthood. Lancelot is in a dilemma, because honour demands that as he has been accused of treason, he must defend himself, and yet he has not the slightest wish to harm Gawain. Lancelot tells his companions that Gawain could not hate him so much that he would cease loving him; we are told that they are highly impressed by this expression of a purely Christian point of view, based on the Gospels, and he rises still further in their estimation as a result. Moreover, Lancelot makes every possible attempt to avert the battle, and is ready to humble himself completely, to the extent of becoming Gawain's liege man and going into exile for a period of ten years. The idea would be that this period of banishment would be the equivalent of the judicial duel and its outcome would finally establish Lancelot's guilt or innocence, without any possible harm to Gawain, but with greater hardship for Lancelot.

Once again, this extreme courtesy of Lancelot's impresses Arthur, but Gawain refuses. At the end of the battle Lancelot shows another outstanding example of chivalry by leaving the battle-field when it becomes apparent that Gawain is beaten, since he has no wish to harm his enemy any further.

Lancelot disappears from the story during the final battle on Salisbury Plain, because he does not fight on Arthur's side. The fault here is Arthur's; when Gawain lies dying he finally repents and forgives Lancelot, and moreover urges Arthur to fetch Lancelot back to fight on his side against Mordred. However, in a tragic decision Arthur declines to send for him, because he has not sufficient faith in Lancelot's new chivalry to be sure that he will not refuse. After Arthur's death, the only honourable course open to Lancelot is to return to Britain and to avenge the king by attacking Mordred's two sons. On the day of the battle, Lancelot hears of Guinevere's death. We know that he has not seen her again since he gave her over at the Joyeuse Garde, and the author has missed the chance of introducing the touching scene of a final meeting between the two lovers; as a result the main theme in the Lancelot story seems rather to fade out at the end.

After Lancelot has killed Mordred's two sons, he has more or less completed his worldly career, and it is as if God takes over control of him. Lancelot gets lost in the forest, wanders along 'as adventure takes him', and arrives at a hermitage to which the Archbishop of Canterbury and his own cousin Bleobleeris had also been brought by adventure – suggesting that it was the destiny of the three men to be brought together in this way. Lancelot's decision to stay with them in the service of God may seem a rapid one, but this act is the logical consequence of the moral advance that we have seen since the Joyeuse Garde episode. Now that everything most important in Lancelot's life, including Guinevere and Arthur, has gone, it might seem too simple for him to give his life up to God; but in the Middle Ages it was considered the normal end of a noble life, and it was certainly fairly common for men and women to renounce this world and devote their last years to prayer. Lancelot spends four years in the hermitage, in penitence; we are told that his soul was finally saved, because at the moment that Lancelot dies, the archbishop has a dream in which he sees Lancelot's soul being taken to heaven by angels. From his good beginning in *The Quest of the Holy Grail*, therefore, Lancelot falls as low as possible at the beginning of the *Death of King Arthur*, and this present book depicts his gradual rise, entirely through his own psychological development, until his assumption at the end.

Compared with the nobility of Lancelot, Arthur seems a really pathetic figure in this romance. Ninety-two years old, he rarely shows up in a good light or makes the right decisions at the right time. It is true that King Arthur is generally very inactive in the so-called 'Arthurian' romances of the Middle Ages. In the poems of Chrétien de Troyes, for example, Arthur and his court merely provide the background against which the chivalric deeds of the great knights are acted out. Arthur himself never takes part in any knightly activities, but is merely a symbol of chivalry, nobility and justice, and moreover is, like the whole of his world, completely ageless. (The author of *The Death of King Arthur* is being unusually down-to-earth in ascribing exact ages not only to the king, but also to Lancelot, Gawain and Guinevere.) At the beginning of the romance here translated, after counting his losses from the Round Table, Arthur announces a tournament at Winchester in a vain attempt, after the Grail quest, to re-create the lost world of knightly adventure. However, despite Lancelot's brilliant performance at Winchester, the king is really unable to halt the decline that has set in. Arthur is pathetic for instance in the way he refuses to believe in Guinevere's adultery, when it would no doubt have been easy for him to find out the truth. When he finally seems inclined to believe the story, he hands over to the villain Agravain the task of catching the lovers together; and he treats Guinevere very cruelly, in a way that recalls the Tristan story as handed down by Béroul, where King Mark sentences Yseut to be burnt after her adultery has been proved with Tristan. In the present book, Arthur decides that Guinevere must also die by fire, because 'a queen is sacred'. However justified Arthur may be in law in disposing of his wife caught in adultery, he nevertheless is lacking in charity and mercy, and is even accused bitterly by his people. He is, however, certainly capable of tender feelings, as can be seen from the episode where he goes to see the bodies of Guerrehet and Gaheriet whom he loved deeply.

From this point on, the weakness of Arthur's character is even more clearly marked. When the order comes from the Pope that he should take his wife back, he meekly accepts it, although he intends to continue his war against Lancelot. When Lancelot hands her over, Arthur seems easily convinced by his claims to innocence, and yet a little later he supports Gawain's insistence that Lancelot should leave Britain. When, later still, Gawain wishes to continue the war against Lancelot in Gaul, Arthur is persuaded by him, even though, as the author comments, he is destined to fail. Arthur's lack of independent thought cannot be entirely due to his great age, because elsewhere we find him fighting just like a young man, and indeed in the final battle on Salisbury Plain he is capable of killing Mordred. So, in *The Death of King Arthur* we see a gradual decline in Arthur's fortune, from the time at the beginning when he is saddened to see that so many of his knights have died in the Quest, and is angry with Gawain for having killed Baudemagus, until his pathetic cry to God at the end, when he sees that all his worldly prowess has passed.

Gawain seems to follow the traditional lines established by Chrétien de Troyes, and indeed already sketched by Wace, as a sort of courtly Don Juan. We have an example of this in his meeting with the girl of Escalot, whom he unsuccessfully begs for her love in the conventional manner. In the same way his great reputation leads women to fall in love with him at a distance; we see this in what is practically the only superfluous episode in the romance, the story of the lady of Beloé, who, when Gawain's corpse is taken past, reveals that she has never loved any other man than him, and who is promptly killed by her husband as a result. For her, Gawain's death is an especially great blow for the female sex, although he is supposed to be seventy-six years old.

Gawain is mostly a sympathetic character in the first part of the romance; at first he is solidly on Lancelot's side, and when he learns of Lancelot's adultery with Guinevere, his friendship for him at first leads him to try to keep the news from the king if possible, though that incurs Arthur's anger. Moreover, when Arthur sentences Guinevere to be burnt at the stake, Gawain expresses his opposition in seeking to withdraw from his feudal ties with the king. It is only after Lancelot involuntarily kills Gawain's brothers Gaheriet and Guerrehet that Gawain becomes Lancelot's enemy, and from this point Gawain's *desmesure* (exaggeration) contributes to the downfall of Arthur's world. He swears to avenge his two brothers, and all his acts from now on are directed towards this end. After Lancelot has left the Joyeuse Garde, Gawain pushes Arthur into a second war as soon as winter has passed, and in this receives his mortal head-wound. He is therefore depicted as bringing on his own suffering, and eventually his death, through his *desmesure*, which refuses to bend even before Lancelot's unheard-of chivalry. It is only when lying wounded that he repents; in speaking to Arthur he refers to his own madness, and shows better judgement than the king in believing that Lancelot would return to help him even now, if he were sent for. This upward moral progression continues when on his death-bed at Dover he begs Lancelot for forgiveness and asks for his own guilt to be recorded in the inscription on his tomb. Like Lancelot, Gawain saves his soul in the end by repentance. Arthur sees in a dream that he is received in heaven through the intercession of the poor, because he has apparently always treated them in a most charitable manner.

The portrayal of Guinevere shows no traces of the clerical anti-feminist manner that we find, even to excess, in *The Quest of the Holy Grail*. In the present text she stands out as a real person, particularly during the first third of the story, when the various turnings in her feelings are described in detail by someone who obviously had a good knowledge of female psychology. However, from the time that Lancelot rescues her from being burnt at the stake, she is portrayed with great reserve. She seems to show no happiness at the thought of being able to stay with Lancelot. Neither does she show any emotion when, as she leaves the Joyeuse Garde, the lovers part; at such a touching moment, the author has not even put any words into her mouth, even though they both realize that they will probably never see each other again. After Lancelot's departure for Gaul, there is no further reference to her love for him, but the fact that her message asking to be rescued from the Tower of London is to be delivered to Lancelot if Arthur is dead, together with all her resistance to Mordred's advances, shows that her love is still very much alive. It is interesting that the portrayal of her love, real, sincere and loyal, lies entirely outside the courtly tradition, since one does not find any of the clichés of courtly love such as abound in Chrétien de Troyes' depiction of the same pair of lovers in *Le Chevalier de la Charrette*.

This brief analysis of the four main characters shows, I think, how the romance is psychologically motivated, and how the protagonists are portrayed as living people with individual personalities. There are not any real 'adventures' in *The Death of King Arthur*; instead, the action moves forward under its own momentum. In *The Quest of the Holy Grail*, the psychology and motives of all the characters are forced into a preconceived dogmatic and theological pattern; however, the author of the present text has no such dogma to put over, despite the fact that he is portraying the advance of his main characters to a state of grace at their deaths – his theology is discreet, and the characters are seen to rise as a result of their own inward moral development, and not as a result of sermons. Perhaps, in showing Lancelot so soon back in sin after returning from the Grail quest, the author is showing how sermons and pious homilies do not really have much effect.

The author of *The Death of King Arthur* tells us about the characters in several ways. There are, for example, the short psychological analyses that we find throughout the text. These analyses are often no more than short comments that reveal the characters' minds. He does not make use of dreams or allegories to this end; in fact, there are few dreams in the present text, and these serve more as warnings – as, for instance, the dreams which King Arthur has before the battle on Salisbury Plain. The author's chief means of portraying his characters' personalities is by the way they speak and act. We have a few monologues: Guinevere in despair because she believes Lancelot has been unfaithful to her, Arthur's surprise at seeing Lancelot's paintings in Morgan's castle, Guinevere repenting that she had doubted Lancelot, and Arthur's prayer after having seen Gawain in his dream. These speeches are not overheard, but there is another kind of monologue, spoken as though no one else were present, but in fact overheard by others. For example: Lancelot's despair when he realizes that he will be unable to attend the tournament at Tanebourc; Lancelot's farewell to the land of Logres, and Arthur's revealing that Mordred is his son when he hears of his treachery. There are many others in the course of the romance. Even more numerous, of course, are the dialogues; for example, those between Guinevere and Bors, Arthur and Morgan, and Arthur and Gawain. Many of these contain important facts about the psychology of the characters.

The romance is very closely structured. For example, the author is skilful in the way he has certain characters present or absent. The absence of Lancelot, incognito, from Arthur's court, makes possible, with all its repercussions, Guinevere's jealousy. Bors and his companions leave Arthur's court after the tournament at Camelot and after the episode of the poisoned fruit, in order to look for Lancelot; they are therefore absent when Mador de la Porte arrives and so cannot offer to defend Guinevere. The author manages to keep up the suspense until the last minute, since Lancelot does not arrive at court until the very day of the battle. Another example: before Arthur visits his sister Morgan's castle, he sends Guinevere back to Camelot; this is because Arthur is going to discover Lancelot's paintings in the castle, and the scene would lose its dramatic effect if Guinevere were there.

The real structure, though, rests in the way that the story gradually but concisely moves towards its inevitable conclusion. It is the adultery of Guinevere and Lancelot which is made the real cause of Arthur's downfall; Lancelot's absence from court causes Guinevere's jealousy; when he returns and champions her against Mador, their love is even greater than before, and thus the episode of the poisoned apple also contributes to the final conclusion. Arthur's shame at seeing Lancelot's paintings, together with the denunciation by Agravain, leads naturally to Lancelot and Guinevere being caught together. Gawain's implacable anger and hatred of Lancelot after Gaheriet's death, by impelling Arthur to leave Britain for Gaul, enables the theme of Mordred's treachery to be introduced naturally. Even the succeeding battle against the Romans plays its part, because in this battle Gawain's head-wound is re-opened, and from this he dies. The wound was inflicted in the first place by Lancelot, in their duel. The author obviously meant Gawain's death to be a punishment for his *outrage* and *desmesure* since his brother's death, and yet he did not want to make Lancelot directly responsible, because Lancelot's love for Gawain and his unwillingness to harm him represent a higher level of chivalry on Lancelot's part.

All the elements are now there; in the first third of the romance the adultery is the theme, but this no longer plays any part once the secondary theme of Gaheriet's death has been introduced. After Gawain's death, the third theme, that of Mordred's treachery, takes over and brings the story to its conclusion. From this point, the end comes quickly. It is interesting to note, for example, that the author has compressed the time-scale by reducing the three final battles described by Geoffrey of Monmouth and Wace into a single one, that held on Salisbury Plain. The epilogue tells of Lancelot's end, as is quite right when the story, despite its title, is really about him and not about Arthur. It is difficult to see how the story could be better structured and motivated.

The text of *The Death of King Arthur* translated here is that published by Professor Jean Frappier, of the Sorbonne.

THE DEATH OF KING ARTHUR

[1]   After Master Walter Map had put down in writing as much as he thought sufficient about the *Adventures of the Holy Grail*, his lord King Henry II felt that what he had done would not be satisfactory unless he told about the rest of the lives of those he had previously mentioned, and the deaths of those whose prowess he had related in his book. So he began this last part; and when he had put it together he called it *The Death of King Arthur*, because the end of it relates how King Arthur was wounded at the battle of Salisbury and left Girflet who had long been his companion, and how no one ever again saw him alive. So Master Walter begins this last part accordingly.

[2]   When Bors arrived at court in the city of Camelot from the faraway lands of Jerusalem, he found much there that brought him great joy, because everyone was very anxious to see him. When he told them about the passing of Galahad and the death of Perceval, they were all very saddened at court, but nevertheless they all consoled themselves as best they could. The king commanded that all the adventures that the companions of the Quest for the Holy Grail had recounted at his court were to be set down in writing; and when he had done this he said:

'My Lords, look among you and count how many of your companions we have lost on this quest.'

They looked and found there were as many as thirty-two missing; and of all these there was not one who had not died in combat.

[3]   The king had heard the rumour that Gawain had killed several of them, and he summoned him before him and said:

'Gawain, I order you, by the oath you swore when I knighted you, to answer the question I am going to ask you.'

'My Lord,' replied Sir Gawain, 'since you have asked me in that manner I shall not fail in any way to tell you, even if it

23

brought me shame as great as ever befell a knight of your court.'

'I want to ask you,' said the king, 'how many knights you think you killed, by your own hand, on this quest.'

Sir Gawain thought for a moment and the king said again:

'By my oath, I want to know, because there are people who are saying that you have killed a very large number.'

'My Lord,' said Sir Gawain, 'you obviously wish to be certain of my great misfortune, and I shall tell you, because I see that I must. I can tell you in truth that I killed eighteen by my own hand, not because I was a better knight than any of the others, but since misfortune affected me more than any of my companions. Indeed, it did not come about through my chivalry, but through my sin. You have made me reveal my shame.'

'Certainly, my nephew,' said the king, 'that was truly great misfortune, and I am well aware that it happened through your sin. Nevertheless, tell me whether you believe you killed King Baudemagus.'

'My Lord,' he said, 'I definitely did kill him – and I have never done anything that I regret as much as that.'

'Indeed, my nephew,' said the king, 'if you have regrets about that it is not surprising; because, may God help me, I regret it too. My court has lost more in him than in the four best knights who died on the quest.'

So spoke King Arthur about King Baudemagus, and as a result Gawain felt worse about the affair than he had done before. And since the king saw that adventures had so declined in the kingdom of Logres that hardly any more took place anywhere, he ordered a tournament to be announced at Winchester, because he nevertheless did not want his companions to cease wearing arms.

[4] But although Lancelot had begun to live chastely as a result of the exhortations of the hermit to whom he had confessed when he had been on the quest for the Holy Grail, and had utterly renounced Queen Guinevere as has already been related, when he returned to court it took him less than a month to become just as deeply and ardently in love as he had ever been, and he fell back into sin with the queen just as

before. What is more, if he had previously indulged in his sin so carefully and so guardedly that no one had been aware of it, now on the contrary he acted so indiscreetly that Agravain, Sir Gawain's brother, who had never greatly liked Lancelot and took more notice of his erring actions than any of the others, realized what was happening. Agravain was so observant that he discovered the whole truth, that Lancelot and the queen loved each other adulterously. The queen was so beautiful that everyone marvelled at her, for at that time she was at least fifty years old but was such a beautiful woman that her equal could not have been found anywhere in the world. Because of this, and since her beauty never failed her, certain knights said that she was the fountain of all beauty.

[5] When Agravain had found out about the queen and Lancelot, he was extremely pleased – more for the harm he thought he would be able to do Lancelot than for an opportunity to avenge the king's dishonour. In that week the day came round for the tournament at Winchester, and a great number of King Arthur's knights attended. However, Lancelot, planning to go in disguise, told all those around him he felt so unwell that he definitely would not be able to go. Despite this, he wanted Bors and Hector and Lionel and their company of knights to attend. They replied that they would not go, because he was so unwell. So he told them:

'I want and command you to go, and you will leave in the morning, while I remain here. By the time you return I shall have recovered completely, if God is willing.'

'My Lord,' they said, 'since it is your wish, we shall go; but we should very much like to have stayed with you and kept you company.'

Lancelot repeated that he did not want them to do that, so thereupon they said no more on the subject.

[6] In the morning Bors left the city of Camelot with his company of knights. When Agravain found out that Bors was going with his knights and that Lancelot was staying behind, he immediately thought that Lancelot's plan was to see the queen after Arthur had left. So he went to his uncle the king and said:

'My Lord, there is something I would tell you about in secret, if I did not think it would distress you. I am only mentioning it to avenge your dishonour.'

'My dishonour?' exclaimed the king. 'Is the matter then so important that my dishonour is involved?'

'Yes, my Lord,' said Agravain, 'and I shall explain why.'

Then he drew him to one side and told him in confidence:

'My Lord, I must tell you that Lancelot and the queen love each other adulterously. Because they cannot meet as they would wish when you are there, Lancelot has stayed behind instead of going to the tournament at Winchester; but he has sent along his knights so that tonight or tomorrow, when you have left, he will be completely free to talk to the queen.'

When King Arthur heard this he could not believe it was true, and in fact was sure that Agravain had invented it.

'Agravain, my nephew,' he said, 'you should never say such a thing, because I could not believe you. I am quite sure that Lancelot could never have had ideas like that, and indeed if he ever did, he was compelled to by the force of love, which neither common-sense nor reason can resist.'

'What, my Lord!' exclaimed Agravain. 'Are you not going to do anything about it?'

'What do you want me to do about it?' he asked.

'My Lord,' said Agravain, 'I should like you to order them to be watched closely until they can be caught together. Then you would know the truth, and next time you would be more ready to believe me.'

'Do what you like about it,' said the king. 'I shall not stop you.'

Agravain said that that was all he was asking for.

[7] That night King Arthur gave considerable thought to what Agravain had said, but he did not let it affect him much, because he did not really believe it was true. In the morning he prepared to leave for the tournament and summoned a great number of his knights to accompany him.

The queen said to him, 'My Lord, I should willingly go to the tournament if it pleased you, and in fact I would very much like to go, because I have heard that many very fine knights will be there.'

'My Lady,' said the king, 'you are not to go this time.'

And so she said no more on the subject. Arthur was quite intentionally making her stay behind in order to put Agravain's accusation to the test.

[8] When the king was on his way to the tournament with his companions, they talked together quite considerably about Lancelot and said that he was not going to attend. And as soon as Lancelot knew that the king had left with the knights who were going to Winchester, he rose from his bed and dressed. Then he went to the queen and said:

'My Lady, if you will permit me, I would like to go to the tournament.'

'Why have you stayed behind after the others?' she asked.

'My Lady,' he said, 'it is because I would like to go alone, and arrive at the tournament completely unrecognized by either friends or strangers.'

'Go, then,' she said, 'if you wish. I give you leave.'

He left her straight away and returned to his quarters, where he stayed until nightfall.

[9] When it was dark, and as soon as everyone in the city of Camelot was asleep, Lancelot went to his squire and said:

'You must ride with me, because I want to go to the tournament at Winchester. The two of us must not travel except at night, because I do not want to be recognized on the way at any price.'

The squire carried out his orders; he made himself ready as quickly as he could, and took Lancelot's best horse, because he realized that his lord wished to bear arms at the tournament. When they were outside Camelot and had joined the right path for Winchester, they rode all night through without taking any rest.

[10] The next day, when it was light, they arrived at a castle where the king had spent the night. Lancelot went there only because he did not want to travel during the day, in case he were recognized. When he arrived beneath the castle, he rode

with his head so low that he could hardly be identified. He did this because some of the king's knights were leaving the castle; and he very much regretted that he had come so early.

[11] King Arthur, who was still looking out of a window, saw Lancelot's horse and recognized it at once because he had given it to him himself, but he did not recognize Lancelot as his head was too low. However, when crossing a street, Lancelot raised his head, and the king noticed him and pointed him out to Girflet:

'Did you see Lancelot just then? Yesterday he was having us believe that he was unwell, and now he is in this castle.'

'My Lord,' said Girflet, 'I will tell you why he did that; he wished to be present at the tournament without being recognized and so he did not want to come with us – that is the honest truth.'

Meanwhile, Lancelot, who was quite unaware of all this, entered a house in the town with his squire, and ordered that his identity should not be revealed to anyone there, if they asked. The king stayed at the window waiting for Lancelot to pass once again, until he realized that he had stopped in the town. Then he said to Girflet:

'We have lost Lancelot; he has found somewhere to stay.'

'My Lord,' replied Girflet, 'that is quite possible. You see, he only rides at night, in order not to be recognized.'

'Because he wishes to remain unnoticed,' the king replied, 'we shall pretend not to have seen him. Be sure that no living soul is told that you have seen him here – I shall not mention it on my side. Then he will be quite able to remain unnoticed, because we are the only people to have seen him.'

And Girflet swore that he would not tell anyone.

[12] So the king left the window with those who were with him, and Lancelot stayed in the house of a rich vavasour who had two handsome strong sons, recently knighted by the hand of King Arthur himself. Lancelot began looking at the two knights' shields and saw that they were all as red as fire without any device on them. That was because it was customary at that time for a newly-dubbed knight to bear a shield of only one colour during his first year; if he did not comply it was an

infringement of the rule of his order. Lancelot said to the lord of the house :

'My Lord, I would very much like to ask you as a favour to lend me one of those shields to wear at the tournament at Winchester, as well as the caparison and the other equipment that go with it.'

'My Lord,' said the vavasour, 'have you not a shield?'

'No,' he replied, 'not one I wish to wear, because if I wore it I should probably be recognized sooner than I would like; so I shall leave it here with my arms, until I return.'

His host said to him, 'My Lord, take whatever you like. One of my sons is unwell and will not be able to bear arms at the tournament, but the other is about to set out.'

Just then the knight who was to go to the tournament came into the room. When he saw Lancelot he was very courteous to him, because Lancelot had the appearances of a fine knight. He asked Lancelot who he was, and the latter replied that he was a foreign knight from the kingdom of Logres, but refused to give him his name or tell him any more about himself. Lancelot would only say that he was going to the tournament at Winchester and that that was why he had come that way.

'My Lord,' said the knight, 'I am glad that you have come, because I wanted to go too. Let us set out together, and we can keep each other company on the way.'

'My Lord,' replied Lancelot, 'I would rather not ride by day, because the heat is too much for me, but if you could wait till evening, I would accompany you. However, I shall not leave before then under any circumstances.'

'My Lord,' said the knight, 'you seem such an excellent knight that I shall do whatever you wish. I shall stay here for the rest of the day out of respect for you, and whenever you decide to go we can leave together.'

Lancelot thanked him for offering to accompany him.

[13] That day Lancelot remained there and was served and provided with everything that a nobleman could desire. The people in his lodging kept asking him who he was, but they were unable to find out anything. However, his squire spoke to the vavasour's daughter, who was very beautiful and pressed

him hard to reveal who his lord was; and when he saw her great beauty, he did not wish to refuse utterly, because that would have seemed an unmannerly thing to do, but said:

'I cannot reveal everything to you, because I should perjure myself and should probably incur my master's anger; but I will certainly tell you all I can without harming myself. In fact he is the finest knight in the world, I can assure you in good faith.'

'May God help me,' said the girl, 'you have said quite enough. You have done me a great favour by saying that.'

[14] Then the girl went straight to Lancelot, knelt before him, and said:

'Noble knight, grant me a gift by the faith you owe to whatever you love most in the world.'

When Lancelot saw such a beautiful and charming girl on her knees before him, he was embarrassed and said:

'Please get up. Be sure there is nothing in the world within my power that I should not do in answer to your request, because you have asked me in such solemn terms.'

She got up and said, 'My Lord, I thank you. Do you know what you have granted me? You have promised to wear my right sleeve on your helmet at the tournament instead of a plume, and to bear arms through love for me.'

When Lancelot heard this request he was annoyed; nevertheless he did not dare to refuse it because he had already promised. However, he was very regretful about having granted what she asked, because he realized that if the queen found out about it, she would be so angry with him that, as far as he could see, he would never find his peace with her. Nevertheless, he decided that he would enter the tournament to keep his promise, for otherwise he would be disloyal if he did not do for the girl what he had promised her. The girl straight away brought him her sleeve attached to a plume, and begged him to carry out great feats of arms at the tournament for her love, so that she could consider that her sleeve had been put to good use.

'I can tell you faithfully, my Lord,' she said, 'that you are the first knight of whom I have ever requested anything, and that I would not have done it even now had it not been for the great goodness there is in you.'

He replied that for her love he would behave in a way that would be beyond reproach.

[15] So Lancelot stayed there all day. In the evening, when it was dark, he left the vavasour's house, and commended him and his daughter to God. He told his squire to carry the shield he had borrowed, and left behind his own. He rode the whole night with his company, until the next morning, a little before sunrise, they came to within one league of Winchester.

'My Lord,' said the squire to Lancelot, 'where do you want us to stay?'

'If anyone knew a place near the tournament where we could stay secretly, I should be very pleased, because I do not want to go into Winchester.'

'In faith,' said the knight, 'you are very fortunate; near here, off the main road to the left, is the house of an aunt of mine. She is a very kind woman and will look after us well. She will be delighted to see us when we arrive at her house.'

'In faith,' said Lancelot, 'I would very much like to go there.'

[16] So they left the main road and went secretly straight to where the lady's house was. When they had dismounted and the lady recognized her nephew, you could not have seen greater joy than hers, because she had not seen him since he had been dubbed a knight.

'My nephew,' she said, 'where have you been since I last saw you, and where have you left your brother? Is he not coming to the tournament?'

'No, my Lady,' he said, 'he cannot – we left him at home a little unwell.'

'And who is this knight,' she asked, 'who has come with you?'

'My Lady,' he replied, 'may God help me, I do not know who he is, except that he seems a good man; and because of the nobility I think there is in him, I am accompanying him to the tournament tomorrow, and we are both bearing the same arms and caparisons of the same kind.'

Then the lady went up to Lancelot and spoke to him with

great respect and honour. Afterwards she escorted him to a bedroom where she made him rest in a very rich bed, because she had been told that he had been riding all night.

Lancelot spent the whole day there and they were given every comfort. That night the squires checked their lords' arms to see nothing was missing. The next day, as soon as dawn came, Lancelot arose and went to hear mass in the chapel of a hermit who lived close by in a wood. When he had heard mass and had said his prayers, as a Christian knight should, he left and returned to his lodging, and then had breakfast with his companions.

Lancelot had sent his squire to Winchester to find out who were going to be supporting those inside the castle, and who were joining those outside. The squire hurried to find out the news and returned quickly to the lodging before Lancelot had begun to put on his arms. When he came to his lord, he said :

'My Lord, there are a great number of people both inside and outside, because knights have come from everywhere, familiar ones and strangers. However, the greater strength is with those inside, since the companions of the Round Table are there.'

'Do you know,' Lancelot asked, 'which side Bors and Lionel and Hector have joined?'

'My Lord, the inside party, and rightly so, because they would not show they were companions of the Round Table if they were not on that side.'

'And who is outside?' asked Lancelot.

'My Lord,' he replied, 'the King of Scotland, the King of Ireland, the King of Wales, the King of North Wales, and many other great men. Still, they have not such good people as those inside, because they are all foreigners, gathered from all sides; they are not used to bearing arms like the knights from the kingdom of Logres, and are not such fine knights.'

Then Lancelot mounted his horse and said to his squire :

'You will not come with me, because if you did you would be recognized, and I should be recognized through you, and I do not want that to happen at any cost.'

The squire said he would naturally stay behind as that was

his lords's wish, although he would rather have gone with him. Then Lancelot departed with his companions and two squires the knight had brought with him. They rode until they came to the tournament-field at Winchester which was already completely covered with jousters, and there were already so many people present that the two sides had formed. However, neither Sir Gawain nor his brother Gaheriet bore arms that day, as the king had forbidden them to do so, knowing well that Lancelot would come; and he did not want them to injure one another if it came to a joust, because he did not want a fight or bad feelings to spring up between them.

[17] Together with a great company of knights the king had climbed to the top of the main tower of the city in order to see the tournament. With him were Sir Gawain and his brother Gaheriet. The knight who had come with Lancelot asked him:

'My Lord, which side shall we fight on?'

'Which of the two,' said Lancelot, 'do you think is in the weaker position?'

'Those outside, I think,' replied the knight, 'because the ones inside are very fine and noble knights and are skilful at bearing arms.'

'In that case,' said Lancelot, 'let us join those outside, because it would not be honourable for us to join the stronger side.'

The other knight replied that he was ready to do whatever Lancelot recommended.

[18] Then Lancelot dug into the stirrups and rode into the ranks. He struck the first knight he met so hard that he knocked both him and his horse to the ground. He struck again to finish his gallop because his lance was not yet broken, and he hit another knight so hard that neither his shield nor his coat of mail could prevent him from receiving a big deep wound in his left side. However, he was not fatally wounded. Lancelot gave him a great thrust and knocked him violently from his horse to the ground. He was quite stunned by the fall and his lance flew into pieces. At this blow several knights present at the tournament stopped to watch, and some said that they had seen the new knight make a fine attack.

'Indeed,' said others, 'that was the finest blow struck today by the hand of a single knight. He will not manage another one like that today.'

Meanwhile, Lancelot's companion spurred on his horse against Hector des Mares who was coming towards him. He struck him and broke his lance on his chest; and Hector struck him back so violently with a short thick lance that he knocked him and his horse down into a heap.

'Now you can see one of the brothers from Escalot Castle on the ground,' everyone said, as wherever they went the brothers were known by the name of their castle because they bore the same arms. The people at the tournament thought Lancelot was one of the two brothers from Escalot because of his arms.

[19] When Lancelot saw his host so violently struck to the ground before him, he was very angry. He spurred on his horse against Hector, holding a good strong lance. However, they did not recognize each other since they had both changed their arms in order to come to the tournament more secretly. Lancelot hit him so hard with all his strength that he struck him to the ground in front of Galegantin the Welshman. Sir Gawain, easily recognizing Hector because he had given him his arms, said to the king when he saw this blow:

'My Lord, that knight with red arms and the sleeve on his helmet is not who I thought it was, I swear it; it is someone else, I am quite sure, because neither of the brothers from Escalot ever dealt such a blow.'

'And who do you think it is?' asked the king.

'I do not know, my Lord,' said Sir Gawain, 'but he is very noble.'

Meanwhile, Lancelot had remounted his companion on his horse and had moved him away from where the crowd was thickest. Bors, who was making his way through the tournament striking down knights and tearing helmets from their heads and shields from their necks, happened to meet Lancelot in the crowd. He did not greet him, because he did not recognize him, but he struck him so hard with all the force of a strong lance that he pierced his shield and his coat of mail and made a big deep wound in his right side with the blade. He came riding very vigorously, and with feet firmly in his stirrups, and struck Lancelot so violently as to knock him and his horse to the ground; and as he fell the lance broke. However, he did not stay long in that position, as his horse was strong and quick and light-footed. His wound did not prevent him from jumping up and remounting, perspiring from humiliation and annoyance. He said to himself that the knight who struck him to the ground was no youth, since he had never come across anyone who had been able to do that before; but no act of kindness the man had ever done in his life would be returned so quickly as this deed, if he were able. Then he took a short thick lance that one of his squires was holding, and he turned towards Bors. Immediately space was cleared for them, as those at the tournament saw that they wanted to joust; and they had fought so well that they were held to be the two champions of the field. Lancelot came galloping as fast as his horse could go, and struck Bors so hard that he knocked him to the ground, with the saddle between his legs, because the strap broke. When Sir Gawain, who knew Bors well, saw him on the ground, he said to the king:

'Indeed, my Lord, if Bors is on the ground there is no great shame in that, because he had nothing on which to hold. The knight who has jousted with him and Hector is a fine one, and, I swear, if we had not left Lancelot ill at Camelot, I would have said that that was him there.'

When the king heard him say this, he realized straight away that it was Lancelot. He smiled and said to Sir Gawain:

'In faith, nephew, whoever that knight is, he has started very well, but it is my opinion that he will do even better later on.'

[20] As soon as Lancelot had broken his lance, he took his sword and began striking great blows to right and left, knocking knights down and killing horses, tearing shields from knights' necks and helmets from their heads, and carrying out feats of prowess in all directions. There was no one watching who did not think it a great marvel.

Bors and Hector, who had got up and remounted, started

acting so valiantly on their side that nobody could justly have reproached them. They carried out such splendid feats of chivalry in front of everyone on the field that most of those on their side were encouraged by their great example of prowess in their attempt to achieve their aim of winning the tournament. They drove Lancelot forward and back, because they were always in front of him, and held him so closely that he had to pass between their hands; that day they deprived him of many fine blows he wished to make. That was not surprising, because he was badly wounded and had lost a great deal of blood, with the result that he did not have complete control over himself, while the others were both knights of great prowess. Yet, whether they wished or not, he performed such deeds of chivalry that those from the city were thrust back inside, and he was regarded as the finest knight at the tournament from both sides. Those inside lost considerably to those outside. When it was time to leave, Sir Gawain said to the king:

'Indeed, my Lord, I do not know who that knight is who is wearing the sleeve on his helmet, but I should say that he is justly the winner of the tournament, and that he should receive the honour and praise for it. I can tell you that I shall never be at ease until I know who he is, because he has carried out too many feats of chivalry for my liking.'

'I do not think I know him,' said Gaheriet, 'but nevertheless I can say that he is the best knight in the world I have ever heard of or seen, except only Lancelot del Lac.'

[21] So spoke Lancelot's friends; and Sir Gawain ordered his horse to be brought to him, because he wanted to go and find out the identity of the knight so that he could become acquainted with him. Gaheriet said he would go too. So they came down from the tower into the courtyard beneath.

As soon as Lancelot saw that those inside the city had lost the tournament, he said to the knight who had come with him:

'My Lord, let us leave here. We cannot do any more good by staying any longer.'

So they departed at great speed, leaving behind on the field

36

the body of one of their squires who had accidentally been killed by a knight with a lance. The knight asked Lancelot which way he wanted to go.

'I should like to be,' he replied, 'in a place where I could stay eight days or more, because I am so badly wounded that riding could do me much harm.'

'In that case,' said the knight, 'let us go back to my aunt's house, where we stayed last night, because we shall be quite peaceful there, and it is not far from here.'

Lancelot agreed. They went through the bushes, because he thought that someone from the king's party might follow them to find out who he was, as many knights, those of the Round Table and others, had seen him that day at the tournament. So Lancelot and the knight and one of their squires rode along at great speed until they came to the house where they had slept the night before. Lancelot dismounted covered in blood, because he had been badly wounded. When the knight saw the wound he was horrified; he summoned an old knight who lived near there and who was specially skilled at healing wounds, to come as fast as possible. This man knew more about the subject, without any doubt, than anyone else who lived in that part of the country. When he had seen the wound, he said that he thought he would be able to cure it, with God's help, but that it would take some time, as it was big and deep.

[22] So Lancelot found help for his wound. In fact he was very fortunate, because if he had delayed at all he could well have died from it. As a result of the wound he received from the hand of his cousin Bors, he lay there for six weeks, without being able to bear arms or leave the house.

But now the story stops speaking of him, and returns to Sir Gawain and Gaheriet.

*

[23] In this part the story tells that when Sir Gawain and Gaheriet had mounted to ride after the knight who had won the tournament, they went the way they thought he had gone. When they had ridden about two English leagues so fast that they could not have failed to catch up with him if he had gone

that way, they met two squires coming along on foot in great grief, carrying in their arms a knight who had just been killed. Sir Gawain and Gaheriet went straight over to them, and asked them if they had met two knights in red arms, one of whom was wearing a lady's or a girl's sleeve on his helmet. They replied that they had not seen a knight that day who was armed as they described, but that they had seen a great many other knights coming from the tournament.

'My Lord,' said Gaheriet to Sir Gawain his brother, 'you can be quite sure now that they have not come this way. If they had, we should have caught up with them a long time ago, because we have ridden quite fast.'

'I tell you truthfully, I am very annoyed that we cannot find them,' said Sir Gawain, 'because he is such a fine knight and such an outstandingly noble man that I should love to know him, and if I had him here with me, I certainly should not stop until I had taken him to Lancelot del Lac so that I could introduce them to each other.'

Then they asked the squires who it was they were carrying.

'My Lords,' they said, 'it is a knight.'

'Who wounded him in that way?' they asked.

'My Lords,' replied the squires, 'a wild boar that he was pursuing at the edge of this forest.'

They described the place, a league away from where they were.

'In faith,' said Gaheriet, 'it is a great pity because he certainly looks like a man capable of being a fine knight.'

[24] Then they left the squires and returned to Winchester, and it was already very dark when they arrived back. When the king saw Sir Gawain come in, he straight away asked him if he had found the knight.

'No, my Lord,' said Sir Gawain, 'he went another way from us.'

The king immediately began to smile, and Sir Gawain looked at him and said:

'Uncle, it is not the first time that this affair has made you smile.'

The king replied, 'It is not the first time that you have asked me, either, and I am sure it will not be the last.'

Then Sir Gawain realized that the king knew who the knight was, and said:

'Oh! my Lord, since you know him, you can tell me who it is, if you please.'

'I shall not tell you now, this time,' said the king, 'because as he wishes to remain unknown, I should be behaving dishonourably if I revealed him to you or anyone else. For this reason I shall remain completely silent for the moment. You will not lose by this; you will find out who he is, but at the right time.'

'In faith,' said Galegantin the Welshman, 'I do not know who he is; but I can tell you truthfully that he left the tournament very badly wounded and bleeding so much that you could have followed his traces, since his blood was running freely from a wound that Sir Bors made in a joust.'

'Is that true?' asked the king.

'Yes, my Lord,' said Galegantin, 'I am telling you the truth.'

'You can be sure,' said the king to Bors, 'that you could never give a knight a wound in all your life that you ought to repent more than this one. If he should die of it, it would be a great pity you ever saw him.'

Hector, who thought that the king had said that out of spite for Bors, jumped forward angrily and full of ill-feeling, saying:

'My Lord, if the knight dies from the wound, let him die, because his death will certainly not cause us any harm or fear.'

At this the king fell silent, and he began to smile through grief and anger at Lancelot's having left the tournament wounded, for he was very worried that his life might be in danger.

[25] That night they spoke a lot about the knight with the sleeve who had won the tournament, and they were very curious to know who he was. However, that was impossible, since they were not to know any more for the moment. The king kept the secret to himself very well, and was not heard to reveal anything until they had returned to Camelot.

The next day they left Winchester, and before they went they had a tournament announced, which was to take place at Tanebourc a month after the following Monday. Tanebourc was a strong and very well-situated castle at the entrance to North Wales. When the king had left Winchester, he rode to the castle called Escalot, the same castle in which he had seen Lancelot. The king stayed in the castle fortress with a large company of knights; however, it happened that Sir Gawain lodged at the house where Lancelot had spent the night, and his bed was made up in the very room where Lancelot's shield hung. That night Sir Gawain did not go to court, as he felt a little unwell, but ate in his lodging with his brother Gaheriet, and Mordred, and with several other knights to keep them company. When they were seated for supper, the girl who had given Lancelot her sleeve asked Sir Gawain to tell her the truth about the tournament, whether it had been a good one and if fine blows had been struck. Sir Gawain told her:

'I can certainly say that the finest blows were struck that I have seen at a tournament for a long time. And it was won by a knight I would like to resemble, because he is the noblest I have seen since I left Camelot. However, I do not know who he is, or what his name is.'

'My Lord,' asked the girl, 'what were the arms of the knight who won the tournament?'

'Completely red ones,' replied Sir Gawain, 'and he wore on his helmet a lady's or a girl's sleeve. I can tell you honestly that if I were a girl I would wish the sleeve were mine, since the man who wore it must love me truly, for in all my life I have never seen a sleeve put to better use than that one.'

When the girl heard what he said, she was very happy, but she did not dare to show it because of the people she was with. So long as the knights were sitting at supper, the girl served them; for it was a custom in the kingdom of Logres at that time that when wandering knights came to the house of any high-born man, if there were a girl living there, the nobler she was the more she was obliged to serve them, and she never sat down at table until they had all finished their meal. So the girl served them until Sir Gawain and his companions had eaten. The girl was so beautiful and so well-made in every way that she could not be surpassed. Sir Gawain watched her with great pleasure as she served them; and he thought that the knight who could have his delight and his comfort with her whenever he wished would be happily born indeed.

[26]   In the evening after supper it came about that the lord of the house went out for a stroll in a meadow behind his house, and he took his daughter with him. When he arrived he found Sir Gawain and his companions who were relaxing there, and they stood up to meet him. Sir Gawain asked him to sit beside him on his right and the girl on his left, and they began to talk about various things. Gaheriet engaged his host in conversation on his side, away from Sir Gawain, and began to ask him about the customs of the castle. The host told him all he knew. Mordred drew away from Sir Gawain because the latter wanted to speak to the girl in confidence, if she would allow him. When Sir Gawain saw the moment was right, he spoke to the girl and sought her love. She asked him who he was.

'I am a knight,' he replied, 'and my name is Gawain, the nephew of King Arthur. I should love you truly if you agreed, in such a way that, so long as our love lasted, I would not love any lady or girl but you, and I would be entirely your knight, and prepared to carry out all your wishes.'

'Ah, Sir Gawain,' the girl replied, 'do not joke with me. I know you are far too rich and too high-born to love a poor girl like me; and yet if you already did love me truly, I can tell you that I should be sorrier for your sake than for any other reason.'

'Why', asked Sir Gawin, 'would you be sorry for me?'

'My Lord,' she replied, 'because even if you loved me so much that your heart would break, you would not be able to obtain my love by any means, because I love a knight whom I would not deceive for anything in the world. I can tell you truthfully that I am still a virgin, and I had never loved any man until I saw him. However, I immediately fell in love with him and begged him to carry out feats of chivalry at the tournament for my love. And he said he would. Moreover he did so well, thanks to God, that a girl who would leave him to take you deserves to lose her reputation, because he is just as fine a knight as you, no less outstanding in arms than you, no less handsome than you, no less noble – and I am not saying this to displease you. So you can be sure that it would be wasted effort to seek my love, because I would not accept any knight in the world but the one I love with all my heart and shall love all the days of my life.'

When Sir Gawain heard her rejecting him so sharply, he became angry and said:

'In that case grant me through courtesy and my love that I may prove against him that I am worthier at arms than he is, and if I am able to conquer him in arms, leave him and take me.'

'What,' she said, 'do you think I would act in that way? In doing that I could bring two of the noblest men in the world to their deaths!'

'What, then,' asked Sir Gawain, 'is he one of the noblest men in the world?'

'My Lord,' replied the girl, 'not long ago I heard him referred to as the finest knight in the world.'

'What is your lover's name?' asked Sir Gawain.

'My Lord,' said the girl, 'I shall not tell you his name, but I shall show you his shield that he left here on his way to the tournament at Winchester.'

'I would very much like to see the shield,' he said, 'because if he is a knight of as great prowess as you say, I cannot help recognizing who it is by it.'

'You may see the shield,' she said, 'whenever you like, since it is hanging in the room where you are sleeping tonight, in front of your bed.'

He replied that in that case he would see it very soon.

[27] Then he got up straight away, and all the others got up too when they saw Sir Gawain wished to go. He took the girl by the hand, and they went into the house, followed by the others. The girl took him to the bedroom, which was so bright with the light of candles and torches that it was as if the whole place were aflame. She at once showed him the shield and said:

'My Lord, there is the shield of the man I most love in the world. Now look and see if you know who the knight is and

42

whether you recognize him; I want to know if you agree that he is the finest knight in the world.'

Sir Gawain looked at the shield and recognized it was Lancelot's. He drew back embarrassed and regretful for what he had said to the girl, because he was frightened that Lancelot might find out. The thought that he could at least make his peace with the girl would be as good as he could ask for. So he said to her:

'For God's sake, please do not be angry for what I said, because I realize I was in the wrong; I certainly agree with you now. You can be sure that the knight you love is the finest knight in the world, and there is no girl anywhere, however truly she might love, who would not be right in leaving me for him. He is a better knight than I am, nobler, more handsome and more charming. If I had known it was he and that you had the heart to love such an outstanding man, indeed I should never have started asking or begging for your love. Nevertheless I can tell you truthfully that of all the girls in the world, you are the one who I wish most of all could love me deeply, if there were not such a great obstacle. And if it is true that Sir Lancelot loves you as much as I think you love him, never was a lady or a girl more fortunate in love. For God's sake I beg you that if I have said anything to displease you, you will forgive me.'

'My Lord,' she replied, 'of course I will.'

[28] When Sir Gawain saw that the girl had promised that nothing of what he had said would be revealed to Lancelot or anyone else, he asked her:

'Please tell me what arms Sir Lancelot bore at the Winchester tournament.'

'My Lord,' she replied, 'he bore a red shield and caparison, and he had on his helmet a silk sleeve I gave him for love.'

'In truth,' replied Sir Gawain, 'those are good signs, because he was there and I saw him just as you described. I now believe even more certainly than before that he loves you truly, because otherwise he would not have worn the sleeve. I think you should have a high opinion of yourself for having such a fine man as your lover. Indeed, I am very glad to hear about it, because he has always been so secretive before everybody that no one has ever known for certain at court that he has been in love.'

'May God help me, my Lord,' she replied, 'I am glad to hear that; for you know that a love affair that is common knowledge can never become truly noble.'

[29] Then the girl left. Sir Gawain escorted her to her own room, and then he went to bed. That night he thought a lot about Lancelot and said to himself that he would not have thought that Lancelot would have aspired to leave his heart in any place that was not nobler and more honourable than all others. 'And yet,' he said, 'I cannot really blame him if he loves this girl, because she is so beautiful and charming in every way that if the noblest man in the world had given her his heart, I think he would have put it to good use.'

[30] That night Sir Gawain slept very little, because he was thinking of the girl and Lancelot, and in the morning, as soon as it was light, he got up, as did all the others, because the king had already summoned Sir Gawain to come up to court, as he wished to leave the castle. When they were all ready, Sir Gawain went up to his host, commended him to God, thanked him for the fine welcome he had given him in his house. Then he went up to the girl and said:

'I commend you to God; please know that I am your knight wherever I am, and that there is no place however distant from which I would not come as soon as possible if you called me to help you. And I ask you, for the sake of God, to greet Sir Lancelot for me, because I think you will see him sooner than I shall.'

The girl replied that as soon as she saw him she would greet him for Sir Gawain. Sir Gawain thanked her and then left on horseback. In the middle of the courtyard he found his uncle King Arthur also on horseback, waiting for him with a great company of knights. They greeted each other, and set out, and rode together talking about many things. After a time Sir Gawain said to the king:

'My Lord, do you know the name of the knight who won the

tournament at Winchester, the one with red arms who wore the sleeve on his helmet?'

'Why do you ask?' said the king.

'Because,' replied Sir Gawain, 'I do not think you know who it was.'

'I do know,' said the king, 'but you do not; and yet you ought to have been able to recognize him from his splendid feats of arms, because no one else could have done as well as that.'

'Indeed, my Lord,' said Sir Gawin, 'it is true that I should have recognized him, because many is the time I have seen him acting with as great prowess, but I did not know who it was because he disguised himself as a new knight. However, I have since found out and now I know quite certainly who he was.'

'And who was he?' asked the king. 'I shall soon know if you are telling the truth.'

'My Lord,' he said, 'it was Sir Lancelot del Lac.'

'That is right,' said the king, 'and he came to the tournament so secretly in order that no knight should refuse to joust with him because he recognized him. He is quite certainly the noblest man in the world and the finest knight alive. If I had believed your brother Agravain, I should have had him put to death, and that would have been such a great crime and dishonour that the whole world would have blamed me for it.'

'Indeed,' replied Sir Gawain, 'what did my brother Agravain say, then? Tell me.'

'I shall tell you,' said the king. 'He came to me the other day and said he was amazed how I could bear to keep Lancelot near me when he was causing me such great shame as to dishonour my wife. He said outright that Lancelot loved her shamefully when my back was turned, and that he had slept with her. According to him, I could be quite sure that he had not remained at Camelot for any other reason than to see the queen freely after I had left for the tournament at Winchester. Your brother Agravain would have had me believe all this, and I would have been dishonoured if I had believed his lies, because I know now that if Lancelot were in love with the queen, he would not have left Camelot while I was away, but would have stayed so as to be able to see her in freedom.'

'Indeed, my Lord,' said Sir Gawain, 'Lancelot stayed behind only so that he could attend the tournament more secretly, and you can still see that that is the truth. Be careful that you never believe any man who brings you that kind of news, because I can assure you that Lancelot never thought of loving the queen in that way. In fact I can tell you truthfully that he loves one of the most beautiful girls in the world, and she loves him too and is still a virgin. We also know that he loved King Pellés' daughter with all his heart,[1] and she was the mother of that splendid knight Galahad who brought the adventures of the Holy Grail to their conclusion.'

'If it were true,' replied the king, 'that Lancelot loved the girl deeply, I could not believe that he would have the heart to be so disloyal to me as to dishonour me through my wife; because treason could not take root in a heart that contains such great prowess, unless through the most powerful sorcery in the world.'

So spoke King Arthur about Lancelot. And Sir Gawain told him that he could be quite sure that Lancelot had never aspired to love the queen immorally, as Agravain had accused.

'I shall go further than that, my Lord,' he said, 'because I feel that Lancelot is so innocent of the whole affair that there is no knight in the world, however good, whom I would not meet in combat to defend Lancelot if he accused him.'

'What can I say?' said the king. 'If everybody kept telling me every day, or even if I saw more than I have seen, I still should not believe it.'

Sir Gawain begged him not to change this true opinion he now held.

[31] Then they stopped talking. They rode on day by day until they arrived at Camelot, and when they had dismounted there were many people who asked for news about the tournament, and about who had won it. However, there was nobody except the king, Sir Gawain and Girflet who could have told them the truth, and they did not yet want to reveal it, as they

46

knew that Lancelot wished to remain unknown. So Sir Gawain said to the queen:

'We do not actually know who it was that won the tournament, as we think it was a foreign knight; but we can tell you that he bore red arms in the jousting, and on his helmet, like a plume, he wore a lady's or a girl's sleeve.'

Then the queen felt sure it was not Lancelot, because she did not think he would bear any token at a tournament that she had not given to him. So she did not inquire any more, except that she asked Sir Gawain:

'Was Lancelot not at the tournament?'

'My Lady,' he replied, 'if he was there and I saw him, I did not recognize him; and if he had been there I think he would have won the tournament. However, we have seen his arms so often that if he had been there, unless he had come in disguise, we should have recognized him easily.'

'I can tell you,' said the queen, 'that he went as secretly as he could.'

'Well, my Lady,' said Sir Gawain, 'if he was there, he was the knight with red arms who won the tournament.'

'He was not,' said the queen, 'be sure of that, because he is not sufficiently attached to any lady or girl to carry a token for her.'

[32]   Then Girflet jumped forward and said to the queen:

'My Lady, I can assure you that the knight with red arms who wore the sleeve on his helmet was Lancelot, because when he had won the tournament and had left, I went after him to find out who he was, and I still was not sure as he was so disguised. I went on till I was able to look him clearly in the face as he was riding along badly wounded with a knight armed just as he was, for they both had arms of exactly the same kind.'

'Sir Gawain,' asked the queen, 'do you think he is right? By the faith you owe my lord the king, tell me what you know, if you do know anything.'

'My Lady,' he said, 'you have begged me in such serious terms that I shall not hide from you anything I know; I can tell you truthfully that it was Lancelot himself who had red arms, who wore the sleeve on his helmet and who won the tournament.'

When the queen heard this, she immediately fell silent, and went into her room crying. She was very upset and said to herself:

'Ah, God, how I have been villainously tricked by the man in whose heart I believed all loyalty to reside, and for whose love I have dishonoured the noblest man alive! Ah, God, who will ever find fidelity again in any man or in any knight, when disloyalty has lodged in the best of all the good ones?'

In that way the queen spoke to herself, because she really imagined that Lancelot had deserted her, and loved the girl whose sleeve he had worn at the tournament. She was so distressed that she did not know what to do next, except that she wanted to take her revenge on Lancelot or the girl, if she could, as soon as she had the opportunity. The queen was deeply hurt by the news that Sir Gawain had brought, because she could not bring herself to believe that Lancelot had the heart to love another woman than her; she was very miserable all day and turned away from laughter and enjoyment.

[33] The next day Bors returned to court, and also Lionel and Hector and their company, from the tournament. When they had dismounted at the king's lodge, where they ate and slept whenever they came to court, Hector began asking various people who had remained with the queen, when the others went to the tournament, where Lancelot had gone, because they had left him there when they departed.

'My Lord,' they said, 'he went from here the day after you left, and he took only a single squire with him. Since then we have neither seen him nor heard news of him.'

[34] When the queen knew that Lancelot's brother and his cousins had come, she summoned Bors before her and said:

'Bors, were you at the tournament?'

'Yes, my Lady,' he replied.

'Did you see your cousin Lancelot?'

'No, my Lady, he was not there.'

'In faith, he was,' insisted the queen.

'He was not, my Lady, save your grace,' he said: 'if he had been there he would not have failed to come and speak to me and in any case I would have recognized him.'

'I tell you that he certainly was there,' said the queen. 'I shall describe him: he was wearing red arms, all of one colour, and on his head he wore a lady's or a girl's sleeve, and it was he who won the tournament.'

'In God's name,' said Bors, 'I certainly hope that it was not my cousin, because the knight you are speaking of, as I have been told, left the tournament suffering very badly from a wound in his left side I gave him in a joust.'

'Cursed be the hour,' said the queen, 'that you did not kill him, because he is so disloyal towards me that I should not have thought him capable of it for anything in the world.'

'How, my Lady?' asked Bors.

She told him all her thoughts, and when she had finished all she wanted to say, Bors replied:

'My Lady, do not believe it is as you imagine, until you know more certainly. May God help me, I cannot believe that he has deceived you in this manner.'

'I tell you for certain', she said, 'that some lady or girl has caught him with a magic potion or spell. Never again will I have anything to do with him, and if by any chance he returned to court, I would prevent him from entering any part of the king's lodge, and I would forbid him ever to be so bold as to set foot here.'

'My Lady,' said Bors, 'you will do as you wish, but still I can tell you that my lord certainly never had any intention of doing that of which you accuse him.'

'He showed that he did, at the tournament,' said the queen; 'I am sorry that the proof is so evident.'

'My Lady,' said Bors, 'if it is as you say, he has never done anything which I regret so much, because he should not transgress against you, of all people, under any circumstances.'

All that week and the next Bors remained in King Arthur's lodge with his company, and they were unusually miserable and pensive because they saw the queen was so angry. During that time no news of Lancelot was brought to court by anyone who had seen him far or near; and King Arthur was most surprised at this.

[35]   One day the king and Sir Gawain were together at the windows of the palace, and were talking about various things, when the king said to Sir Gawain :

'Nephew, I keep wondering where Lancelot can be staying so long. It is a long time since I have known him be absent from my court for such a while as on this occasion.'

When Sir Gawain heard this, he smiled and said to the king:

'My Lord, you can be sure that he is not bored where he is, because if he were, he would not be long returning; and if he is enjoying himself, no one should be surprised at that, because even the richest man in the world ought to be happy if he had left his heart in the place where I think Lancelot has left his.'

When the king heard this, he was very anxious to know more, and so he begged Sir Gawain, by his faith and the oath he had sworn to him, to tell him the truth.

'My Lord,' said Sir Gawain, 'I shall tell you the truth as far as I know it; but it must be kept a secret between the two of us, because if I thought it would be told elsewhere, I should not say anything.'

The king said that he would not repeat any of it.

'My Lord,' said Sir Gawain, 'I can tell you that Sir Lancelot is staying at Escalot because of a girl he loves. She is quite certainly one of the most beautiful girls in the kingdom of Logres, and she was still a virgin when we were there. Because of the great beauty I saw in her, I begged her for love not very long ago, but she rejected me, saying that she was loved by a finer and more handsome knight than I was. I was very curious to know who this could be. I pressed her to tell me his name, but she kept refusing. However, she said she would show me his shield, and I replied that that would be good enough for me. So she showed me it, and I recognized it straight away as Lancelot's. I asked her, "Tell me, for love's sake, when this shield was left here." She replied that her lover had left it when he went to the tournament at Winchester, that he had borne her brother's arms which were completely red, and that the sleeve he had worn on his helmet was hers.'

[36] The queen was leaning pensively at another window and overheard all that the king and Sir Gawain were saying. She came forward and asked:

'Nephew, who is that girl you find so beautiful?'

'My Lady, it is the daughter of the vavasour of Escalot, and if he loves her it is not surprising, because she is endowed with very great beauty.'

'Indeed,' said the king, 'I could not imagine him giving his heart to a lady or a girl unless she were of very high birth. I am sure he is not staying for that reason, but is lying sick or wounded, if I am not mistaken about the injury in his side that his cousin Bors gave him at the tournament at Winchester.'

'In faith,' said Sir Gawain, 'that could well be, and I do not know what to think, except that if he were ill he would have let us know or at least he would have sent a message to his brother Hector and his cousins who are staying here.'

That day the king, the queen and Sir Gawain talked a great deal together, and the queen left them as distressed as she could possibly be, because she believed that Gawain was telling the truth about Lancelot and the girl. She went straight to her room and summoned Bors to her; and he came at once. As soon as the queen saw him, she said:

'Bors, now I know the truth about your lord, your cousin; he is staying at Escalot with a girl he loves. Now we can say that you and I have lost him, because she has so ensnared him that he could not leave if he wished. That was said just now before the king and me by a knight whose word you would always believe; and I can tell you that he affirmed it was true.'

'Indeed, my Lady,' replied Bors, 'I do not know who it was, the knight who told you that, but even if he were the most truthful in the world, I am certain he was lying when he suggested such a thing, because I know that my lord has such a noble heart that he would not deign to do what he is said to have done. I would beg you to tell me who it was that spoke to you about this, because whoever he may be I shall make him admit before tonight that it is a lie.'

'I am not going to speak any more about the matter,' she said, 'but you can be sure that I shall never forgive Lancelot.'

'Indeed, my Lady,' said Bors, 'that is a pity; since you have taken to hating my lord so much, our men have no reason to stay here. For that reason, my Lady, I take my leave of you and commend you to God, because we shall leave in the morning. After we have set out, we shall search for my lord until we find him, if it pleases God; and when we have found him, we shall stay in that part of the country, if he wishes, at some nobleman's house. If he does not wish to stay there, we shall go away to our lands and our men who are longing to see us because we have not been with them for a long time. And I can tell you, my Lady,' continued Bors, 'that we should not have stayed in this country as long as we have, if it had not been through love for our lord, and he would not have remained so long after the quest for the Holy Grail except for you. You know for certain that he loved you more loyally than any knight ever loved a lady or a girl.'

When the queen heard this she was as distressed as she could be, and could not stop the tears coming to her eyes. When she spoke she said that the hour should be cursed that ever brought such news to her, 'for I have been badly treated,' she said. Then she spoke again to Bors.

'What, my Lord,' she said, 'are you then leaving me in this way?'

'Yes, my Lady,' he said, 'because I must.'

Then he left her room and went to his brother and Hector. He told them what the queen had said to him, and they were all distressed. They did not know whom to blame for the situation, but they all cursed the hour that Lancelot first became acquainted with the queen. Bors said to them:

'Let us take leave of the king and depart from here. Then we can search for our lord until we find him. If we are able to take him to the kingdom of Gaunes or the kingdom of Banoic, we shall never have done anything so worthwhile, because then we should be at peace, if he could bear to be away from the queen.'

Hector and Lionel agreed on this, and they went to the king, asking for leave to go to seek Lancelot. He gave it most regretfully, because he cherished their company, especially that of

Bors who at that time had a greater reputation, led a better life and practised finer chivalry than any other knight in the kingdom of Logres.

[37] The next day King Ban's descendants[2] left the court, and they rode straight to Escalot. When they arrived, they asked for news of Lancelot wherever they expected to find some information, but they were quite unable to see anyone who could tell them anything. They sought high and low, but the more they asked the less they found out. They rode in that way for eight days without discovering anything. When they took stock of this, they said:

'We are wasting our time, because we shall not find him before the tournament; but he will quite certainly go to that if only he is in this part of the country and able to do as he wishes.'

For that reason they stayed at a castle called Athean, a day's ride away from Tanebourc, and there were only six days to go before the tournament. The King of North Wales was staying nearby in a retreat of his, eight leagues from Athean, and as soon as he heard that relatives of King Ban were there, knights who were the most famous in the world and of the greatest prowess and chivalry, he went to see them, because he very much wanted to make their acquaintance. He also hoped, if it was possible, that they would join his side at the tournament against King Arthur and his company. When they saw that the king had come to see them, they considered it an act of great nobility on his part, and they welcomed him courteously, as they knew how. They invited him to stay there the night with them, and the next day he persuaded them to go back with him to his retreat. The King of North Wales kept them at his lodge with great joy and honour until the day of the tournament, and begged them until they promised to be on his side in the jousting. The king was very happy at this promise and expressed his thanks.

But now the story stops telling of Bors and his company, and returns to Lancelot, who lay ill at the house of the aunt of the new knight from Escalot.

*

[38]   Now the story tells that when Lancelot arrived there, he was put to bed because of his illness; and he lay there a month or more as a result of the wound his cousin Bors had given him during the tournament at Winchester. The knight who had been with him at the time felt sure that he would die of it. He was very sad about this, since he had seen so much good in Lancelot that he thought more highly of him because of his chivalry than of all other knights he had ever seen, although he did not yet know it was Sir Lancelot. When he had stayed there more than a month, it happened that the girl who had given him the sleeve came, and when she saw that he had not yet recovered, she was very sad and asked her brother how he was.

He replied, 'He is getting better, thanks be to God, but less than a fortnight ago I did not think he would get over his injury, except through death. His wound has been very difficult to cure, and that is why I was sure he would die of it.'

'Die!' exclaimed the girl, 'God protect him from that! Indeed that would be a grievous shame, because after his death there would be no truly noble knight left in the world.'

'Do you then know who he is?' asked the knight.

'Yes, my Lord,' she replied, 'very well. He is Sir Lancelot del Lac, the finest knight in the world; I was told by Sir Gawain, King Arthur's nephew.'

'Indeed,' said the knight, 'by my faith, I can well believe that it is he; because I have never seen a man perform so many feats of arms as he did at the tournament at Winchester, nor was a lady's or a girl's sleeve ever better employed or more respected than yours.'

The girl stayed there with her brother until Lancelot had recovered somewhat, so that he was well enough to leave; and when he was almost back to normal in health and appearance, the girl, who had stayed with him night and day, loved him so deeply, because of all the good things that were told of him and the beauty she saw in him, that she felt she simply would not survive if she did not obtain his love. Thus the girl loved Lancelot as strongly as was humanly possible.

When she could no longer keep her thoughts to herself, she

came to him one day, dressed and adorned in the most beautiful manner possible, wearing the most splendid dress she could find, and indeed full of the greatest earthly beauty. She came before Lancelot and said:

'My Lord, would not any knight be unchivalrous if I begged for his love and he rejected me?'

'If his heart were free and he could do with it as he wished,' replied Lancelot, 'he would indeed be most unchivalrous to reject you; but if however he were not in a position to bestow himself or his heart freely, and so rejected you, no one could blame him. I shall speak for myself straight away, for, may God help me, if it were true that you deigned to offer me your heart, and I were free to do as I liked with my own, just as many other knights are, I should certainly consider myself very fortunate if you deigned to offer me your love; for, may God help me, it is a long time since I have seen a lady or a girl more deserving to be loved than you.'

'What, my Lord,' said the girl, 'is your heart not so freely yours that you can do with it as you wish?'

'I certainly do with it as I wish,' replied Lancelot, 'because it is exactly where I want it to be, and I would not wish it to be anywhere else, since it could not be as well placed in any other spot than where I have left it; and may God grant that it never leaves that place of its desire, because if it did I could not live a single day at peace as I do now.'

'Indeed, my Lord,' said the girl, 'you have said enough for me to know a part of your mind, and I am very sad that that is how it is, for from what you have told me you could kill me with a single word. However, if you had spoken a little less openly, you would have set my heart in a tender optimistic mood, so that hope would have made me live in all the joy and sweetness that an amorous heart can experience.'

[39] Then the girl went to her brother and straight away revealed to him all her thoughts. She told him that she loved Lancelot so deeply that she was close to death if he did not grant her what she desired. Her brother was very distressed and said:

'Sister, you will have to find another object for your desires, because you will never attain this one. I know that he has left his heart in such a high place that he would not deign to lower himself by loving such a poor girl as you, even if you are one of the most beautiful women in the world. If you wish to love someone, you will have to place your heart a little lower, because you will never be able to pluck the fruit from such a high tree.'

'Indeed, brother,' said the girl, 'that grieves me, and I wish he meant no more to me than any other knight or than he did before I saw him. But now that cannot be, for it is my destiny to die for him, and I shall die, as you will see.'

In these terms the girl spoke about her death, and it came about exactly as she said, because she could not help dying for the love of Lancelot, as the story will recount later on.

[40] That same day it happened that a squire from Northumberland was staying there, and Lancelot summoned him before him and asked where he was going.

'My Lord,' he said, 'I am going to Tanebourc where the tournament is arranged for the day after tomorrow.'

'Which knights will be there?' asked Lancelot. 'Do you know?'

'My Lord,' he replied, 'the knights of the Round Table will be there, and those who were at the tournament at Winchester, and it is said that King Arthur is bringing Queen Guinevere to see the jousting.'

When Lancelot heard that the queen would be there, he was so distressed that he thought he would die of grief, and he began to grow excited and spoke so loudly that all those who were with him heard him:

'Ah, my Lady, you will not see your knight there, because all I can do is languish here. Ah, knight that gave me this wound, God grant that I may meet you so that I may discover who you are! Indeed, I would not spare you from a violent death for the whole world.'

Then his great grief made him stretch out. As he did so, he burst his wound, and blood broke out in as great a spurt as from an animal shot in the heart by a huntsman. He immediately lost consciousness.

When his doctor saw this, he said to the squire:

'You have killed him with your news.'

He had Lancelot undressed and put to bed, and did his best to stop his wound bleeding, because otherwise he would soon have died.

[41] All that day Lancelot did not open his eyes or say a word; in fact he was as if half dead. The next day he gathered together all the strength he had and pretended that he felt no more pain and was completely cured. He said to his doctor:

'Master, thanks to God and yourself, you have taken such great care and trouble over me that I feel healthy and well enough to ride without doing myself any harm. Therefore I should like to ask the lady of the house and my companion, this knight here, who has paid me so much honour during my illness, to grant me leave to go and see the tournament, because all the flower of the world's fine chivalry will be there.'

'Ah, my Lord,' said the good man, 'what are you saying? Indeed, even if you were riding the most gently-moving horse in the world, you can be sure that nothing could prevent you from dying before you had ridden as much as an English league, because you are still so weak and ill that I do not see how anyone but God could cure you completely.'

'Ah, master,' said Lancelot, 'for the love of God, will you not say anything else?'

'Certainly not,' said the doctor, 'except that you are sure to die if you leave here in this condition.'

'In faith,' said Lancelot, 'if I do not go to the tournament that is being held at the castle of Tanebourc, I shall not be able to recover because I shall die of grief; and if I have to die I would rather die on horseback than languishing here.'

'You will do whatever your heart instructs you,' replied the good man, 'because you obviously will not change your plans for anything I say; and since you do not wish to follow my advice, I am going to leave you and your companions completely, because if you die on the way I do not want it to be said that it is my fault, and if you recover, which God grant, I do not want to be either praised or blamed for it.'

'Ah, master,' said Lancelot, 'are you going to abandon me,

after all the treatment and help you have given me in my illness until now? How could you find the heart to do that?'

'In faith,' said the doctor, 'I am obliged to leave you, because I would not want such a noble man and fine knight as you to die while in my keeping.'

'My dear friend,' said Lancelot, 'are you really saying truthfully that I should certainly die if I left here now to go to the tournament at Tanebourc?'

'I can tell you in all honesty,' replied the good man, 'that if all the world were on your side except only God, you would not be able to ride two leagues without killing yourself. However, if you stay here with us another fortnight, I promise you that within that time, with the help of God, I shall make you so healthy and well that you will be able to ride wherever you want without danger.'

'Master,' said Lancelot, 'I shall remain because of your promise, but I shall be as grieved and angry as it is possible to be.'

Then Lancelot turned to the squire standing beside him who had brought the news about the tournament. He had asked the squire to stay till the next day to accompany him, because he really expected to go to the tournament with him. He said:

'My friend, now you may go, because it seems that I have to stay here. When you arrive at the tournament at Tanebourc and see Sir Gawain and my lady Queen Guinevere, greet them on behalf of the knight who won the tournament at Winchester, and if they ask you how I am, do not tell them anything of my condition or where I am.'

The squire said he would willingly take the message. Then he mounted his horse and departed, and rode until he arrived at the tournament. He was acquainted with the King of North Wales, and he went to his lodge and stayed there the night before the tournament was due to begin.

When night had fallen, Sir Gawain came to the King of North Wales' lodge. He went to his court and stayed there to see and to talk to Bors and his companions. They welcomed him with great joy and splendour. The squire was serving wine, and when he was kneeling before Sir Gawain to pour him some, he began to smile broadly, because he remembered the knight and the foolish thing he had wanted to do in order to be at the tournament. When Sir Gawain saw him smile, he took note of it and was sure there was a good reason behind it. So he drank some wine, and then he said to the squire:

'I beg you to answer the question I am going to ask you.'

The squire said he would answer it willingly, if he could.

'I want to ask you,' said Sir Gawain, 'why you began smiling just now.'

'In faith,' replied the squire, 'I just remembered the most foolish knight I have ever seen or heard about, who was almost mortally wounded, and, ill as he was, wished to come to the tournament, whether his doctor wanted him to or not. He was still so sick that it was very difficult to get a word out of him. Do you not think that was the greatest madness?'

'Ah, dear friend,' said Sir Gawain, 'when did you see the knight you are talking about? I can tell you that I know him to be a very noble knight, and I am sure that if he were in good health he would not lightly let himself be prevented from coming here. Now may God give him health, because it is indeed a great pity when a noble knight has an illness which stops him carrying out acts of prowess.'

'In God's name, my Lord,' the squire replied, 'I do not know who he is, but I can tell you that I heard him referred to as the finest knight in the world. Also, when I left him this morning, he asked me to greet you on behalf of the knight who won the tournament at Winchester, and he also sends many greetings to my lady the queen.'

When Sir Gawain heard this, he knew at once that it was Lancelot. He said to the squire:

'Dear friend, tell me where you left the knight to whom you are referring.'

'My Lord,' replied the squire, 'I cannot tell you, because I promised not to.'

'At least you have told us,' said Sir Gawain, 'that he is injured.'

'My Lord,' replied the squire, 'if I told you that, I regret it, because I have revealed more to you than I should have done; but nevertheless I beg you for love's sake that if you see my lady the queen before I do, you will greet her from the knight I have spoken of.'

Sir Gawain said he would willingly do that.

[42] The three cousins had heard everything that the squire had said, and were dismayed – they realized it was Lancelot he was talking about and who had sent greetings to the queen and Sir Gawain. They pressed the boy to tell them where he had left him, but he replied that he would not say any more however much they begged him.

'At least,' they said, 'you can tell us where you left him.'

He named a place other than the true one.

They said that when they left the tournament they would search for him until they found him.

[43] On the next day the knights of four kingdoms assembled on the field beneath Tanebourc against those of the Round Table. Many fine jousts were made with the lance and many splendid blows struck with the sword, and you could have seen the field full of foreign knights who had come to fight against those of the kingdom of Logres and those of the Round Table, whose prowess and boldness were famous. However, out of all those present it was King Ban's descendants, and Sir Gawain and Bors, who were the most outstanding.

When the king saw and knew that Lancelot had not been present, he was very sad, because he had come more in order to see and speak to Lancelot than for any other reason. So in that very place, following the general feeling of most of those present, he had another tournament proclaimed, to be held in a month's time on the field at Camelot. All agreed about this. In that way the tournament was ended and no more was done on that occasion.

[44] That day the king asked Bors and his companions to come to court, but he said he would not until he had some certain information about Lancelot. The king did not dare to insist.

Sir Gawain told the queen what the squire had said about Lancelot, and how he was prevented from coming to the tournament by his doctor because he was too ill. However the queen was unable to believe that he had been ill for so long, and was certain that the girl whom Sir Gawain had praised so highly was the real reason for his delay, and that he had remained with her. She was sure that that was the only explanation why he had stayed away from court so long, and she hated him so much for it that there was no shame that she would not willingly have inflicted on him. However, she so much regretted the departure of Bors and his companions from court because of Lancelot's absence, and she was so distressed that she had lost them, that she did not know what to do. She would very much have liked them to return, if that were possible, because she so much liked their company for the great delight it brought her that she esteemed no one else as much as she did them. And when she was holding her privy council she said from time to time that she did not know any knight in the world so worthy of or so suited to ruling a great empire as Bors of Gaunes; because of her love for him she very much regretted that all his companions had not remained at court.

The king stayed at Tanebourc to rest, and he summoned Bors and all his companions who were staying with the King of North Wales to come and see him; but they replied that they would not go and would not enter his court until they had found certain news of Lancelot.

The day after he had summoned them, the king left Tanebourc and rode towards Camelot with the men from his lodge. The same day Bors left the King of North Wales with his companions, and Sir Gawain went with them, saying that he would never leave them until they had found Lancelot.

They rode to the place where the boy had told them that he had left him, but when they arrived they could not find anyone who was able to give them any news of him. Then Sir Gawain said to Bors:

'My Lord, I would suggest that we should go to Escalot, because I know a lodge in that castle where I think we shall find the news we are seeking.'

'My Lord,' replied Bors, 'I wish we were there already, because I am impatient to find my cousin.'

So they went on from there and rode till evening, and slept that night beside a copse. The next day as soon as it was light they mounted and rode on in the cold; and they continued day after day until they arrived at Escalot. Sir Gawain dismounted at the lodge where he had once stayed, and he took Bors to the room were he had left Lancelot's shield. He found it still hanging there, and he said:

'My Lord, have you ever seen that shield before?'

Bors replied that he had left that shield behind at Camelot when he went to the tournament at Winchester.

Then Sir Gawain asked the lord of the house to come and talk to him, and he came straight away. Sir Gawain said to him:

'My Lord, I ask you as a favour, and beg you by the faith you owe whatever it is you love most in the world, to tell me where the knight who left that shield is now; because I am quite sure that you know where he is, and that you can tell us if you wish. If you refuse to answer despite our pleas, be sure that we shall cause you harm and that we shall fight you if we have an opportunity.'

'If I thought,' said the good man, 'that you wanted to know for his good, I would tell you, but otherwise I certainly would not.'

'I swear to you,' said Sir Gawain, 'by whatever I hold from God, that of all the people in the world we are the men who most love him from the bottom of our hearts, and who would do most for him; and because we have not seen him for a long time and do not know if he is in sickness or health, we are searching for him and have been for more than a week.'

'Stay here tonight,' said the good man, 'and tomorrow, when you wish to leave, I will tell you where you can find him; and if you like I will give you one of my boys here who will show you the right path.'

[45] That night the companions stayed there and were received with great joy and splendour. They were happier than they usually were because of the news they had heard.

The next day, as soon as they saw it was light, they arose, and when they came to the hall they found their host already awake too. The knight who was lying ill there when Láncelot arrived had now recovered, and said he would go with them and keep them company to the place where they would find the knight they were seeking. They replied that they would be delighted if he did.

So they mounted and all left together. They commended their host to God, and rode so fast that in the evening they arrived at the lady's house where Lancelot had been staying. By then he had recovered so much that he was able to go for walks. When they arrived there, they dismounted at the door, and Lancelot was strolling and having a pleasant time in the courtyard with the good man who had set himself to curing him. After him walked the knight who had been with him at the tournament, and who had always kept him company during his illness, because he had not left him by night or by day.

When the others had dismounted in the courtyard and Lancelot recognized them, you do not need to ask whether he was delighted. He ran straight away to Bors and wished him welcome, and to Hector, Lionel, and Sir Gawain. He was especially pleased to see Sir Gawain. Then he said:

'My Lords, welcome.'

'My Lord, God bless you; the great desire we had to see you, and our worries because you were not at the tournament at Tanebourc, made us set out to search for you. Now everything has turned out well, thanks to God, because we have found you with less difficulty than we had expected. But, for God's sake, tell us how you are, and what you have been doing, because we heard the other day that you were very ill.'

'Indeed,' he replied, 'thanks to God, I am much better now, because I am well on the way to recovery. But I have certainly been very ill and suffered great pain, and I have also been in danger of death, so I have been led to understand.'

'My Lord,' said Bors, 'where do you think the illness took you?'

'I know,' he replied, 'that it was at the tournament at Winchester, because of a serious wound that a knight gave me in a joust; the injury was more dangerous than I thought, and I am still suffering from it, because I am still not well enough to be able to ride tomorrow in comfort.'

'My Lord,' said Sir Gawain, 'because your health is now

improving, I am not worried about your past suffering, because you no longer care about that now, but tell me when you think you will be well enough to come to court.'

'Indeed,' he replied, 'if it pleases God, very soon.'

The doctor who had been looking after him said to Sir Gawain:

'My Lord, I can tell you that he will quite certainly have recovered within a week, so that he will be able to ride and bear arms just as vigorously as he did a little while ago at the tournament at Winchester.'

They replied that they were very pleased at that news.

[46] The next day, as they were sitting at dinner, Sir Gawain laughingly asked Lancelot:

'My Lord, did you ever know who the knight was who gave you that wound?'

'Indeed, no,' replied Lancelot, 'but if I could ever find out and by chance I came across him at a tournament, I do not think any favour he ever did me would be so quickly repaid, because before he left I should make him feel whether my sword could cut steel, and if he drew blood from my side, I would draw as much or more from his head.'

Then Sir Gawain began clapping his hands as joyfully as could be, and said to Bors:

'Now we shall see what you are going to do, because you have not been threatened by the most cowardly man in the world, and if he had threatened me like that, I should not be happy until I had made my peace with him.'

When Lancelot heard this, he was quite perplexed, and said:

'Bors, was it you who wounded me?'

Bors was so unhappy that he did not know what to say, because he did not dare to admit it, nor could he deny it. But he replied:

'My Lord, if I did it, I am very sorry, and no one should blame me for it; because if you were the knight I wounded, as Sir Gawain is alleging, you were so disguised that I would never have recognized you in those arms – they were like those of a new knight, whereas you have been bearing arms for more than twenty-five years. That was the reason why I did not recognize you. I think you should not bear me a grudge for what I did.'

He replied that he did not, because that was the way it had happened.

'In God's name, brother,' said Hector, 'I congratulate you for that day, because you made me feel the hard ground at a time when I had no need of it.'

Lancelot replied, laughing, 'Brother, however much you complain about what I did that day, I shall complain even more, because now I know that you and Bors are the two knights who most prevented me from doing as I wished at that tournament, as you were so often in front of me and only intended to injure and dishonour me. I think I would have won the tournament, but the two of you prevented me; and I can tell you that nowhere have I ever found two knights who caused me as much trouble or who made me suffer as much as you two. But you will not hear me speak of it again like this, and I forgive you.'

'My Lord,' said Sir Gawain, 'now you know just how well they can strike with lances and swords.'

'Indeed I do,' he said, 'I found that out for myself, and I still have very clear signs to show for it.'

[47] They spoke a great deal about the incident; and Sir Gawain was pleased to speak about it because he saw Bors was as ashamed and abashed as if he had committed the greatest misdeed in the world. So they remained there the whole week in great joy and happiness, glad to see that Lancelot was maintaining his recovery. All the time they were there Bors did not dare to reveal to him what he had heard the queen say, because he feared he might be too greatly tormented if he were told the cruel words the queen had spoken about him.

But now the story stops telling about them and returns to King Arthur.

[48] This part of the story tells how when King Arthur had left Tanebourc with the queen, he rode the first day until he came to a castle of his called Tauroc. That night he stayed there with a great company of knights, and the next morning he commanded the queen to go on to Camelot.

The king stayed at Tauroc for three days, and when he left he rode until he came to a certain forest. In this forest Lancelot had once been kept in prison for two winters and a summer, in the castle of Morgan the Faithless,[3] who still lived there with a large number of people who kept her company at all seasons. The king entered the forest with his retinue; he did not feel very well. They strayed on until they completely lost the right path, and they continued until it was dark. Then the king stopped and asked his retinue:

'What are we going to do? We have lost our way.'

'My Lord,' they said, 'it would be better for us to stay here than to move on, because we should only put ourselves to more trouble, as there are no houses or castles in this forest so far as we know. We have plenty of food, so let us set up your tent in this meadow and rest now, and tomorrow, if it pleases God, when we set out again we shall find a road that will lead us out of this forest as we wish.'

The king agreed with this; and as soon as they had begun to put up the tent, they heard a horn quite close by which was blown twice.

'In faith,' said the king, 'there are people near here. Go and see who they are.'

Sagremor the Foolish mounted his horse, and went directly to where he had heard the sound of the horn. He had not gone very far when he found a tower, great and strong and closely crenellated, and enclosed all around with a very high wall. He dismounted and went up to the gate, and called. When the porter heard there was someone at the gate, he asked who he was and what he wanted.

'I am Sagremor the Foolish,' he said, 'a knight sent by my Lord King Arthur who is close by in this forest; and he informs the people in this castle that he wishes to stay here tonight. So make ready to receive him as you should, because I shall bring him to you straight away with all his retinue.'

'My Lord,' said the porter, 'I beg you to wait a moment so that I may speak to my lady, who is up in her room, and I shall return to you at once and give you her reply.'

'What,' said Sagremor, 'is there no lord here?'

'No,' he replied.

'Then go quickly and return quickly,' said Sagremor, 'because I do not want to wait here long.'

The boy went upstairs to his lady, and he repeated the message to her just as Sagremor had told it, that King Arthur wished to stay there for the night. As soon as Morgan heard this news, she was delighted and said to the boy:

'Go back quickly and tell the knight to bring the king here, because we shall receive him as well as we possibly can.'

He went back to Sagremor and told him what his lady had instructed. Then Sagremor left the gate and returned to the king, and said:

'My Lord, you are fortunate, because I have found you a lodging where you will be entertained tonight as you wish, so I have been told.'

When the king heard this, he said to those with him:

'Let us mount and ride straight there.'

They all mounted, Sagremor led the way, and when they came to the gate they found it open. So they entered and saw that the place was beautiful, delightful, rich and splendidly kept; they thought they had never seen such a fine and well-arranged castle in their lives. There were such a great number of candles there, producing such intense light, that they were all amazed how this could be, and there was no wall that was not covered in silk cloth.

The king asked Sagremor:

'Did you see any of this decoration just now?'

'Indeed, no, my Lord,' he replied.

And the king made a sign of the cross out of astonishment, because he had never seen any church or abbey more richly hung with tapestries than the courtyard there.

'In faith,' said the king, 'if there were great wealth inside, I should not be surprised, because there is an excess of it out here.'

King Arthur dismounted, as also did all the others in his retinue. When they entered the great hall, they met Morgan, and with her at least a hundred people, ladies and knights, who were in her company. They were all dressed so richly that never, at any feast he had ever held in his life, had King Arthur seen people so richly adorned as they all were in the hall. When they saw the king enter, they all cried with one voice:

'My Lord, be welcome here, because no greater honour has ever befallen us than that you wish to stay here.'

The king replied, 'May God grant you all joy.'

Then they took him into a room which was so rich that he was sure he had never seen any that was so beautiful and delightful.

[49] As soon as the king had sat down and washed his hands, the tables were set, and all those who had come in the king's retinue were asked to sit down, provided they were knights. The girls began to bring food, as if they had had a month's warning of the arrival of the king and all his companions. Moreover the king had never seen in his life a table as plentifully adorned with rich vessels in gold and silver as this one, and if he had been in the city of Camelot and had done everything possible to ensure a rich meal, he would not have had any more than he had that night at that table, nor would he have been served better or more elegantly. They all wondered where such great plenty could come from.

[50] When they had eaten just as much as they wished, the king, in a room near by, listened to all the different musical instruments he had ever heard of in his life, and they all sounded together so sweetly that he had never heard music that was so gentle and pleasant to the ear. In this room the light was brilliant; before long he saw two very beautiful girls come in carrying two large burning candles in golden candlesticks. They came up to the king and said:

'My Lord, if it pleases you, it is now time for you to rest, because the night is well advanced and you have ridden so far that we think you must be exhausted.'

The king replied, 'I would like to be in bed already, because I have great need of sleep.'

'My Lord,' they said, 'we have come to accompany you to your bed, since we have been commanded to do so.'

'Certainly,' replied the king.

So he got up straight away, and the girls went to the very

same room where Lancelot had once spent such a long time. In that room Lancelot had depicted the whole story of his love for Queen Guinevere. The girls put Arthur to bed there, and when he was asleep they left him and returned to their lady.

Morgan thought a great deal about King Arthur, because she intended him to know the whole truth about Lancelot and the queen, and yet she feared that if she told him everything and Lancelot heard that the king had found out from her, nothing in the world could guarantee that he would not kill her. That night she pondered over the question, whether to tell him or to remain silent; because if she told him she would be in danger of death should Lancelot find out, and if she kept the affair secret, she would never again have such a good opportunity of telling him as now. She kept thinking about this until she fell asleep.

In the morning, as soon as it was light, she arose and went to the king, greeted him very courteously, and said:

'My Lord, I beg you for a reward for all the services I have rendered you.'

'I shall grant you it,' said the king, 'if it is something in my power to give.'

'You can certainly give it to me,' she said, 'and do you know what it is? It is that you stay here today and tomorrow. You can be sure that if you were in the finest city you possess, you would not be better served or more at ease than here, because there is no wish you could express that would not be satisfied.'

And he said he would stay, because he had promised her her reward.

'My Lord,' she said, 'of all the houses in the world, you are in the one where people were most longing to see you; I can tell you that there is no woman anywhere who loves you more than I do, and so I should, unless human love did not exist.'

'My Lady,' said the king, 'who are you that you love me so much, as you say?'

'My Lord,' she said, 'I am the person closest to you in blood. My name is Morgan, and I am your sister. You ought to know me better than you do.'

He looked at her and recognized her, and jumped up from

the bed as joyful as it was possible to be. He told her that he was very happy about the adventure that God had granted him.

'You see, my sister,' said the king, 'I thought you were dead and had left this world; and since it has pleased God that I should find you alive and well, I shall take you back to Camelot when I leave here, and from now on you will live at court and will be a companion for my wife Queen Guinevere. I know she will be very happy and joyful when she hears the news about you.'

'Brother,' she said, 'do not ask that of me, because I swear to you that I shall never go to court, for when I leave here I shall most certainly go to the Isle of Avalon, which is the dwelling-place of the ladies who know all the magic in the world.'

The king dressed and sat down on his bed. Then he asked his sister to sit beside him, and he began to ask her how she was. She told him a part, and kept a part secret from him. They remained talking there until Prime.

[51] That day the weather was very fine; the sun had risen splendid and brilliant and its light penetrated all parts of the room, so that it was even brighter than before. They were alone, because they took pleasure in talking together, just the two of them. When they had asked each other many questions about their past lives, it happened that the king began looking around him and saw the pictures which Lancelot had painted long before, when he was a prisoner there. King Arthur knew his letters well enough to be able to make out the meaning of a text, and when he had seen the inscriptions with the pictures that explained their meaning, he began to read them. So he found out that the room was illustrated with all Lancelot's deeds of chivalry since he had been made a knight. Everything that Arthur saw he remembered from the news that had constantly been brought to court about Lancelot's chivalry, as soon as he had accomplished each of his acts of prowess.

[52] Thus the king began to read of Lancelot's deeds in the paintings he saw; and when he examined the paintings which related the meeting arranged by Galeholt,[4] he was completely astounded and taken aback. He looked again and said under his breath:

'In faith, if these inscriptions tell the truth, then Lancelot has dishonoured me through the queen, because I can see quite clearly that he has had an association with her. If it is as the writing says, it will be the cause of the greatest grief that I have ever suffered, since Lancelot could not possibly degrade me more than by dishonouring my wife.'

Then he said to Morgan:

'My sister, I beg you to tell me the truth about what I am going to ask you.'

She replied that she would be pleased to, if she could.

'Swear that you will,' said the king.

And she swore it.

'Now I am going to ask you,' he said, 'by the faith you owe me and have just pledged me, to tell me who painted these pictures, if you know the truth, and not to refuse for any reason.'

'Ah, my Lord,' said Morgan, 'what are you saying and what are you asking me? Certainly, if I told you the truth and the man who did the paintings found out, no one except God could guarantee that he would not kill me.'

'In God's name,' he said, 'you must tell me, and I promise you as a king that I shall never blame you for it.'

'My Lord,' she replied, 'will you not spare me from telling you for any reason?'

'Certainly not,' said the king. 'You must tell me.'

'In that case I shall tell you without lying about anything,' replied Morgan. 'It is true, though I do not know whether you know it yet, that Lancelot has loved Queen Guinevere since the first day that he received the order of chivalry, and it was for love of the queen that he performed all his acts of prowess when he was a new knight. You could have known this at the castle of the Douloureuse Garde⁵ when you first went there and could not enter because you were stopped at the river; each time you sent a knight he was unable to go inside. But as soon as Kay went, since he was one of the queen's knights, he was allowed in, and you did not notice this fact as well as some people did.'

'It is true,' said the king, 'that I did not notice it, but all the same it did happen exactly as you say. However, I do not know whether it was for love of the queen or of me.'

'My Lord,' she replied, 'there is more to come.'

'Tell me,' said the king.

'My Lord,' she said, 'he loved my lady the queen as much as any mortal man can ever love a lady; but he never revealed the fact himself or through anyone else. His love spurred him on to perform all the deeds of chivalry you see depicted here.

[53] 'For a long time he only languished, just like anyone who loves and is not loved in return, because he did not dare to reveal his love. Eventually he met 'Galeholt, the son of the Giantess, the day he bore black arms and won the tournament organized by the two of you, as you can see related in these pictures here. When he had made peace between you and Galeholt in such a way that all honour fell to you, and when Galeholt saw that Lancelot's strength was declining daily because he could not eat or drink, so deeply did he love the queen, he kept pressing him until in the end he admitted that he loved the queen and was dying for her. Galeholt begged him not to despair, because he would arrange matters so that Lancelot could have what he desired from the queen. And he did just as he promised; he implored the queen until she gave in to Lancelot, and, with a kiss, granted him her love.'

'You have told me enough,' said the king, 'because I can clearly see my shame and Lancelot's treachery; but tell me now who painted these pictures.'

'Indeed, my Lord,' she replied, 'Lancelot did them, and I shall tell you when. Do you remember two tournaments held at Camelot, when the companions of the Round Table said they would not go to a joust where Lancelot was on their side, because he always carried off the prize? And when Lancelot knew, he turned against them, making them leave the field and forcing them to retreat into the city of Camelot Do you remember that?'

'Yes,' replied the king. 'I can still see that tournament in my mind, because never in any place that I have been to have I seen a knight carry out so many feats of arms as he did that day. But why do you speak about that?'

'Because', she replied, 'when he left court on that occasion he was lost for more than a year and a half, and no one knew where he was.'

'Yes,' said the king, 'that is true.'

'In fact,' she said, 'I held him prisoner for two winters and a summer, and during that time he painted the pictures you can see here. I should still be keeping him in prison, and he would never have escaped all the days of his life, if it had not been for what he did, the greatest sorcery that a man ever carried out.'

'What was that?' asked the king.

'In faith,' she replied, 'he broke the bars of that window with his bare hands.'

And she showed him the bars, which she had had repaired since. The king said that it was not the work of a man, but of a devil.

He looked carefully at the paintings in the room, and he thought deeply about them. For a long time he did not say a word. After he had thought for some time, he said:

'Agravain told me about this the other day, but I did not believe him, as I thought he was lying. However, what I have seen here makes me far more certain than I was before. For that reason I can tell you that I shall never be satisfied until I know the whole truth. If it is as these pictures witness, that Lancelot has brought me such great shame as to dishonour me through my wife, I shall never rest until they are caught together. Then, if I do not inflict such justice on them as will be spoken of for evermore, I promise that I shall never again wear a crown.'

'Indeed,' said Morgan, 'if you did not punish them, God and the whole world should certainly hold you in shame, because no true king or true man can tolerate being dishonoured in this way.'

The king and his sister spoke a great deal about the matter that morning and Morgan kept urging him to avenge his shame without delay; and he promised her as a king that he would do so with such vigour that it would always be remembered, if he could manage to catch them together.

'It will not be long', said Morgan, 'before they are caught together, if you go about it carefully.'

'I shall make sure', said the king, 'that if one loves the other adulterously as you say, I shall have them caught together before the end of the month, if Lancelot should return to court by then.'

[54] That day the king remained with his sister, and the next day and the whole week; she hated Lancelot more than any other man because she knew the queen loved him. All the time the king was with her she never stopped urging him to avenge his shame when he returned to Camelot, if he had the opportunity.

'My sister,' said the king, 'you do not need to ask me, because not for half my kingdom would I fail to do what I have resolved.'

The king stayed there the whole week, since the place was beautiful and pleasant, and full of game which he spent all his energy hunting. But now the story stops telling of him and Morgan, except to say that he did not allow anyone to enter his room while he was there, save only Morgan, because of the paintings which made his shame so evident, and he did not want anyone else apart from himself to know the truth, because he feared the dishonour too much, and feared also that the news would spread. Now the story stops telling of him and returns to Lancelot and Bors and their companions.

[55] Here the story tells that Bors and Sir Gawain and the other companions stayed with Lancelot until he had completely recovered and regained all the strength he had had before. As soon as he felt he was better and could bear arms without danger, he said to his doctor:

'Do you not think that I can now do what I like with my body without doing any harm to the wound I have had so long?'

'I can tell you truthfully,' said the good man, 'that you are completely cured and that you do not need to worry any more about any illness you have had.'

'I am pleased at that news,' replied Lancelot, 'because now I can go when I like.'

[56] The companions celebrated that day very joyfully. In the evening Lancelot told the lady of the house that he would be leaving the next morning, and he thanked her for the fine company and the hospitality he had been given in her house. Then he made such a great gift of money to her and to the man who had cured his wound that they were able to live comfortably for all the days of their lives. That same day the two brothers from Escalot begged Lancelot for permission to join his company as knights of his banner, because they did not wish to leave him for another lord. He was pleased to receive them, because they were both fine and noble knights, and he said:

'My Lords, I am pleased to accept you as my companions, but I shall often go very far from you, and you will not hear any news of me until I return.'

'My Lord,' they replied, 'that does not matter, provided we can be associated with you and you accept us as your knights.'

He said he would willingly do that, and that he would give them lands and inheritances in the kingdom of Banoic or in the kingdom of Gaunes. And so they became his knights.

[57] That same day the girl who was the sister of the two brothers from Escalot came to Lancelot and said:

'My Lord, you are going, and it is doubtful whether you will come back; and because no messenger telling of his lord's need should be believed as well as his lord himself, I shall tell you of my need, which is very great. I want you to know that I am on the way to death if I am not turned away from it by you.'

'To death?' asked Lancelot. 'You certainly will not die if there is any way I can help you.'

Then the girl began crying bitterly, and said to Lancelot:

'Indeed, my Lord, I can say that it is a pity I ever saw you.'

'Why?' asked Lancelot. 'Tell me.'

'My Lord,' she replied, 'as soon as I saw you, I loved you more than it is possible for a woman's heart to love a man, because since then I have not been able to eat or drink, rest or sleep, but have been tormented in my thoughts all the time, and have suffered every pain and every grief by night and by day.'

'It was madness,' said Lancelot, 'to expect so much of me, especially since I told you that my heart was not my own, and that if I could have done as I wished with it, I should have considered myself fortunate for a girl like you to deign to love me. After I had told you that, you should not have expected anything from me, because you ought to have known what I meant – that I would not love you or any other woman, except the one with whom I have left my heart.'

'Ah! my Lord,' said the girl, 'shall I not receive any other help from you in my misfortune?'

'Certainly not,' replied Lancelot, 'because I cannot do anything about it even if it is a matter of life and death.'

'My Lord,' she said, 'I am sorry you have said that. You can be sure that I have arrived at death's door, and my heart will be separated from its love for you through death. And that will be the reward for the good company my brother has been to you ever since you arrived in this part of the country.'

Then the girl left him and took to her bed. The result was that she never got up again, but died, as the story will relate.

Lancelot, who was most upset and angry at what he had heard the girl say, was unusually quiet and reserved that night. All his companions were surprised at this, because they were not accustomed to seeing him so sad.

[58] That evening Bors sent the knight who had cured Lancelot to the King of North Wales, asking him to be sure to be grateful to him, because he had done him a great service. The next day, as soon as it was light, Lancelot left with all his company and commended the lady of the house to God.

When they had got under way, they rode day after day until they came to the city of Camelot and dismounted in the courtyard of the principal palace. When Lancelot entered, the queen was at the windows, and as soon as she saw him she left the window at which she was leaning and went into her room. When Sir Gawain had dismounted, he went straight away to the queen's room and found her sitting on her bed; her looks were those of an angry woman. Sir Gawain greeted her, and she stood up as he came and welcomed him.

'My Lady,' he said, 'we have brought you Lancelot del Lac, who has been absent from this part of the country for a long time.'

She replied that she could not speak to him then, because she felt too unwell.

Sir Gawain left her room and returned to his companions, saying:

'My Lords, I have to tell you that the queen is unwell; we cannot speak to her. But let us rest here until the king comes. If we are bored we can go hunting, as there are plenty of forests near here.'

And they all agreed to this.

[59] That night Bors spoke to the queen and asked her what was wrong with her.

'I am not ill at all,' she said, 'but I have no wish to enter that hall while Lancelot is there, because I have not eyes with which to see him, or a heart that would allow me to speak to him.'

'What, my Lady,' said Bors, 'do you then hate him so much?'

'Yes, indeed,' she replied. 'At the moment there is nothing in this world I hate as much as I hate him, nor have I ever in my life loved him as much as I hate him now.'

'My Lady,' said Bors, 'that is a great pity for us and all our lineage. It grieves me that things have turned out like this, for many will suffer without deserving it. Moreover Destiny arranged the love between you, as I saw it arranged, in such a way that it could only be to our disadvantage. I know that my lord cousin, who is the noblest and most handsome man in the world, has every confidence at present that he can surpass anyone else, if one thing does not prevent him, and that is your anger. Beyond all doubt this would turn him away from all worthy adventures, because if he knew what you have said here, I do not think I should be able to reach him before he killed himself. I think it is a great pity that he, the finest of the best, loves you so deeply, while you hate him.'

'If I hate him mortally,' said the queen, 'he has deserved it.'

'My Lady,' said Bors, 'what can I say? I have certainly never

77

seen any noble man that loved a woman for a long time, who
was not finally held to be dishonoured, and if you reflect on the
ancient deeds of the Jews and the Saracens, you could learn
about many who history affirms were dishonoured by a
woman. Consider the story of King David: you will read that
he had a son, the most beautiful creature that God ever made,
who waged war against his father under the instigation of a
woman, and died a shameful death. So you can see that the
most handsome of the Jews died because of a woman. Then
you can see in the same story that Solomon, to whom God gave
wisdom beyond the comprehension of a mortal mind, and also
knowledge, denied God for a woman and was dishonoured and
deceived. Samson, who was the strongest man in the world,
died through a woman. Noble Hector and Achilles, who in
arms and chivalry surpassed all other knights in ancient times,
were both killed, and more than a hundred thousand with them,
all because of one woman whom Paris took by force in Greece.
In our time too, it is less than five years since the death of
Tristan, the nephew of King Mark, who loved fair Yseut so
faithfully that he never did anything to harm her in all his life.
What more can I say? No man ever became deeply involved in
love who did not die as a result. I can tell you that you would
be doing something worse than all the other women, because
you would be destroying in the body of a single knight all the
virtues through which a man can rise in worldly honour and
be called noble – I mean beauty and prowess, valour and
chivalry, and gentility. My Lady, you can maintain all these
virtues in my lord so perfectly that none are lost, because you
know he is the most handsome man in the world, and the
noblest, and the boldest and finest knight we know; and moreover he comes from such outstanding lineage on both his
father's and his mother's sides that no man of higher birth is
known in the world. But just as he is now clothed and covered
in all good virtues, in the same way you would strip and de-
prive him of them. One could say truthfully that you would be
removing the sun from among the stars, that is to say the
flower of the world's knights from King Arthur's men. You can
see quite clearly, my Lady, that you would be damaging this

kingdom and many others much more than one lady ever did through one knight. That is the great power for good we expect from your love.'

The queen replied to these words and said to Bors:

'If what you say were to happen now, no one would stand to lose as much as I should, because I would lose body and soul. Now leave me in peace, because for the present moment you will not receive any other reply from me.'

'My Lady,' said Bors, 'I tell you that you will never hear me mention the matter again, unless you speak of it first.'

Then Bors left the queen and went up to Lancelot; and he said to him secretly, when he had drawn him some way away from the others:

'My Lord, I strongly recommend we should leave here, because I do not think we are welcome.'

'Why?' asked Lancelot.

'My Lord, my Lord,' said Bors, 'my lady the queen has just forbidden you and me and all those who come in your name to enter her lodge.'

'Why?' asked Lancelot. 'Do you know?'

'Yes, I certainly do know,' he replied, 'and I shall tell you when we are away from here.'

'Let us mount, then,' said Lancelot, 'and you will tell me what the reason is, because I am impatient to know.'

[60] Then Lancelot came to Sir Gawain and said:

'My Lord, we must depart, my companions and I, as I have to see to some affairs I cannot leave. When you see my lord the king, greet him from me, and tell him I shall come back as soon as I can.'

'In God's name,' said Sir Gawain, 'you cannot leave here in that way – you must wait for my lord the king.'

But Lancelot said that he would not. Then he mounted with his companions, and Sir Gawain accompanied him for some time. Sir Gawain said:

'My Lord, in this field at Camelot there will soon be a great and marvellous tournament. Be sure you are there, because there will be few knights from the kingdom of Logres who will not be present.'

Lancelot said he would come, if it was possible for him to do so.

So they parted, and Sir Gawain returned to Camelot, angry because Lancelot had left so soon. Lancelot rode until he arrived at the forest of Camelot, and when they had entered it, he asked Bors to tell him why the queen was angry with him.

'My Lord,' he said, 'I shall tell you.'

Then he began to tell him about the sleeve he wore at the tournament at Winchester, 'and it is because of that that the queen is very angry and says she will never forgive you.'

When Bors had told him the whole story, Lancelot stopped and began to cry very bitterly, and no one could get a word out of him. After he had been like this for quite some time, he replied:

'Ah, Love! those are the rewards for serving you; because a man who offers himself completely to you cannot escape with less than death, and such is the price you pay to someone who loves you faithfully. Ah! Bors, my cousin, you who know my heart as well as I do, and know for certain that I would not be unfaithful to my lady for anything in the world, why did you not defend me before her?'

'My Lord,' said Bors, 'I did everything in my power, but she would not agree with anything I said.'

'Now advise me, then,' said Lancelot, 'and tell me what I can do, because if I cannot find my peace with her, I shall not survive very long. If she had forgiven me for causing her unhappiness and anger, I would have gone joyfully, but in the state in which I am at present, since I have her anger and her ill-feelings and have not leave to speak to her, I do not think I can live very long, because my grief and anger will pierce my heart. For that reason I am asking you, my friend, to advise me, because I do not see what I can do for myself after what you have just said.'

'My Lord,' said Bors, 'if you can tolerate not being near her or seeing her, I can tell you truthfully that you will not see a month pass, if she does not see you or receive any news about you, without her being even more anxious to have you in her company than you ever were to be with her, and desiring you more; you can be sure that she will send someone to find you, whether you are near or far. That is why my advice is that you should spend your time enjoying yourself in this part of the country, attending all the tournaments that you hear announced. You have with you your fine and noble retinue, and a good many of your kinsmen; you should be pleased about this, because they will accompany you, if you wish, anywhere you want to go.'

He said that he agreed with what Bors advised, but that he did not need any companions. He wished to go alone except only for a squire he would take with him until he decided to dismiss him.

'But you, Bors,' he said, 'you will go away until you see me or a messenger I send to look for you.'

'My Lord,' said Bors, 'I am very sorry that you are leaving us like this and going off through this part of the country with such little company, because, if any misfortune should befall you tomorrow, how should we know?'

'Do not worry,' he replied, 'for He who up till now has permitted me to be victorious wherever I have been will not allow by His grace any harm to befall me wherever I am; and if anything did happen to me, you would know sooner than anyone else, be sure of that.'

[61] Then Lancelot went back to his company, who were waiting for him in the middle of the field. He told them he had to go away to see to something and that he could not take many companions with him. He took a squire called Hanguis and told him to follow him; Hanguis said he would willingly go with him, and was delighted.

So in that way he left his close friends, and they said to him:

'My Lord, make quite sure you are at the tournament at Camelot, and so armed that we can all recognize you.'

He replied that he would be there, if he were not prevented by some great obstacle. Then he called Bors and said:

'If I am at the tournament, I shall bear white arms without any other colours, and in that way you will be able to recognize me.'

Then they separated and commended each other to God. But now the story stops telling about them all and returns to King Arthur.

*

[62] Now the story relates that after the king had stayed with his sister Morgan for as long as he wished, he left with a great company of people. When he was out of the forest, he rode until he came to Camelot. On arriving, and finding out that Lancelot had spent only one day at court, he did not know what to think, because he was sure that if Lancelot loved the queen adulterously as had been alleged, he could not be absent from the court and turn his back on it for as long as he did. This was a thing which went a long way to set the king's mind at rest, and which led him to discount what he had heard his sister Morgan say. However, there was never again a time that he was not more suspicious of the queen than he had been before, because of what he had learnt.

The day after the king arrived at Camelot, it happened that at dinner time Sir Gawain was eating at the queen's table, and many other knights were there also. In a room beside the hall there was a knight called Avarlan who mortally hated Sir Gawain, and had a poisoned fruit with which he hoped to kill him. So he decided that if he sent it to the queen, she would sooner give it to Sir Gawain than to anyone else; and if he ate it, he would die straight away.

The queen took the fruit, because she was not on her guard against treachery, and she gave it to a knight who was a companion of the Round Table, called Gaheris de Karaheu. Gaheris, who had a very great affection for the queen, accepted it through love for her and started eating it. As soon as he had swallowed some of it, he immediately fell dead before the eyes of the queen and all those who were at table. They all jumped up straight away and were dumbfounded by what had happened. When the queen saw the knight lying dead before her, she was so distressed by this misadventure that she could not decide what to do, because so many noble men had seen what

had happened that she could not deny it. The news was
to the king by a knight who had been eating in the qu
room.

'My Lord,' he said, 'something extraordinary has just ha
pened in there; my lady the queen has killed a knight through
the greatest misdeed in the world. He was a companion of the
Round Table and the brother of Mador de la Porte.'

And he related what had happened. The king made a sign of
the cross out of surprise, and jumped up from the table to see
whether what he had been told was true or not; so did all the
others who were in the hall. When the king came to the room
and found the dead knight, he said that it was a real misfortune
and that the queen had committed a great crime if she had
done it intentionally.

'In fact,' said someone there, 'she has deserved death if she
really knew that the fruit of which the knight has died was
poisoned.'

The queen did not know what to say, so stunned was she by
the unfortunate event, except that she replied:

'May God help me, I regret what has happened a hundred
times more than I am glad, and had I thought that the fruit I
gave him was treacherous, I would not have given it to him
for half the world.'

'My Lady,' said the king, 'however you gave it to him, the
deed is wicked and criminal, and I very much fear that you
acted out of greater anger than you admit.'

Then the king said to all those who were round the body:

'My Lords, this knight is dead, unfortunately; now see that
you treat his body with as great honour as should be paid to
such a noble man. For indeed he was a noble man and one of
the best knights at my court, and in all my life I have never
seen a more loyal knight than him. And I regret his death
much more than many people might think.'

Then the king left the room and went back to the main
palace and made the sign of the cross over and over again out
of surprise at the knight's tragic death. The queen left after the
king, and went into a meadow with a great company of ladies

and girls, and as soon as she arrived there, she began to grieve bitterly, and said that God had forgotten her when through such ill-fortune she killed a man as noble as him.

'And, may God help me,' she said, 'when I gave him the fruit to eat just now I did it with the best of intentions.'

[63] The queen was very sad about what had happened, and her ladies enshrouded the body as well and as richly as they could. They honoured it as it was right to honour the body of a good man, and the next day it was buried at the entrance of St Stephen's Cathedral in Camelot. And, when as beautiful and as rich a tomb as could be found in the country had been placed there, the companions of the Round Table put on it, by common consent, an inscription which read, 'HERE LIES GAHERIS LE BLANC OF KARAHEU, THE BROTHER OF MADOR DE LA PORTE, WHOM THE QUEEN KILLED WITH POISON'. The inscription accused the queen of the knight's death. King Arthur was very sad, and so were all those who were with him; in fact they were so melancholy that they spoke very little of the matter until the tournament.

But now the story stops telling of King Arthur and his company, and returns to Lancelot, to relate the event which prevented him from going to the tournament held in the meadow at Camelot.

*

[64] Here the story recounts that when Lancelot had left Bors and his brother Hector, he rode up and down in the forest of Camelot, and stayed each night with a hermit who had once confessed him. The hermit treated Lancelot as honourably as he could. Three days before the tournament Lancelot called his squire and said:

'Go to Camelot and bring me a white shield with three diagonal red bands and a white caparison; I have borne those arms so often that if Bors comes to the tournament he will easily be able to recognize me. I am doing it for him rather than for anyone else, because I certainly do not want him to wound me, or to wound him myself.'

The squire left Lancelot to go to the city to fetch the arms he described, and Lancelot went out for a ride in the forest, unarmed except for his sword. That day it was very warm and because of the heat Lancelot dismounted from his horse, took off its saddle and reins, and tied it to an oak-tree close by. When he had done this he went to lie beside a spring and fell asleep straight away because the place was cool and fresh whereas until then he had been very hot.

As it happened, the king's huntsmen were hunting a large stag and had pursued it in the forest. It came to the fountain to quench its thirst, because it had been chased one way and another for some time. When it had arrived at the fountain, an archer riding a large horse a long way ahead of the others came close to the stag and aimed at it, in order to strike it in the middle of its breast; but it happened that he missed the stag, as it jumped forward a little. However, the shot was not a complete failure, because it struck Lancelot so violently in the left thigh that the blade went right through it, as did also part of the shaft. When Lancelot felt that he was wounded, he jumped up in great pain and distress, and seeing the huntsman coming towards the stag as fast as he could drive his horse, he cried:

'Scoundrel, worthless fool, what harm have I done you that you should injure me while I am asleep? You will regret it, I can tell you, and you will certainly be sorry that you happened to come this way.'

Then Lancelot drew his sword and tried to attack him, wounded as he was. When the other man saw him coming and knew it was Lancelot, he turned in flight as fast as he could, and when he met his companions, he said:

'My Lords, do not go any further if you do not wish to die, because Sir Lancelot is at that spring and I wounded him with an arrow when I tried to shoot the stag; I fear that I may have injured him mortally and that he may be following me.'

[65] When the others heard this, they said to their companion:

'You have acted very badly, because if he is hurt and the king finds out, we shall be dishonoured and punished; and if the king himself does not act, no one except God could protect us against his kinsmen when they know what has befallen him here.'

Then they turned and fled through the forest.

Lancelot, who had remained, badly wounded, by the spring, painfully drew the arrow from his thigh and saw that the wound was big and deep, because the blade of the arrow was very broad. So he cut a strip off his tunic to bind the wound, which was bleeding profusely; and when he had staunched it as well as he could, he went to his horse and put on its saddle and reins. Then he mounted in great pain, and with considerable difficulty arrived back at the hermitage where he had recently been staying since he had left Bors. When the hermit saw him so badly injured, he was astounded, and asked him who had done it.

'I do not know,' he replied, 'who the blackguards are that have done this to me, but I know they are from the retinue of my lord King Arthur.'

Then he told him how he had been wounded and in what circumstances.

'Certainly, my Lord,' said the hermit, 'that was sheer misfortune.'

'I do not care so much for myself,' said Lancelot, 'as for the fact that I shall not be able to go to the tournament at Camelot; and in the same way I was prevented from going to the other one at Tanebourc recently, because of another wound I had at that time. That is the thing that most dismays me and that I regret most – because I was not at the other tournament. I particularly wanted to be at this one.'

'Since it has happened like this,' said the hermit, 'you will have to put up with it, because if you went this time, you would not do anything that would be to your honour. So you had better stay here, if you take my advice.'

And he said that he would indeed stay, whether he wished to or not, because he had no choice.

Thus Lancelot remained there because of the circumstance of his wound. He was very miserable and felt that he would die of anger. In the evening, when his squire came back and found him so badly injured, he was astounded. Lancelot told him to put down the shield and the caparison he had brought, and said that he was now forced to stay there. And he was there for a whole fortnight before he could ride as he wished.

Now the story stops telling about him and returns to King Arthur.

◆

[66] In this part the story tells that King Arthur stayed at Camelot after Gaheris' death until the tournament; and on the stated day you could have seen twenty thousand men in the field at Camelot, on one side and on the other, of such quality that there was not one who was not held to be a fine and noble knight. Once they had assembled, you could have seen a great many knights knocked down if you had been there. On that day Bors of Gaunes was the outstanding knight, and on each side every man said that Bors had surpassed him.

The king, who knew him well, went up to him and said:

'Bors, I am taking you with me; you must come in and stay with us, and you will remain in our company as long as you wish.'

'I cannot possibly come,' replied Bors, 'because my lord cousin is not here; if he were, I would willingly stay as long as it pleased him to remain with you, and, may God help me, if I had not expected to find him at this tournament I should not have come, because he told me, when he left me recently, that he would be here without fail unless some obstacle forcibly prevented him from coming.'

'You will remain with me,' said the king, 'and wait till he returns to court.'

'My Lord,' said Bors, 'I should stay in vain, because I do not think you will see him for some time.'

'Why will he not come, then?' asked the king. 'Is he angry with us?'

'My Lord,' replied Bors, 'you will not find out any more from me; ask someone else if you want to know the truth.'

'If I knew anyone at court who would tell me it, I would ask them,' said the king, 'but because I know no one, I must be patient and wait for the return of the man about whom I am asking you.'

Then Bors left the king, and went with his brother and Hector and his companions. Sir Gawain accompanied them for some distance and said to Bors:

'I am very surprised that Lancelot was not at this tournament.'

'Indeed,' said Bors, 'I am sure he is ill or imprisoned somewhere, because if he were free to do so I know he would have come.'

Then they took leave of each other, and Bors went the way he expected to find the King of North Wales, saying to his brother and Hector:

'I am only worried that my lord is grieving for the queen, who is angry with him. Cursed be the hour that their love ever began, because I fear that many things may yet become even worse as a result.'

'Indeed,' said Hector, 'if ever I was right about anything, you are going to see the greatest war of your life take place between our kinsmen and King Arthur, and all as a result of the same thing.'

Thus Lancelot was a subject of conversation among those who loved him most and who were the most concerned about him.

[67] When Sir Gawain had left them he rode until he came to Camelot; and after he had dismounted and gone up to the palace, he said to the king:

'My Lord, you can be quite certain Lancelot is ill, because he did not come to the tournament; at the moment there is nothing I would like to know as much as how he is, because I am wondering if he is wounded or whether he has stayed behind because of some other kind of illness.'

'Indeed,' said the king, 'if he is unwell, I am sorry he is not here, because his presence here and that of his companions enhances my court so much that no one can estimate its true value.'

King Arthur spoke in this way about Lancelot and King Ban's

kinsmen, and he remained there with a great company of knights.

On the third day after the tournament it happened that Mador de la Porte arrived at court. No one there was bold enough to tell him about his brother, because they all realized he was such a valiant knight that, as soon as he heard the truth, he would certainly not let anything prevent him from avenging his brother to the best of his ability. The next day he happened to go to the cathedral in Camelot, and when he saw the tomb which had recently been placed there, he thought it must belong to one of the companions of the Round Table, and he went over to it to see whose it was. When he saw the inscription that read, 'HERE LIES GAHERIS OF KARAHEU, THE BROTHER OF MADOR DE LA PORTE, WHOM THE QUEEN KILLED WITH POISON', he was astounded and aghast, and he could not really believe it was true. Then he looked behind him and saw a Scottish knight who was a companion of the Round Table. He immediately called him and begged him by the fidelity he owed him to answer truthfully what he was going to ask him.

'Mador,' said the knight, 'I know what you are going to ask me. You want me to say whether it is true that the queen killed your brother. In fact it is just as the inscription says.'

'Indeed,' said Mador, 'that is a great tragedy, because my brother was very noble, and I loved him dearly as one brother should another. I shall seek to avenge him as best I can.'

Mador grieved deeply for his brother, and remained there till high mass had been sung. When he knew that the king was seated at table, he left his brother's tomb in tears and went into the hall up to him, speaking so loud that all those present could hear him, and beginning his speech thus:

'King Arthur, if you uphold what is right as a king should, maintain justice in your court so that if anyone wishes to accuse me I shall act as you please according to it, and if I wish to accuse anyone present, I shall be given justice as the court will ensure.'

The king replied that he could not deny him that, and that

whatever Mador might say, he would see that justice was done to the best of his ability.

'My Lord,' said Mador, 'I have been your knight for fifteen years and I hold fiefs from you; now I shall return you your homage and your land, because I no longer wish to hold any fief from you.'

Then he went forward and ritually divested himself of all the land he held from the king, and after he had done this, he said:

'My Lord, now I request you as a king to grant me justice concerning the queen who killed my brother; if she wishes to deny and disavow that she has acted treacherously and dishonourably, I shall be pleased to prove my case against the finest knight she wishes to represent her.'

When he had said this there was a great noise in the court and many said among themselves:

'The queen is in a sorry plight now, because she will not find anyone to fight against Mador; everyone knows quite certainly that she killed the knight as she has been accused.'

The king was deeply distressed about the accusation, because he could not deny the knight justice, and justice would obviously call for the queen's death. He summoned her to come before him to reply to Mador's charge, and she came full of sadness and anger, because she was well aware that she would not find a knight to fight for her, as they all knew that she had quite definitely killed Gaheris.

The tables were removed, and a great number of knights and barons were present. The queen came forward with her head bowed, and she clearly looked distressed. She was escorted on one side by Sir Gawain and on the other by Gaheriet, the most outstanding in arms of all Arthur's kinsmen except only Sir Gawain. When she was standing before the king, he said:

'My Lady, this knight is accusing you of the death of his brother and says that you killed him treacherously.'

She lifted her head and asked:

'Where is this knight?'

Mador rushed forward and said:

'Here I am.'

'What?' she asked. 'Are you saying that I killed your brother treacherously and knowingly?'

'I am saying', he replied, 'that you killed him wickedly and faithlessly, and if there were present here a knight bold enough to be prepared to defend you against me in battle, I should be ready to kill or defeat him tonight or tomorrow or any day proposed by the people in this court.'

[68]   When the queen saw that he was boldly putting himself forward to prove her treachery against the very finest knight present, she began to look around her to see if anyone would offer to defend her against the accusation. When she saw that no one there was coming forward, but that they were all looking down and listening, she was so distressed and confused that she did not know what would become of her, or what she should say or do. Nevertheless, despite all her grief and fear, she replied:

'My Lord, I beg you to treat me with justice according to the procedure in your court.'

'My Lady,' said the king, 'the procedure in my court is such that, if you admitted the deed of which you are accused, you would be sentenced to death; but we certainly cannot deny you forty days' grace so that you may decide what to do, and to see whether within that time you can find a knight who would fight a duel for you and defend you against the accusation.'

'My Lord,' said the queen, 'can I not expect any other attitude from you?'

'No, my Lady,' said the king, 'because I should not wish to act unjustly for you or for anyone else.'

'My Lord,' she replied, 'I shall accept the forty days' grace, and if it pleases God, I shall find a knight during that time who will fight for me; if I have not found one by the fortieth day, do with me as you please.'

The king granted her respite, and when Mador saw that the matter had so turned out, he asked the king:

'My Lord, are you being just to me in granting the queen so much grace?'

'Yes, quite certainly,' replied the king.

'In that case I shall go,' he said, 'and I shall be back on that day, if God preserves me from death and imprisonment.'

'I can tell you,' said the king, 'if you are not ready to do then what you have offered, you will never be listened to again.'

He replied that he would be there, if death did not prevent him, 'because no prison could stop me from seeing to this affair.'

[69] So Mador left the court and went away in such great grief for his brother that all who saw him were astounded. The queen remained there sad and perplexed, because she knew she would never find any knight prepared to fight for her except one of King Ban's kinsmen, and these would not fail her for any reason if they were present. However, she had so firmly sent them away and estranged them that she felt guilty about what she had done. Now she repented it so bitterly that there was nothing in the world, short of dishonouring herself, that she would not have done to enable them to be present once again as they had been not long before.

[70] The day after the accusation was made, it happened about noon that a boat decked in very rich silk cloth arrived beneath the tower at Camelot. The king had dined with a great company of knights, and was at the windows of the hall, looking down the river. He was very pensive and sad because of the queen; he was well aware she would receive no help from the knights present there, since they had all seen clearly that she had given Gaheris the fruit from which he died, and as they all knew it openly, there was no one who dared to risk himself against such odds. When the king, pondering over this, saw the rich and beautiful boat arrive, he pointed it out to Sir Gawain and said:

'Gawain, that is the most splendid boat I have ever seen. Let us go and see what is inside.'

'Let us go,' said Sir Gawain.

Then they went down from the palace, and when they had reached the river, they saw the boat so finely apparelled that they were both astounded.

'In faith,' said Sir Gawain, 'if that boat is as beautiful inside as it is outside, it would be a marvel; it is almost as if adventures were beginning again.'

'I was about to say the same thing,' said the king.

The boat was covered like a vault, and Sir Gawain lifted up a corner of the cloth and said to the king:

'My Lord, let us go aboard, and we shall see what is there.'

So the king jumped aboard straight away, and then Sir Gawain, and when they were inside, they found a beautiful bed in the middle of the boat, adorned with all the riches that can adorn a bed, and in it lay a girl who was not long dead. To judge from how she still looked, she must have been very beautiful.

Then Sir Gawain said to the king:

'Ah! my Lord, do you not think Death was wicked and horrible, to enter the body of such a beautiful girl as she was not long ago?'

'Yes,' said the king, 'I think this was a girl of great beauty, and it is a pity that she died so young. Because of the great beauty I see in her, I should very much like to know who she was and who her parents were.'

They looked at her for some time, and when Sir Gawain had considered her closely, he recognized her as the beautiful girl whom he had begged for her love, but who had said that she would never love anyone but Lancelot. Then he said to the king:

'My Lord, I know who this girl was.'

'And who was she?' asked the king. 'Tell me.'

'Certainly, my Lord,' said Sir Gawain. 'Do you remember the beautiful girl about whom I spoke to you the other day, the one I said Lancelot loved?'

'Yes,' said the king, 'I remember it well; you explained that you had sought her love, but that she had completely rejected you.'

'My Lord,' said Sir Gawain, 'this girl is the one we were speaking of.'

'That certainly makes me very sad,' said the king. 'I should very much like to know the circumstances of her death, because I think she died of grief.'

[71]   While they were speaking, Sir Gawain looked beside the girl and saw a very rich purse hanging from her belt, which did not seem to be empty. He took it, opened it straight away, and took out a letter which he handed to the king. The king started reading it and found that it said as follows:

'To all the knights of the Round Table, greetings from the girl from Escalot. I will address my complaint to all of you, not because you could ever put it right, but because I know you to be the noblest and most joyous people in the world. I am telling you quite plainly that I came to my end through loving faithfully. If you ask for whom I suffered the pains of death, I shall reply that I died for the noblest man in the world, and also the wickedest: Lancelot del Lac. He is the wickedest as far as I know because however much I begged him with tears and weeping he refused to have mercy on me, and I took it so much to heart that as a result I died from loving faithfully.'

This was what was in the letter, and when the king had read it to Sir Gawain, he said:

'Indeed, young woman, you can truly say that the man you died for is the wickedest and most valiant in the world, because the wicked way he has treated you is so terrible that everyone ought to blame him for it. Certainly, I, who am a king and should not do anything unjust, would not have allowed you to die for the finest castle I possess.'

'My Lord,' said Sir Gawain, 'now you can see that I was maligning him when I said the other day that he was staying with a lady or a girl he loved, and you were right when you said he would not deign to degrade his heart by loving someone so low-born.'

'Now tell me,' said the king, 'what we should do with this girl, because I do not know what is best; she was a virtuous woman, and one of the most beautiful girls in the world. Let us pay her the great honour of burying her in the Cathedral of Camelot, and put on her tomb an inscription which tells the truth about her death, so that our descendants may remember her.'

Sir Gawain said he agreed with all this.

While they were looking at the letter and the girl, and were lamenting her misfortune, the barons had come down from the palace to the foot of the tower to see what there was in the boat. The king ordered the boat to be uncovered and the girl to be taken out and carried up to the palace; many people came to see her. The king began telling Sir Yvain and Gaheriet the girl's story, and how she died because Lancelot would not grant her his love. They told the others, who were very eager to hear the truth, and the news spread so far one way and another that the queen heard all the details about what had happened. Sir Gawain said to her:

'My Lady, my Lady, now I know I was not telling the truth about Sir Lancelot, when I told you he loved the girl from Escalot and that he was staying with her; because without doubt if he had loved her as much as I suggested, she would not now be dead, but Lancelot would have granted her all she sought from him.'

'My Lord,' she replied, 'many good men are maligned, and it is a pity because they often suffer more as a result than is supposed.'

[72] Then Sir Gawain left the queen, and she was even more miserable than before, calling herself an unhappy woman, wretched and lacking all sense, and saying to herself:

'You miserable creature, how did you dare to think that Lancelot could have been so inconstant as to love another woman than you? Why have you so betrayed and deceived yourself? Do you not see that all the people in this court have failed you and left you in such great danger that you will not escape alive unless you find someone to defend you against Mador? You have failed everyone here, so that no one will help you, because they all know that you are in the wrong and Mador in the right, and for this reason they are all abandoning you and allowing you to be led basely to your death. Nevertheless, despite the blame attached to you, if your lover were here, the most faithful of all, who has already rescued you from death in the past, I know he would deliver you from this danger that threatens you.

'Ah! God,' she exclaimed, 'why does he not know the distress now affecting my heart, for my own sake and for his?

Ah! God, he will not know in time, and I shall have to die shamefully. That will make him suffer so much that he will die of grief, as soon as he has heard that I have passed away from this world, because no man has ever loved a woman as much or as loyally as he has loved me.'

[73] The queen lamented in this way and grieved, and blamed and rebuked herself for what she had done, because she ought to have loved and held dear above all others the man she rejected and sent far away from her.

The king had the girl buried in the Cathedral of Camelot, and commanded a very rich and beautiful tomb to be placed over her grave, with an inscription reading: 'HERE LIES THE GIRL FROM ESCALOT, WHO DIED FOR LOVE OF LANCE-LOT'. This was very richly done in letters of gold and azure.

But now the story stops telling of King Arthur and the queen, and returns to Lancelot.

*

[74] The story relates now that Lancelot remained with the hermit until he had more or less recovered from the injury caused by the huntsman. One day after Terce he mounted his horse, because he wished to go for a ride in the forest. He left the hermitage and started along a narrow path. He had not ridden very far when he found a very beautiful spring beneath two trees, and beside the spring was lying an unarmed knight: he had put down his arms beside him and tied his horse to a tree. When Lancelot saw the knight asleep, he thought he would not wake him but would let him rest, and when he awoke, talk to him and ask him who he was. So he dismounted, tied up his horse fairly close to the other, and lay down on the other side of the spring.

It was not long before the other knight was awakened by the noise of the horses fighting, and when he saw Lancelot before him, he was very curious to know what adventure had brought him there. They sat up and greeted each other, and asked each other who they were. Lancelot did not want to reveal who he was when he saw the other man did not recognize him, but replied that he was a knight from the kingdom of Gaunes.

'And I am from the kingdom of Logres,' said the other.

'Where are you from?' asked Lancelot.

'I have come from Camelot,' he replied, 'where I left King Arthur with a great company of people, but I can tell you that more of them are angry than joyful because of an adventure which took place there recently, and it happened to the queen herself.'

'My lady the queen?' asked Lancelot. 'For God's sake tell me what it was, because I should very much like to know.'

'I shall tell you,' said the knight. 'Not long ago the queen was eating in her room together with a great company of ladies and knights, and I myself was dining with her that day. After we had had the first course, a boy came to her room bringing a fruit which he presented to the queen. She gave it to a knight to eat, and he died as soon as he had put it in his mouth. There was a great shout and everyone came to see what had happened so unexpectedly. When they saw the knight dead, there were many who blamed the queen for it. They buried the body and said no more about the subject to her.

'The other week it happened that Mador de la Porte, the knight's brother, came to court, and when he had seen his brother's tomb and knew for certain that he had died because of the queen, he went before the king and accused the queen of treachery. The queen looked all around her to see if there were any knights present who would come forward to defend her, but there was none so bold as to be prepared to throw down the gage of battle. The king gave the queen forty days' grace, on the condition that, if by the fortieth day she had not found anyone prepared to accept Mador's challenge, she would be sentenced to death. That is the reason why people at court are so distressed, because she certainly will not find a knight prepared to fight for her.'

'Tell me, then, my Lord,' said Lancelot, 'when my lady the queen was accused as you say, were not any of the knights of the Round Table present?'

'Yes, a good many of them,' replied the knight. 'All the king's five nephews were there, Sir Gawain and Gaheriet and the other brothers; also Sir Yvain the son of King Urien, Sagremor the Foolish, and many other fine knights.'

'How was it, then,' asked Lancelot, 'that they allowed my lady the queen to be dishonoured in their presence, without any of them defending her?'

'In faith,' said the knight, 'none of them would have been so bold. They were right, too, as they did not want to act disloyally for her sake, since they were all quite certain she had killed the knight. In my opinion they would have been dishonest if they had knowingly offered to defend an unjust cause.'

'And do you think,' asked Lancelot, 'that this Mador will ever return to court to take up the matter?'

'Yes, indeed,' replied the knight. 'I know he is going back on the fortieth day to uphold the accusation he has made, and I am sure the queen will be dishonoured, because she will not find a knight valiant enough to dare to take up his shield to defend her.'

'I think she will,' said Lancelot, 'because all the kindnesses she has shown towards foreign knights would be in vain if she could not find anyone ready to fight to defend her; and I can tell you there are some people in the world who would rather put themselves to death than fail to rescue her from this danger. Please tell me when the forty days will be up.'

The knight told him.

'Then I can tell you,' said Lancelot, 'that there is a knight in this country whom even King Arthur's honour would not prevent from being at court that day, and defending my lady the queen against Mador.'

'You can be sure,' said the knight, 'that the man who involves himself in this adventure will derive no honour from it, because if he won the battle everyone at court would know he had erred against justice and loyalty.'

Thereupon they stopped talking and said no more about the subject. However, they stayed there till Vespers, and then the knight went to his horse, mounted, took leave of Lancelot, and commended him to God.

When the knight was some way away from him, Lancelot

saw an armed knight coming, and a squire with him. He kept his eyes on him until he recognized it was his brother Hector des Mares. He was delighted to see him, walked to meet him, and shouted loud enough for him to hear:

'Hector, welcome! What adventure brings you here?'

When Hector saw him, he dismounted, straight away took off his helmet, and greeted him in turn, as happy as it was possible to be.

'My Lord,' he said, 'I was going to Camelot to defend my lady the queen against Mador de la Porte, who has accused her of treachery.'

'You will stay with me tonight,' said Lancelot, 'and until I have completely recovered. When it is time for the battle we shall go to court together, and if the knight who has made the accusation does not find anyone to defend my lady then, he never will.'

[75] They both agreed on this, and then Lancelot mounted his horse, and Hector too. They went straight to the hermitage where Lancelot had been staying. When the hermit saw Hector, he was very happy not only for love of Lancelot, but also because he had seen him in the past. That night Hector was very eager to know who had wounded Lancelot. Lancelot told him everything as it had happened, and his brother was very surprised. They stayed there a week, until Lancelot had completely recovered from the wound caused by the huntsman, and so was as healthy and well as he had ever been. Then he left the hermitage and began to ride through the country accompanied only by Hector and two squires, so secretly that it was hardly possible to recognize who he was. One day they happened to meet Bors, who was riding in an attempt to discover where he might find Lancelot. That same week he had parted from his brother Lionel and left him with the King of North Wales, who had asked him to stay to keep him company.

When Lancelot and Bors met, the two cousins were delighted. Bors drew Lancelot to one side and said:

'Have you heard the news about how my lady the queen has been indicted before the king?'

'Yes,' he replied, 'I have been told all about it.'

'My Lord,' said Bors, 'I can tell you that I am pleased, since, as she cannot find anyone to defend her, she will be forced to make her peace with you so that one of us can fight against Mador.'

'Even if she should always hate me so much that I never found my peace with her,' replied Lancelot, 'I should not want her to be dishonoured while I lived, because of all the ladies in the world she is the one who has paid me the greatest honour ever since I have been bearing arms. I shall risk myself to defend her, but not as boldly as I have fought in other battles, because I know for certain, from what I have been told, that I shall be in the wrong and Mador will be in the right.'

That night the cousins slept at a castle called Alfain, and from then there were only four days left until the battle.

Lancelot said to Hector and Bors:

'You will go to Camelot and stay there till Tuesday, because that is my lady's day. Between now and then ask my lady if I can ever be at peace with her, and come to see me when I have won my battle, if it pleases Our Lord that I should have that honour, to tell me what you have found her attitude to be.'

They said they would willingly do that.

In the evening they left Lancelot, and he utterly forbade them to mention to a living soul that he was coming to court.

'But nevertheless,' he said, 'so that you will recognize me when I come, I shall tell you that I shall be wearing white arms and a shield with one diagonal band; by that you will recognize me, although other people will not know who I am.'

They they both left Lancelot, and he stayed in the castle in the company of a single squire whom he ordered to prepare the kind of arms he had described.

But now the story stops telling of him and returns to his cousin Bors.

*

[76] In this part the story relates that when the two cousins had left Lancelot, they rode until they arrived at Camelot at None; this was quite possible since Alfain was only four Eng-

lish leagues from Camelot. When they had dismounted and disarmed, the king went forward to meet them, because they were two of the knights he esteemed most in the world. Sir Gawain and all the noblest men present went to meet them too. They were received with as great honour as should be paid to such knights.

But when the queen heard that they had come, she was more delighted at their arrival than she had ever been before. She said to a girl who was with her:

'Now that those two have come I am quite sure I shall not die alone, since they are so noble that they will risk their bodies and souls rather than allow me to be put to death in any place at which they are present. Blessed be God who has brought them here at this moment; otherwise things would have turned out very badly for me.'

[77] While she was saying this, Bors arrived, very anxious to speak to her. As soon as she saw him come in, she stood up to greet him and bade him welcome.

He replied, 'God give you joy.'

'I am assured of joy,' she replied, 'because you have come, and yet I expected to be far removed from it. However, now I think I shall soon regain it through God and through you.'

He replied, as if he did not know what she was talking about:

'My Lady, how is it that you have lost all joy, and can regain it only through God and through me?'

'What, my Lord?' she replied. 'Do you not know what has happened to me since you last saw me?'

He replied that he did not.

'No?' she said. 'Then I shall tell you everything truthfully.'

So she told him the truth as it had happened, without omitting anything. 'Now Mador is accusing me of treachery, but there is not a knight here valiant enough to dare to defend me against him.'

'If knights are failing you, my Lady, it is not surprising.' he replied, 'because you have failed the finest knight in the world. So it will not be unjust, I think, if things turn out badly for you, because you have driven the finest knight we know of to his death, and for that reason I am more pleased about this misfortune that has befallen you than I have been about anything for a long time. Now you will know and recognize how much one loses when a noble knight is lost, because if he were present, nothing in the world would prevent him from undertaking the battle against Mador, although he would know he was in the wrong. But, thank God, you are driven to the point where you will not find anyone to fight for you, and as a result I think you risk receiving every dishonour.'

'Bors,' said the queen, 'whoever fails to help me, you will not desert me, I know.'

'My Lady,' he replied, 'God forbid that you receive any help from me, because as you have taken away from me the man I loved above all others, I ought not to help you, but do all I can to harm you.'

'What,' said the queen, 'have I taken him away from you?'

'Yes,' he replied, 'so that I do not know what has become of him, and since I told him news of you I do not know where he has gone any more than if he were dead.'

[78] Then the queen was greatly distressed and began to cry bitterly. She was so miserable that she did not know what was to become of her. When she spoke, she said, so loudly that Bors could hear:

'Ah, God, why was I ever born when I have to end my life in such great suffering?'

Then Bors left her, having taken his revenge on her by what he had said. When he had left her room and she saw that there was nothing to bring her any comfort, she began to grieve just as much as if she could see the person she most loved in the world lying dead before her. She said, under her breath:

'Dearest friend, now I know that King Ban's kinsmen did not love me except for your sake, because they have failed me now that they think you have left me. Now I can see that in my need I am going to miss you very much.'

[79] The queen was in great sadness and wept night and day. She never stopped lamenting; instead her grief became greater every day. The king was very unhappy because he could not find a knight to enter the battle-field as a challenge to Mador.

Each one said he would not undertake to do it because he knew the queen was wrong and Mador right. The king spoke to Sir Gawain on the subject and said:

'Sir Gawain, I beg you for God's sake and for love of me to undertake the battle against Mador, to defend the queen against his accusation.'

He replied, 'My Lord, I am quite prepared to carry out your wishes, but grant me as a king that you advise me honourably, as one should a loyal knight. We know perfectly well that the queen killed the knight as she is accused. I saw it and so did many others. Now tell me if I can defend her honourably; because if I can I am ready to enter the battle-field for her, and if I cannot, I will tell you that I would not enter it even if she were my mother, because the person is not yet born for whom I should like to dishonour myself.'

The king could get no other reply either from Sir Gawain or from the other knights present, because they were all determined not to act dishonourably either for the king or for anyone else. As a result the king was very sad and miserable.

The night before the battle was due to take place, you could have seen in Camelot all the highest-ranking men in the kingdom of Logres, because they had assembled to see what the result of the duel would be for the queen. That night the king spoke angrily to the queen and said:

'My Lady, I do not know what to say about you. All the good knights of my court have failed me, and as a result you can be sure that tomorrow will bring you a base and shameful death. I would rather have lost all my land than that this should have happened during my lifetime, because I have never loved anyone in this world as much as I loved you and still do love you.'

When the queen heard this she burst into tears, and so did the king, and when they had lamented together for some time, the king said to her:

'Did you ask Bors or Hector to undertake the battle for you?'

'No,' replied the queen, 'because I do not think they would have done so much for me, as they do not hold any fiefs from you but come from a foreign country.'

'Still, I suggest that you should ask each of them,' said the king, 'and if both of them should fail you, then I do not know what to say or advise.'

And she said that she would ask them, to find out what would happen.

[80] Then the king left her room as distressed as could be, and the queen straight away commanded Bors and Hector to come and speak to her. They came immediately. When she saw them arrive, she fell at their feet and said, in tears:

'Ah, noble knights, renowned for your valour and high birth, if you ever loved the man called Lancelot, come to my help in my need, not for my sake but his. If you are unwilling to do this, you must know that by tomorrow evening I shall be shamed and basely dishonoured, because all the knights of this court will finally have failed me in my great need.'

When Bors saw the queen so anxious and so unhappy, he took pity on her; he raised her up from the ground, and said, in tears:

'My Lady, do not be so dismayed. If tomorrow by Terce you have not a better champion than I should be, I shall enter the battle for you against Mador.'

'A better champion?' asked the queen. 'Where could one come from?'

'My Lady,' said Bors, 'I cannot tell you that, but what I have told you I shall keep to.'

When the queen heard this, it made her very happy, because she immediately thought it must be Lancelot about whom he was talking and who was to come to rescue her. Bors then straight away left the queen, with Hector, and they went to a large room in the palace where they usually slept when they came to court.

[81] The next day at Prime the palace was full of barons and knights who were all awaiting Mador's arrival. Many of them were very anxious about the queen, because they did not think she would find a knight to defend her. Shortly after Prime, Mador arrived at court, together with a great company of knights who were all his kinsmen. He dismounted, and then went up to the palace completely armed except for his helmet,

his shield and his lance. He was a remarkably big man, and full of such great strength that there was scarcely a stronger knight at King Arthur's court.

When he came before the king, he repeated his challenge about the battle that he had given before, and the king replied:

'Mador, the queen's case must be settled according to the principle that if she does not find anyone today who is prepared to defend her, we shall do with her what the court will decide. Now remain here until Vespers, and if no one comes forward by then to undertake the battle, your accusation is upheld and the queen is found guilty.'

He replied that he would wait; then he sat down in the middle of the palace, with all his kinsmen around him. The hall was remarkably crowded, but they all kept so quiet that there was not a sound. They stayed like that for a long time after Prime.

[82] A little before Terce, Lancelot arrived fully armed, lacking nothing that a knight ought to have; however he came quite alone, without any knight or sergeant. He bore white arms and had a diagonal band of red on his shield. When he arrived at court he dismounted and tied up his horse to an elm tree there, and hung his shield from it. Then he went up to the palace without removing his helmet, and appeared before the king and the barons without a soul there recognizing him, except only Hector and Bors.

When he came near the king, he spoke loud enough for all those present to hear him, and said to him:

'My Lord, I have come to court because of something unbelievable I have heard related in this country. Some people have led me to understand that a knight is to come here today to accuse my lady the queen of treachery. If this is true, I have never heard of such a mad knight, because we all know, friends and strangers, that in the whole world there is no lady as worthy as she. I have therefore come because of the value I know there is in her, prepared to defend her if there is a knight present who is accusing her of treachery.'

[83] At this, Mador jumped forward and said:

'My lord knight, I am ready to prove that she dishonourably and treacherously killed my brother.'

'And I am ready,' said Lancelot, 'to defend her and prove she never had dishonour or treachery in mind.'

Mador took no notice of this and threw down his gage before the king; Lancelot did the same, and the king received them both.

Then Sir Gawain said to the king:

'I think now that Mador was in the wrong, because, however his brother died, I would swear on the relics of the saints that to my knowledge the queen never had dishonour or treachery in mind. It could soon turn out badly for Mador if this other knight has any prowess in him.'

'I do not know who the knight is,' said the king, 'but I think he is going to win and that is what I should like.'

[84] Then the palace began to empty; everybody, high and low, went down to the jousting-field outside the town, where battles were generally fought in a very beautiful place. Sir Gawain took the knight's lance and said he would carry it on to the field; Bors took his shield. Lancelot mounted at once and entered the field. The king summoned the queen and said:

'My Lady, here is a knight who is risking his life for you. You must know that if he is vanquished, you will be sentenced to death, and he will be dishonoured.'

'My Lord,' she replied, 'may God be on the side of justice as truly as I never had dishonour or treachery in mind.'

Then the queen took her knight, accompanied him on to the field and said:

'My Lord, act in God's name, and may Our Lord help you today.'

Then the knights faced each other, spurred on their horses and came together as fast as they could drive their horses. They struck each other so violently that their shields and coats of mail could not protect them from receiving deep wounds. Mador fell from his horse to the ground, and was quite shaken by the fall as he was big and heavy. However, he soon stood up, although rather lacking in confidence, as he had found his enemy to be strong and fierce at jousting.

When Lancelot saw him standing, he thought it would be unchivalrous to attack him from horseback, so he dismounted and let his horse wander where it wanted. Then he drew his sword, protected his head with his shield, and went to attack Mador where he found him. He gave him such powerful blows on his helmet that he was quite stunned; however, he defended himself as best he could and struck Lancelot hard many times in return. But all this did him no good, because before mid-day had passed Lancelot had wounded him so badly that he was bleeding in more than a dozen places.

Lancelot had harassed and tormented Mador so much on all sides that those present saw clearly that he had lost, and would die if this was what his adversary wanted. They all praised the man fighting Mador, because they thought that they had not seen such a noble knight for a long time.

Lancelot, who knew Mador well and had no wish for him to die, because they had once been companions in arms, saw that he had driven him to the point where he could kill him if he wished, and took pity on him.

'Mador,' he said, 'you are defeated and dishonoured, if that is my will; and you can see that you are a dead man if this battle continues. Therefore I suggest you abandon your accusation, before any harm comes to you, and I shall make sure for you that my lady the queen forgives you for having accused her, and that the king acquits you completely.'

[85] When Mador heard the courtesy and the nobility of his opponent's offer, he recognized straight away that it was Lancelot. He knelt before him, took his sword and handed it to him, saying:

'My Lord, take my sword, and I shall put myself entirely at your mercy. I can tell you that I do not feel myself dishonoured, because I certainly could not compare myself with such a noble knight as you; you have shown that both here and elsewhere.'

Then he said to the king:

'My Lord, you have tricked me by setting Sir Lancelot against me.'

When the king heard it was Lancelot, he did not wait till he had left the field, but instead ran forward to him and embraced him, armed as he was. Sir Gawain came forward and unlaced his helmet. Then you could have seen around him the greatest joy of which you had ever heard tell. The queen was acquitted of Mador's accusation, and she now considered herself silly and foolish for having been angry with Lancelot.

One day it happened that the queen was alone with Lancelot, and they began to talk of various things. The queen said:

'My Lord, I mistrusted you quite wrongly about the girl from Escalot, because I know for sure that if you had loved her as much as various people led me to understand, she would not now be dead.'

'What, my Lady?' asked Lancelot. 'Is she dead, then, that girl?'

'Yes, indeed,' replied the queen, 'and she lies inside St Stephen's Cathedral.'

'That is certainly a great shame,' he said, 'because she was very beautiful. I am very sorry, may God help me.'

They spoke at length about this, and about other things. And if Lancelot had loved the queen before, from now on he loved her more than he had ever done in the past, and so did she him. They acted, however, with such a lack of discretion that many people at court discovered the truth about them, and even Sir Gawain knew it for certain, as did all his four brothers.

It happened one day that all five of them were in the palace, talking in confidence about the matter. Agravain was much more concerned than any of the others. While they were discussing the subject, the king happened to come out from the queen's room, and when Sir Gawain saw him he said to his brothers:

'Be quiet, here comes my lord the king.'

Agravain replied that he would not keep quiet for him, and the king overheard this and said to him:

'Agravain, tell me what you are talking about so loudly.'

'Ah!' said Sir Gawain, 'for God's sake let us say no more on the subject; Agravain is being more unpleasant than usual, and you should not be interested to know, because no good could come of it for you or any noble man.'

'In God's name,' said the king, 'I wish to know.'

'Oh, no, my Lord,' said Gaheriet, 'that is quite impossible, because there is nothing in what he is saying but fables and the most disloyal lies in the world. For that reason I beg you as my liege lord to stop asking.'

'By my head,' said Arthur, 'I will not. I will go as far now as to request you, on the oath you swore to me, to tell me what you were arguing about just now.'

'It is remarkable how anxious you are to hear about it,' said Sir Gawain. 'Indeed, even if it made you angry with me and you expelled me, poor and exiled, from this country of yours, I still should not tell you, because if you believed it, even if it were the greatest lie in the world, more harm could come of it than has ever come about in your time.'

Then the king was even more distressed than before, and he said that he would know, or he would have them all put to death.

'In faith,' said Sir Gawain, 'you will never know from me, because all I would finally receive would be your hatred, and neither I nor anyone else could fail to regret it.'

Then he left the room, and so did Gaheriet. The king kept calling them, but they would not return. They went away as sadly as could be, saying to each other that it was a pity the subject had ever been raised, because if the king discovered the truth and had a conflict with Lancelot, the court would be destroyed and dishonoured, because Lancelot would have on his side all the strength of Gaul and many other countries.

[86] So the two brothers went off, so miserable that they did not know what to do. The king, who had stayed with his other nephews, took them into a room near a garden. Then he closed the door on them, and asked and begged them by the faith they owed him to tell him what he wanted to know. First he turned to Agravain, but he said he would not tell him. Let him ask the others! They too said that they would not speak.

'If you will not tell me,' said the king, 'either I shall kill you or you will kill me.'

Then he ran to a sword lying on a couch, drew it from its scabbard, and went up to Agravain saying that he would not fail to kill him if he did not tell him what he so much desired to know. He raised the sword high to strike his head, and when Agravain saw he was so angry, he shouted:

'Ah, my Lord, do not kill me! I will tell you. I was saying to my brother Sir Gawain, and to Gaheriet and my other brothers you can see here, that they were disloyal traitors for having so long permitted the scandal and dishonour which Sir Lancelot del Lac is causing you.'

'What,' said the king, 'is Lancelot dishonouring me? What are you talking about? Tell me, because I have never suspected he might be bringing me shame, since I have always honoured and loved him so much that he should never cause me any dishonour.'

'My Lord,' said Agravain, 'he is so loyal to you that he is dishonouring you through your wife and has committed adultery with her.'

When the king heard this, his colour changed and he turned pale. He said:

'That is unbelievable.'

Then he began thinking and said nothing for a long time.

'My Lord,' said Mordred, 'we have hidden it from you as long as we could, but now it is right that the truth should be known and that we should tell you. So long as we hid it from you, we have also been disloyal and guilty of perjury; now we are freeing ourselves of the blame of that. We are telling you truthfully that it is as we say; now you must see how your dishonour can be avenged.'

As a result of this the king was so pensive and sad and distraught that he did not know what to do. However, when he spoke, he said:

'If you have ever loved me, find a way to catch them together, and if I do not take my revenge on them as one should on traitors, I shall never want to wear a crown again.'

'My Lord,' said Guerrehet, 'advise us, then, because it is a fearsome undertaking to bring so noble a man as Lancelot to his death. He is strong and bold, and his kinsmen are powerful in every way. That means, as you are well aware, that if Lancelot dies, King Ban's kinsmen will wage such a great and vigorous war against you that the most powerful men in your kingdom will find it difficult to withstand it. You yourself, if God does not defend you, could be killed, because they will be more intent on avenging Lancelot than saving themselves.'

'Don't worry about me,' said the king, 'but do as I tell you. Let them be caught together, if you can arrange it; I am commanding you to do this on the oath you swore to me when you were made companions of the Round Table.'

They agreed to do this because he so desired it, and they all three swore it. Then they left the room and went into the palace.

[87] That day the king was more pensive than usual, and it was quite evident that he was angry. At None Sir Gawain came, together with Gaheriet, and when they saw the king, they could tell from his face that the others had told him about Lancelot. For that reason they did not turn towards him, but instead went to the windows of the palace. The hall was quiet; no one present dared to say a word because they saw the king was angry.

At that moment an armed knight arrived who said to the king:

'My Lord, I can tell you news from the tournament at Karahés. The knights from the kingdom of Sorelois and from the Waste Land have lost everything.'

'Were there any knights present from here?' asked the king.

'Yes, my Lord, Lancelot was there and was the winner everywhere.'

The king frowned and lowered his head when he heard this news, and began to think. When he had thought for some time, he got up and said, loud enough for many to hear:

'Ah, God, what grievous shame it is that treason ever took root in such a noble man!'

The king went to his room and lay down sadly on his bed. He knew perfectly well that if Lancelot were caught in adultery and put to death, there would be such a great torment in the country as had never before been caused by the death of a single knight. And yet it was better that Lancelot should die than that a king's dishonour should not be avenged before his death.

Then he commanded his three nephews to come to him, and when they were present, he said:

'My Lords, Lancelot is returning from that tournament. Now explain to me how he may be caught in the act you revealed to me.'

'I certainly do not know,' said Guerrehet.

'In God's name,' said Agravain, 'I will tell you. Announce to all your sergeants that you are going hunting the next morning, and tell all your knights to accompany you except Lancelot. He will be pleased to stay, and I am quite sure it will happen that as soon as you have left for the hunt, he will go and sleep with the queen. We shall stay behind to establish the truth for you, and we shall be hiding here in a room to catch him and to keep him until you return home.'

The king readily agreed to this.

'But be careful', he said, 'that not a soul knows about it, until it is done as you have described.'

During this conversation Sir Gawain arrived, and when he saw them talking together so confidentially, he said to the king:

'My Lord, God grant that nothing but good may come to you out of this discussion, because I fear it may harm you more than anyone else. Agravain, my brother, I beg you not to begin anything you cannot conclude, or to say anything about Lancelot if you do not know it for certain, because he is the finest knight you have ever seen.'

'Gawain,' said the king, 'depart from here, because you are a man I shall never trust again. You have behaved badly towards me, since you knew my dishonour and permitted it without informing me.'

'My treason certainly never did you any harm,' replied Sir Gawain.

Then he left the room and saw Gaheriet, and said:

'Despite everything, Agravain has told the king what we did not dare to tell him. You can be sure that it will cause a great deal of harm.'

'In that case,' said Gaheriet, 'I will have nothing to do with it; someone as noble as Lancelot will never be accused of that crime by me. Now let us leave Agravain with what he has started. If good comes of it, may he benefit; but if it turns out badly, he cannot say we had anything to do with it.'

[88] Then they left and went to Gaheriet's lodging. As they were going down through the town they met Lancelot and his companions. As soon as they saw one another from a distance, they were very happy.

'Sir Lancelot,' said Gaheriet, 'I want to ask you a favour.'

Lancelot agreed readily, provided it was something he could do.

'Thank you,' said Gaheriet. 'I want you to come and stay with me tonight together with your company. I can assure you that I am asking this more for your own good than to annoy you.'

When Lancelot heard him say this, he agreed. They turned round and went down to Gaheriet's lodge just as they were.

Then squires and sergeants rushed forward to disarm Lancelot and the others who had come from the tournament. At supper time, they all went to court together, because they dearly loved Lancelot. When he arrived, Lancelot was extremely surprised that the king, who usually gave him such a fine welcome, did not say a word to him this time, but turned his face aside as soon as he saw him coming. He did not realize that the king was angry with him, because he did not think he could have heard the news that he had been told. Then he sat down with the knights and began to enjoy himself, but not as much as he usually did, because he saw the king was so pensive.

After supper, when the table-cloths had been removed, the king summoned his knights to go hunting the next morning in the forest of Camelot. Then Lancelot said to the king:

'My Lord, I shall accompany you there.'

'My Lord,' replied the king, 'you can stay behind this time, because I have so many other knights that I can quite do without your company.'

Then Lancelot saw that the king was angry with him, but he did not know why; and he was very sorry about it.

[89] In the evening, when it was time to go to bed, Lancelot

left with a great company of knights; and when they were at their lodge, Lancelot said to Bors:

'Did you see the look King Arthur gave me? I think he is angry with me for some reason.'

'My Lord,' said Bors, 'he has heard about you and the queen. Now be careful what you do, because we risk fighting a war which will never come to an end.'

'Ah,' said Lancelot, 'who was it that dared to talk about it?'

'My Lord,' replied Bors, 'if a knight spoke about it, it was Agravain, and if it was a woman, it was Morgan, King Arthur's sister.'

That night the two cousins talked a lot about the subject. The next day, as soon as it was light, Sir Gawain said to Lancelot:

'My Lord, I am going hunting with Gaheriet. Are you coming?'

'No,' replied Lancelot, 'I am staying behind, because I am not in a position to go as I wish.'

Sir Gawain and Gaheriet followed the king to the hunt. And as soon as the king had left, the queen called for a messenger, and sent him to Lancelot, who was still in bed. She commanded him to come to her without fail.

When Lancelot saw the messenger, he was very pleased, and told him to return, because he would follow him. Then he dressed and got ready, and wondered how he could go secretly so that no one would know. He asked Bors' advice, and Bors begged him for God's sake not to go.

'If you go, you will suffer for it; my heart, which has never been apprehensive for you before, tells me so.'

But Lancelot replied that he was determined to go.

'My Lord,' said Bors, 'as you wish to go, I shall tell you the best way to take. There is a garden which stretches as far as the queen's room; go through it. You will find the quietest and least frequented path of which I know. But I beg you for God's sake not to fail for any reason to take your sword with you.'

Then Lancelot did as Bors had described, and went along the garden path which led up to King Arthur's house. When he was near the tower, Agravain, who had placed his spies everywhere, knew he was coming, since a boy had told him:

'My Lord, Sir Lancelot is coming this way.'

He told him to be quiet.

Then Agravain went to a window looking out over the garden and watched Lancelot hurrying towards the tower. Agravain had a great company of knights with him; he took them to the window and pointed out Lancelot, saying:

'There he is. Now make sure, when he is in the queen's room, that he does not escape.'

They replied that there was no chance of his fleeing, since they would surprise him when he was naked.

Lancelot, who did not suspect that he was being watched, went to the door of the room leading on to the garden, opened it, and went in, passing from room to room until he came to where the queen was expecting him.

[90] When Lancelot was inside, he locked the door after him, as it was not his lot to be killed on that occasion. Then he took off his shoes and undressed and climbed into bed with the queen. However, he had not been there long when those who were looking out to capture him came to the door of the room. When they found it locked, they were all confounded, and realized that they had failed in what they had set out to do. They asked Agravain how they could enter, and he instructed them to break down the door, as it was the only way.

They knocked and banged until the queen heard, and said to Lancelot:

'My friend, we have been betrayed.'

'What, my Lady?' he said, 'What is it?'

Then he listened and heard all the noise of the men who were trying to force the door, but were unable to.

'Ah, my friend,' said the queen, 'now we are dishonoured and dead; the king will know all about you and me. Agravain has laid a trap for us.'

'Do not worry, my Lady,' said Lancelot. 'He has arranged his own death, because he will be the first to die.'

Then they both jumped up from the bed and dressed as best they could.

'My Lady,' asked Lancelot, 'have you a coat of mail here or any other armour with which I could protect myself?'

'No,' replied the queen. 'Our misfortune is so great that we must both die, you and I. I am sorrier for your sake, may God help me, than for mine, because your death will be a much greater loss than mine. And yet, if God should grant that you escaped from here alive and well, I know there is no one yet born who would dare to put me to death for this crime while he knew you were alive.'

When Lancelot heard her say this, he went to the door not fearing anything, and shouted to those who were striking it:

'Wait for me, you evil cowards. I am going to open the door to see who will come in first.'

Then he drew his sword, opened the door, and told them to come forward. A knight called Tanaguin who hated Lancelot mortally put himself before the others, and Lancelot, raising his sword, struck him so violently with all his force that neither his helmet nor his iron coif could save him from being split to the shoulders. Lancelot wrenched out his sword, and struck him dead to the ground. When the others saw what had happened to him, they all drew back and left the doorway quite empty. Seeing this, Lancelot said to the queen:

'My Lady, the battle is over. When it pleases you I shall go, and shall not be prevented by any man here.'

The queen said she wanted him to be in safety, whatever might happen to her. Then Lancelot looked at the knight he had killed, who had fallen inside the door of the room. He pulled him nearer and closed the door. Then he disarmed him and armed himself as well as he could. Having done that, he said to the queen:

'My Lady, since I am armed, I should now be able to go safely, if it pleases God.'

She told him to go if he could.

He went to the door, opened it, and said that they would never hold him. Then he rushed among them, brandishing his sword, and struck the first man he met to the ground so violently that he was unable to get up again. When the others saw this, they drew back and even the boldest of them let him pass.

Seeing that they were leaving him alone, he passed through the garden and went back to his lodging. There he found Bors, who was very worried that he might not be able to return as he wished, because he had realized that King Arthur's kinsmen had been spying on Lancelot in order to be able to catch him in some way. When Bors saw his lord coming fully armed, although he had left unarmed, he knew there had been a fight. He went to meet Lancelot, and asked:

'My Lord, what has made you arm yourself?'

Lancelot told him how Agravain and his two brothers had spied on him, because they wished to catch him with the queen, and how they had taken many knights with them.

'And they nearly caught me, too, since I was not prepared for them, but I defended myself vigorously, and with the help of God I managed to escape.'

'Ah, my Lord,' said Bors, 'now things are turning out for the worse, because what we have hidden for so long is now in the open. Now you will see the beginning of a war that will never end during our lifetimes; because if until now the king has loved you more than any man, from now on he will hate you even more, since he knows that you have wronged him so much by dishonouring him through his wife. Now you must decide what we are going to do, as I am quite certain that from now on the king will be my mortal enemy. However, may God help me, I am most sorry for our lady the queen, who will be put to death because of you. I should be happier if it were possible for us to decide how she can be rescued from the danger she is in, and brought to safety.'

[91] While they were discussing this, Hector arrived. When he heard what had come about, he was sadder than anyone, and said:

'The best thing I can see is for us to leave and enter the forest out there, but taking great care not to let the king find us, because he is there at present. When it is time for our lady the queen to be judged, she will certainly be taken out there to be put to death. Then we will rescue her, whether those who think they are taking her to her death agree or not. When we have got her with us, we shall be able to leave the country and go to the kingdom of Banoic or the kingdom of Gaunes. If we can manage to lead her to safety, we shall not fear King Arthur or all his power in any way.'

Lancelot and Bors agreed with this plan; they ordered their knights and sergeants to mount, and were thirty-eight in all. They rode until they had left the town and arrived at the edge of the forest, where they knew it was thickest, so that they would be unlikely to be noticed while it was light.

Then Lancelot called one of his squires and said:

'Go straight to Camelot and find out what is happening to my lady the queen and what they plan to do with her. If they have condemned her to death, come and tell us straight away, because despite all the trouble or difficulties we might have in rescuing her, we shall not fail to save her from death as best we can.'

Then the boy left Lancelot, mounted his horse, went by the quickest route to Camelot, and arrived at King Arthur's court.

But now the story stops telling of him, and returns to Sir Gawain's three brothers at the moment when Lancelot escaped from them after they had found him in the queen's room.

*

[92] Now the story relates that, when Lancelot had left the queen and fled from those who were hoping to catch him, the men at the door of the room, seeing that he had gone, went in and caught the queen. They insulted and taunted her more than they should have done, saying that now they had proof and that she would not escape with her life. They treated her with a total lack of respect, and she heard them as distressed as could be, weeping so bitterly that the wicked knights should have had pity on her.

At None the king returned from the hunt. When he had dismounted in the courtyard, he was immediately told the news that the queen had been caught with Lancelot; he was much saddened and asked whether Lancelot had been captured.

'No, my Lord,' they replied, 'he defended himself very vigorously. No other man could have done what he did.'

'Since he is not here,' said King Arthur, 'we shall find him at his lodge. Take a large number of armed men and go and capture him. When you have caught him, come to me, and I shall deal with him and the queen together.'

Then as many as forty knights went to get armed, not because they wanted to but because they had no choice, since the king had commanded them in person. When they arrived at Lancelot's lodge, they did not find him there, and all the knights were pleased about this, because they knew that if they had found him there and had tried to take him by force, they could not have avoided a great and violent battle. So they went back to the king and told him that they had missed Lancelot, because he had left some time previously and had taken all his knights with him. When the king heard this, he said he was very angry, and because he was not able to take his revenge on Lancelot, he would take it on the queen in such a way that it would be spoken about evermore.

'My Lord,' asked King Yon, 'what do you intend to do?'

'I intend,' replied King Arthur, 'that severe justice should be taken on her for this crime she has committed. And I command you first of all, because you are a king, and then the other barons present here, to determine among you how she should be put to death, because she will not escape with her life, and even if you yourself took her side and said she should not die, she would die nevertheless.'

'My Lord,' said King Yon, 'it is not the normal custom in this country for a man or a woman to be sentenced to death after None. But in the morning, if we have no alternative but to make a judgment, we shall do it.'

[93] Then King Arthur fell silent, and was so despondent that he could not eat or drink the whole evening, and did not wish the queen to be brought before him. In the morning at Prime, when the barons had assembled in the palace, the king said:

'My Lords, what must we do with the queen according to true justice?'

The barons drew aside and discussed the matter. They asked Agravain and the two other brothers what ought to be done, and they said it was their judgment that justice called for her to be put to a shameful death, because she had committed great treachery by sleeping with another knight in place of such a noble man as the king.

'And it is our judgment that she has deserved death by this one thing.'

All the others were obliged to agree with this, because it was obvious that it was what the king wanted. When Sir Gawain saw that the decision of the court meant that the queen's death sentence was confirmed, he said that, if it pleased God, his grief would never allow him to see the death of the lady who had paid him the greatest honour of any in the world. Then Sir Gawain went up to the king and said:

'My Lord, I return to you whatever fiefs I hold from you, and I shall never serve you again in all my life if you tolerate this treachery.'

The king did not say a word in reply, because his attention was elsewhere; and Sir Gawain straight away left the court and went to his lodging, lamenting as much as if he saw everyone dead before him. The king commanded his sergeants to light a great and powerful fire in the jousting-field of Camelot, in which the queen would be burnt, because a queen who was guilty of treachery could die in no other way, given that she was sacred. Then a great noise of shouting arose in the city of Camelot, and all the people were as grief-stricken as if she were their mother. Those who had been ordered to prepare the fire made it so great and impressive that everyone in the city could see it.

The king commanded the queen to be brought forward, and she came, crying bitterly. She was wearing a dress of red taffeta, a tunic, and a cloak. She was so beautiful and so elegant that she surpassed any other woman of her age one could have found in the world. When the king saw her, he felt such great pity for her that he was unable to look at her, but commanded her to be taken from him and dealt with as the court had decided in its judgment. Then she was led out of the palace and down through the streets.

When the queen had left the court and the city's inhabitants could see her coming, then you could have heard people on all sides, shouting:

'Ah, my Lady, more kindly and courteous than all others, where will the poor people ever find pity now? Ah, King Arthur, you who have treacherously sought her death, you can still repent, and the traitors who have arranged this can die in shame!'

That is what the city-people were saying as they followed the queen, weeping and shouting as if they were out of their minds.

The king commanded Agravain to take forty knights and to go and guard the field where the fire had been lit, so that if Lancelot came he would be powerless against them.

'My Lord, do you then wish me to go?' he asked.

'Yes,' replied the king.

'Then command my brother Gaheriet to come with us.'

The king commanded him, but he said he would not go. However, the king threatened him so much that finally he promised to go. So he went back to fetch his arms and all the others did too. When they were armed and had left the city, they saw that they were in fact eighty, all together.

'Listen, Agravain,' said Gaheriet, 'do you think I have come to fight with Lancelot if he wants to rescue the queen? I tell you I shall not fight with him; I would rather he kept the queen for the rest of his life than she should die here.'

[94] Agravain and Gaheriet went on talking until they were near the fire. Lancelot was in hiding with all his men at the edge of the forest, and as soon as he saw his messenger return, he asked him what news he was bringing back from King Arthur's court.

'Bad news, my Lord,' he said. 'My lady the queen has been sentenced to death, and there is the fire they are getting ready to burn her in.'

'My Lords,' he said, 'let us mount! There are some people

who expect to put her to death but who will die themselves. May God grant, if ever he heard the prayer of a sinner, that I first find Agravain, who caught me in that trap.'

Then they counted themselves to see how many knights they were, and they found they were thirty-two in number. Each one mounted his horse, and took shield and lance. They rode to where they saw the fire.

When the men in the jousting-field saw them coming, they all shouted together:

'There is Lancelot, flee, flee!'

Lancelot, who was riding ahead of all the others, went to where he saw Agravain, and shouted:

'Coward, traitor, you have come to your end.'

Then he struck him so hard that no armour could save him from having a lance thrust through his body. Lancelot, a man of valour and strength, gave him a mighty blow that knocked him to the ground from his horse. As he fell, the lance broke.

Bors, who came riding as fast as he could urge his horse to gallop, shouted to Guerrehet to defend himself because he was challenging him mortally, and he turned his horse towards him and struck him so violently that no armour could prevent him from thrusting the blade of his lance into his chest. Guerrehet fell from his horse to the ground in such a condition that he had no need of a doctor. The others put their hands to their swords and began to fight. But when Gaheriet saw that his two brothers were down, you do not need to ask whether he was angry, because he realized they were dead. Then he turned towards Meliadus the Black, who was actively helping Lancelot and avenging the queen's disgrace. He struck him so hard that he knocked him into the middle of the fire; then he put his hand to his sword, because he was a man of great valour, and struck another knight to the ground at Lancelot's feet.

Hector, who was taking note of all this, saw Gaheriet, and said to himself:

'If that man lives much longer, he can do us a lot of harm, as he is so valiant; it is better I should kill him than that he should do us more harm than he has done already.'

Then Hector spurred on his horse, went up to Gaheriet,

brandishing his sword, and struck him so violently that his helmet flew off his head. When Gaheriet felt his head unprotected, he felt quite lost, and Lancelot, who was making a tour of inspection round the ranks, did not recognize him. He struck him so hard on his head that he split it to his teeth.

[95] When King Arthur's men saw this blow and saw Gaheriet fall, they were quite dispirited; and their opponents pressed them so hard that out of the whole group of eighty there only remained three. One of these was Mordred and the other two were from the Round Table.

When Lancelot saw that there was no one left from King Arthur's household to hold him back from anything, he went up to the queen, and said:

'My Lady, what is to be done with you?'

She was delighted by this happy outcome that God had sent her, and said:

'My Lord, I should like you to place me in safety somewhere outside King Arthur's control.'

'My Lady,' said Lancelot, 'climb on to a palfrey and come with us into the forest. There we shall come to a decision on what it is best to do.'

And she agreed with this.

[96] Then they put her on a palfrey and went into the thickest part of the forest. When they were deep within it, they checked to see if they were all there, and they saw that they had lost three of their companions. Then they asked one another what had happened to them.

'I saw three of our men die at Gaheriet's hand,' said Hector.

'What?' said Lancelot, 'was Gaheriet present, then?'

'My Lord,' said Bors, 'what are you asking? You killed him.'

'In God's name,' said Hector, 'you killed him.'

'Now we can be sure,' said Lancelot, 'that we shall never be at peace with King Arthur or with Sir Gawain, because of their love for Gaheriet. We shall see the beginning of a war that will never come to an end.'

Lancelot was very angry at Gaheriet's death, because he was one of the knights he most loved in the world.

Bors said to Lancelot:

'My Lord, we ought to decide how my lady the queen is to be led to safety.'

'If we could manage,' replied Lancelot, 'to take her to a castle I once conquered, I do not think she need fear King Arthur. The castle is remarkably strong and so placed that it cannot be besieged. If we were there and had provisioned it well, I would summon to me knights near and far I had often served in the past; there are a great many in the world that would support me by the oath they have sworn, to come to my aid.'

'Where is this castle of which you speak,' asked Bors, 'and what is it called?'

'It is called,' said Lancelot, 'the Castle of the Joyeuse Garde; but when I conquered it, at the time when I had only recently been dubbed a knight, it was called the Douloureuse Garde.'

'Ah, God!' exclaimed the queen. 'When shall we be there?'

[97] They all agreed with Lancelot's idea, and set out along the main path through the forest, saying that however many men might follow them from King Arthur's household, they would all be killed. They rode until they arrived at a castle in the middle of the forest, called Kalec. The lord of it was an earl who was a fine knight of great strength and who loved Lancelot above all men.

When he knew Lancelot had arrived, he was delighted and received him very courteously, treating him with all the honour that he could. He promised to help him against all men, even King Arthur, and said:

'My Lord, I would like to give this castle to you and my lady the queen; I think you ought to accept it, because it is very strong and if you wish to stay here you will not have to worry about anyone, or about anything King Arthur can do.'

Lancelot thanked him, but said that he definitely could not stay there.

Then they left the castle and rode day after day until they were four leagues from the Joyeuse Garde. Lancelot sent messengers ahead to say they were coming, and when the people in the castle knew, they went to meet him as joyfully as if he were God himself, and welcomed him with even more honour than they would have done King Arthur. When they knew he wanted to stay there, and why he had come, they swore to him on the saints that they would lay down their lives to help him. Then Lancelot summoned the knights of the district and they came in great numbers.

But now the story stops telling of them and returns to King Arthur.

*

[98] Now the story relates that when King Arthur saw Mordred returning in flight through the city of Camelot with so few companions, he was amazed how this could be. He asked those who were coming towards him why they were fleeing.

'My Lord,' said a boy, 'I have bad news to tell you and all those present here. My Lord, I have to tell you that of all the knights that were leading the queen to the fire only three have escaped. One of them is Mordred and I do not know who the other two are; I think all the others are dead.'

'Ah!' said King Arthur, 'was Lancelot there, then?'

'Yes, my Lord,' he replied, 'and that is not all he has done, because he has rescued the queen from death and taken her away with him. He has disappeared with her into the forest of Camelot.'

The king was so shaken by this news that he did not know what to do. At this point Mordred came in and said to the king:

'My Lord, things have gone badly for us. Lancelot has got away and taken the queen with him, after defeating us all.'

'They will not be able to go much further, if I can help it,' said the king.

Then he commanded knights and sergeants and all those who were with him to arm, and they mounted as soon as they could. They left the city covered in steel, rode up to the forest, and went up and down to see if they could get any news about the people for whom they were searching. But, as it happened, they found no one. The king then suggested they should divide and go different ways in order to find them more easily.

'In God's name,' said King Caradoc, 'I do not think that is a good idea, because if they separate and Lancelot finds some of them, since he has a great company of strong and bold knights with him, those he meets will undoubtedly pay with their lives, for he will kill them.'

'What shall we do, then?' asked King Arthur.

'Send your messengers to all the seamen in this country's ports, telling them that none should be so bold as to allow Lancelot to pass. In that way he will be forced to stay in this country whether he wishes to or not, and thus we shall easily be able to find out where he is. Then we shall be able to attack him with so many men that he will be captured without difficulty, so that you can take your revenge on him. That is what I advise.'

Then King Arthur called his messengers and sent them to all the ports in the land, forbidding anyone to be so bold as to let Lancelot pass.

When he had sent off his messengers, he returned to the city. As he came to the place where his knights were lying dead, he looked to the right and saw his nephew Agravain, whom Lancelot had killed, lying there. He had been struck in the body by a lance, and the blade had passed right through him. As soon as the king saw him he recognized him, and he was so heartbroken that he could not hold himself in his saddle, but fell to the ground in a swoon on top of the body. When he got his breath back after a time and could speak, he said:

'Ah, my nephew, the man who struck you in that way really hated you; everyone should know that the man who deprived my kinsmen of such a knight as you has brought great grief to my heart.'

He took off Agravain's helmet and looked at him; then he kissed his eyes and his mouth, which by now were cold. After this he had him carried back to the city.

[99] The king was dreadfully grief-stricken and made a tour of the field in tears; he went on looking until he found Guerrehet, whom Bors had killed. Then you could have seen the king in great distress. He struck his hands together, which were still armed, as he was wearing all his armour except his helmet. He lamented greatly and said that he had lived too long

when he saw those he had brought up in great affection die in such a tragic way. While he was grieving and had Guerrehet placed on his shield so that he could be carried back to the city, he went on looking round. Then to the left he saw the body of Gaheriet whom Lancelot had killed – this was Arthur's favourite nephew except for Gawain.

When the king saw the body of the man he had loved so much, there was no grief that a man can suffer for another that Arthur did not feel. He ran up to him as fast as he could and embraced him very closely. He swooned again and all the barons were frightened that he might die in front of them. He was unconscious for as long as a man could walk half a league; when he came to he said, loud enough for all to hear:

'Ah, God! Now I have lived too long! Ah, death! If you delay any longer I shall consider you too slow in coming. Ah, Gaheriet! If I must die of grief, I shall die for you. My nephew, it is a pity the sword was ever forged that struck you, and cursed be the man who struck you, because he has destroyed both me and my race.'

The king kissed his eyes and his mouth, bloody as they were, and grieved so much that all those watching were astonished. In fact, there was no one there who was not sad, because they all loved Gaheriet greatly.

[100] At all this noise and shouting Sir Gawain came out from his lodge, because he believed that the queen was dead and that the lamentation was for her. When he had arrived out in the streets and the people there saw him, they said:

'Sir Gawain, if you want to know great grief and see the destruction of your own flesh and blood, go up into the palace, and there you will find the greatest pain you ever experienced.'

Sir Gawain was quite confounded by this news, and did not say a word in reply, but went along the streets with his head bowed. He did not think the great grief would be over his brothers, because he knew nothing about that yet, but thought it was over the queen. As he was going through the town, he looked to the right and to the left, and saw everyone weeping together, young and old. As he went past, everybody said to him:

'Sir Gawain, go and know your great grief.'

When Sir Gawain heard what they were all saying, he was more dismayed than before, but he did not let it be seen. When he arrived at the palace, he saw everyone there lamenting as much as if they had seen the deaths of all the princes in the world.

Seeing Sir Gawain come in, the king said:

'Gawain, Gawain, know your great grief, and mine too; for here is your brother Gaheriet, the most valiant of our race, lying dead.'

He showed him to Sir Gawain, still all bloody in his arms, lying against his chest. When Sir Gawain heard this he had not the strength to answer a word or to remain standing, but lost consciousness and fell to the ground in a swoon. The barons were so grieved and distressed by this that they thought they would never again feel joy. When they saw Sir Gawain fall in that way, they took him in their arms and cried bitterly over him, saying:

'Ah, God! This is a terrible tragedy in every way.'

When Sir Gawain regained consciousness, he got up and ran to where he saw Gaheriet lying; then he took him from the king and pressed him hard against his chest, and began to kiss him. As he kissed him he fainted again, and fell to the ground in a swoon for a longer time than before. When he came to, he sat near Gaheriet and looked at him. Seeing how hard he had been struck, he said:

'Ah, brother, cursed be the arm that struck you in that way! Dear brother, the man who struck you certainly hated you. Brother, how did he have the heart to put you to death? Dear brother, how could Fortune allow you to suffer such a base and ugly death when she had endowed you with all good qualities? She used to be so kind and friendly to you and raised you up in her principal wheel. Brother, she has done this to kill me, to make me die of grief for you. It would certainly be quite fitting if I did, and I would not object, because now that I have seen your death, I no longer wish to live, except until I have taken my revenge on the traitor who did this to you.'

[101]   Sir Gawain said this, and would have said more, but his

heart was so afflicted that he could not say another word. When he had been silent for some time, grieving as much as was humanly possible, he looked to the right and saw Guerrehet and Agravain lying dead in front of the king on the shields on which they had been brought in. He recognized them straight away, and said, loud enough for everyone to hear:

'Ah, God! I have truly lived too long, when I see my flesh and blood killed so grievously.'

Then he fell on them several times, and was so affected by the great grief he had in his heart that the barons who were present there feared that he might die in their hands. The king asked his barons what he could do for Gawain, saying:

'If he stays here for long, I think he will die of grief.'

'My Lord,' they replied, 'we suggest that he should be carried from here, put to bed in another room and watched over until his brothers are buried.'

'Let us do that, then,' said the king.

So they took Sir Gawain, who was still unconscious, and they carried him into another room. He lay there in such a state that no one could get a word, good or bad, out of him.

[102] That night there was such great lamentation in the city of Camelot that there was nobody who was not in tears. The dead knights were disarmed and enshrouded, each according to his lineage. Coffins and tombs were made for them all. For Guerrehet and Agravain two coffins were made which were as beautiful and rich as those suitable for a king's sons; their bodies were placed in them, one beside the other, in St Stephen's Cathedral, at that time the principal church of Camelot. Between the two tombs the king ordered another to be made, even finer and more splendid than the others, and Gaheriet's body was placed in it next to his two brothers. At the moment that he was let down into the earth you could have seen many tears. All the bishops and archbishops of the country came, and all the high-born men, and they paid the dead knights the greatest honour that they could, especially Gaheriet, because they had been such good men and fine knights. They had an inscription put on his tomb saying, 'HERE LIES GAHERIET, KING ARTHUR'S NEPHEW, WHO

WAS KILLED BY LANCELOT DEL LAC'. They put on the other two tombs the names of those who had killed them.

[103] When all the clergy who had come there had conducted the burial service as was fitting, King Arthur returned to his palace and sat among his barons, as sad and pensive as could be. He would not have been so distressed if he had lost half his kingdom. All the other barons were in the same state. The hall was crowded with high-ranking barons, and they were all as quiet as if there had not been a soul there.

Seeing them so still, the king spoke loud enough for everyone to hear, and said:

'Ah, God! For so long you have allowed me to live in great honour, and now in a short time I have been so afflicted by real misfortune that no man has ever lost as much as I have. Because when it happens that someone loses his land through force or treason, that is something which it is quite possible to regain later; but when one loses one's closest friends whom one cannot recover by any means in the world, then the loss is irreversible, then the damage is so great that it cannot possibly be put right.This has befallen me not through God's justice, but through Lancelot's pride. If our grievous loss had come about through Our Lord's vengeance, then we should have found some honour in it and been able to suffer it easily; but instead it has happened through the man we have brought up and enriched in our country over a long period, as if he had been one of our very flesh and blood. It is he who has caused us this loss and this dishonour. You are all my men, and have sworn fidelity to me and hold fiefs from me; therefore I require you on the oath you have sworn to me, to help me, as one should help one's liege lord, so that my dishonour may be avenged.'

[104] Then the king fell silent and waited quietly for the barons to reply. They began to look at one another, urging one another to speak up. When they had been silent for a long time, King Yon stood up and said to the king:

'My Lord, I am your bondsman, and I must counsel you with our honour and yours in mind. It is certainly to your honour to avenge your shame. However, anyone who cared about the good of your kingdom would not I think declare war on King

Ban's kinsmen, because we know for a fact that Our Lord has raised King Ban's race above all others. Therefore, at present, so far as I know, there are no men anywhere in the world who are so noble that, if they declared war on them, they would not be the worse for it, provided only that you were not among them. For this reason, my Lord, I beg you for God's sake not to begin fighting them if you do not think you are definitely superior, because I certainly believe they would be very difficult to defeat.'

There was a great deal of shouting in the palace because many of them reproached and criticized King Yon for what he had said, and accused him openly of having spoken out of cowardice.

'I certainly did not say that,' he replied, 'because my fear was greater than that of any of you; but I know for a fact that when the war has begun, if they can manage to return to their country safe and well, they will be far less worried about your attacks than you think.'

'Indeed, Sir Yon,' said Mordred, 'I have never heard as noble a man as you give advice as bad as that; I think the king should go to war, and take you whether you want to go or not.'

'Mordred,' replied King Yon, 'I shall go more willingly than you. May the king set out when he wishes.'

'You are arguing quite uselessly,' said Mador de la Porte. 'If you want to declare war, you will not have far to go, because I have been told that Lancelot is between here and the sea in a castle he once conquered when he was beginning to seek adventures, called the Joyeuse Garde. I know the castle very well, because I was once imprisoned there, and feared I should die, until Lancelot released me and my companions.'

'I know that castle well, too,' said the king. 'Tell me if you think he has taken the queen with him.'

'My Lord,' said Mador, 'you can be sure the queen is there, but I do not recommend you to go, because the castle is so strong that it is in no danger of a siege from any side, and those inside are so noble that they would have little fear of your attacks. However, if they saw an opportunity to do you some harm, they would do it without hesitation.'

When the king heard this, he said:

'Mador, you are right about the strength of the castle, and about the self-assurance of those inside. However, you are perfectly aware, as are all those present, that since I first wore a crown I have never waged a war that I did not bring to an end to my honour and to that of my kingdom. For this reason you can be sure that nothing would make me hold back from fighting the men who have caused me such a great loss among my close friends. And now I summon those present here, and I shall call all those who hold lands from me, far and near. When they have assembled we shall leave the city of Camelot, in a fortnight's time. And because I do not want any of you to draw back from this undertaking, I require all of you to swear on the saints that you will continue fighting until our shame has been avenged to the honour of all of us.'

[105] Then the saints' relics were brought, and everyone in the palace, poor and rich together, swore that oath. When they had all sworn to keep up the fight, the king summoned through his messengers all those who held fiefs from him, far and near, to be present at Camelot on the stated day, because he then wanted to set out with all his forces to go to the castle of the Joyeuse Garde. Thereupon they all agreed and prepared to go to the district enclosed by the Humber. Thus they decided on the war that was later to turn to King Arthur's disadvantage; however superior they were at the beginning, they were beaten in the end.

But Rumour, which spreads so quickly through the world, arrived at the Joyeuse Garde the very next day after the matter had been discussed, since a boy, a sergeant of Hector des Mares, left court immediately and took the news there.

When he arrived, they were anxiously awaiting information from court. He told them that the war had been decided upon, and had been so affirmed that there could be no going back on it, because all the most powerful men at court had taken an oath, and afterwards all others who held fiefs from the king had been summoned.

'Have things then come to this?' asked Bors.

'Yes, my Lord,' replied the messenger, 'before long you will see King Arthur and all his forces.'

'In God's name,' said Hector, 'it is a pity they are coming, because they will repent it.'

[106] When Lancelot heard this news, he took a messenger and sent him to the kingdom of Banoic and to the kingdom of Gaunes, ordering his barons to stock their fortresses with provisions, so that, if it happened that he left Great Britain and had to return to the kingdom of Gaunes, he could find the castles strong and defensible to hold out against King Arthur, if need should be. Then he summoned all the knights he had served in Sorelois and in the Foreign Land, to help him against King Arthur. Because he was so highly regarded everywhere, so many men came that if Lancelot had been a king with a territory of his own, most people would not have thought it possible that he could have assembled such great chivalry as he did on that occasion.

But now the story stops telling of him and returns to King Arthur.

*

[107] Now the story relates that on the day King Arthur had summoned his men to Camelot, they came in such great numbers on foot and on horseback that no man had ever seen such great chivalry. Sir Gawain, who had been ill, was now better, and on the day they assembled there, he said to the king:

'My Lord, before you set out, I suggest that out of these barons here you choose as many good knights as were killed the other day when the queen was rescued, and that you promote them to the Round Table in place of those who died, so that we have the same number of knights as before, that is a hundred and fifty. I can tell you that if you do this your company will be more worthy in all ways and will be feared more.'

The king was quite in agreement with what he suggested, and commanded that it should be done, as nothing but good could come of it. Then straight away he called the high-ranking barons and ordered them on the oaths they had sworn him to elect as many of the best knights as were necessary to complete the Round Table, and that they should not refuse anyone for reasons of poverty. They said they would be pleased to do this.

So they drew apart and sat down in the main hall of the palace. They counted how many were missing from the Round Table, and found that the number was seventy-two. Therefore they straight away elected that number and installed them in the seats of those who had died, or had been with Lancelot. But no one was so bold as to sit in the Perilous Seat.[6] The knight who sat at Lancelot's place was called Elianz; he was the finest knight in the whole of Ireland and a king's son. In Bors' seat sat a knight called Balynor, the son of the King of the Strange Isles; he was a very fine knight. Hector's seat was occupied by a Scottish knight, powerful in arms and in the number of his friends; Gahariet's place was taken by a knight who was the nephew of the King of North Wales.

When they had done this on the recommendation of Sir Gawain, the tables were set and they all sat down. That day, seven kings who held fiefs from Arthur and were his liege men served at the Round Table and at the king's table. Then the knights who were to set out for the war prepared their departure, and worked well into the night before they were completely ready.

[108] In the morning, before sunrise, many thousands of men left Camelot, intending to harm Lancelot. As soon as King Arthur had heard mass in Camelot Cathedral, he mounted with his barons, and they rode until they came to a castle called Lamborc. The next day they travelled as far as they had done the first day; and they rode day after day until they came to within half a league of the Joyeuse Garde. Because they saw the castle was so strong that it was in no danger from attack, they camped in tents beside the river Humber; but this was a long way from the castle. All that day they saw to settling the camp; they had stationed armed knights in front of them so that, if it should happen that the people in the castle came out to fight, they would be as well received as one should receive one's enemy. That was how they camped.

However, their adversaries, who had foresight, had sent a great number of men the night before into a nearby forest, to surprise Arthur's army when the occasion arose, and rush out and attack them in front of the castle. Therefore the people in the castle were not at all dismayed when they saw the siege begin, but said to one another that they would leave the enemy in peace for the first night and attack them the next day, if they saw an opportunity. The group of men sent into the forest consisted of forty knights, led by Bors and Hector. The people in the castle had told them that when they saw a red flag raised above the fortress, they were to make a frontal attack on King Arthur's men; those who had remained in the castle would make a sortie at the same moment, so that Arthur's men would be assailed on two sides.

[109] All day the men in the wood kept a look out on the castle in case they should see the red flag which was their sign to attack, but they did not see it because Lancelot could not allow Arthur's army to be attacked on the first day. Instead he let them rest all day and all night, so that there was no fighting at all. As a result, Arthur's men felt more confident than before, and said among themselves that if Lancelot had had large forces, nothing would have stopped him from coming out to attack them and the whole army, because no true knight would willingly suffer injury from his enemy.

When Lancelot saw how the castle was besieged by King Arthur, the man he had most loved in the world and whom he now knew to be his mortal enemy, he was so saddened that he did not know what to do, not because he feared for himself but because he loved the king. He called a girl, took her into a room, and said to her in secret:

'Go to King Arthur and tell him from me that I cannot understand why he is waging war on me, because I did not imagine I had wronged him so much. If he says it is because of my lady the queen whom he has been led to believe I have dishonoured, tell him I am ready to prove I am not truly guilty of that wrong, by fighting one of the best knights in his court. Moreover, for his love, and to regain his good will which I have lost through unfortunate circumstances, I shall put myself under the jurisdiction of his court. If he has begun the war because of the death of his nephews, tell him I am not so guilty of their death that he should feel such mortal hatred for me, because those who died brought their deaths upon themselves. If he will not agree with these two things, tell him I shall meet his strength with mine, and that I shall be as sad as it is possible to be at this anger between us, sadder in fact than anyone could imagine. The king should know that because the war has been started, I shall defend myself with all my power. I assure him, because I hold him to be my lord and my friend – although he has not come here as my lord but as my mortal enemy – that he need have no fear of me concerning his own safety, because I shall always guarantee him to the best of my ability against those seeking to harm him. Tell him all this from me.'

The girl replied that she would willingly carry that message. [110] Then the girl went to the castle gate and left secretly; it was Vespers and King Arthur was sitting at supper. When she came to the army, no one tried to hold her back, because they saw it was a girl carrying a message. So they took her to King Arthur's tent. Recognizing the king among his barons, she went up to him and said what Lancelot had told her to say, just as he had directed.

Sir Gawain, who was close to King Arthur and heard the message, spoke before any of the other companions at court had uttered a word on the matter, and said in front of all the barons:

'My Lord, you are near to avenging your dishonour and the injury Lancelot has done you through your friends; and when you left Camelot, you swore to annihilate King Ban's kinsmen. I have told you this, my Lord, because you have a good opportunity to avenge your dishonour; if you made peace with Lancelot you would be shamed and your line abased, so that you would never again have any honour.'

'Gawain,' said the king, 'things have gone so far that while I am alive, whatever Lancelot may say or do, he will never be at peace with me. Of all the men in the world he is the one I ought most easily to forgive a great crime, since without any doubt he has done more for me than any other knight; but in the end he has made me pay too dearly for it, by taking away from me my dearest friends and those I loved most, excepting only you. For this reason there will never be peace between him and me, and he will never have it, I promise you as a king.'

Then the king turned towards the girl and said:

'You can tell your lord that I certainly will not do what he asks, but instead I assure him of a mortal war.'

'That is a greater pity for you than for anyone else,' replied the girl. 'You, who are one of the most powerful kings in the world and the most famous, will be destroyed and brought to death as a result of the war; you know that death often deceives wise men. And you, Sir Gawain, who ought to be the wisest, are in fact the most foolish of all, far more foolish than I thought, because you are seeking your own death as you can see quite clearly. Now think: do you not remember what you once saw in the Adventurous Palace of the Rich Fisher King, at the time you witnessed the battle of the serpent and the leopard?' If you had remembered correctly the marvels you saw and the interpretation of them the hermit gave you, this war would never have taken place as long as you could have avoided it. But your wickedness and your misfortune are pursuing you in this undertaking. You will repent when it is too late to put things right.'

Then the girl turned towards the king and said:

'My Lord, because I can only expect war from you, I shall go back to my lord and tell him what your reply is.'

'Go, then,' he said.

[III] So the girl left the army and went to the castle where they were waiting for her. She entered, and when she was before her lord and had told him that it was quite impossible to make peace with King Arthur, Lancelot was very angry, not because he feared him, but because he loved him deeply. Then he went into a room and began to think very hard. In his thoughts he sighed loudly, and the tears came to his eyes and ran down his face.

When he had been in this state for some time, the queen

happened to come into the room, and found him so pensive that she stood in front of him for a long while before he saw her. Seeing he was so deep in thought, she spoke to him and asked him why he was looking so miserable; he replied that he was thinking hard about not being able to find peace or mercy from King Arthur.

'My Lady,' he said, 'I am not saying that because we fear he could do us any great harm, but because he has treated me with so many honours and so many kindnesses that I should very much regret it if anything should happen to him.'

'My Lord,' she replied, 'you must take note of his strength. In any case, tell me what you intend to do.'

'I intend,' he said, 'that we should fight tomorrow, and to whomever God gives the honour, may he have it, because I shall do everything in my power to ensure that the army at present besieging the castle is soon removed. Since it has come about that I shall never have any peace or love from them, I shall never spare any of them, except King Arthur himself.'

At that point they finished their conversation and Lancelot went into the great palace and sat among his knights, and pretended to be more joyful than in fact he was in his heart. He ordered that the tables should be set and that everyone should be served as richly as if they were at King Arthur's court.

After those present had eaten, his closest friends asked him:

'What are we doing tomorrow? Are you not planning to attack the army?'

'Yes,' he said, 'before Terce.'

'If we stay shut in here for much longer,' they said, 'our enemies will think we are cowards.'

'Do not dismay;' said Lancelot, 'since we have not attacked yet, they are more confident than they were before, and fear us less. They think that if we have not yet gone out it is because we have no men inside. However, if it pleases God, before Vespers tomorrow they will know if I am alone in here, and they will repent, if I can make them, having started this war. We shall quite definitely make a sortie tomorrow and attack them, and therefore I am asking you all to be equipped, so that we can sally out when we see the best opportunity.'

They all agreed this was a good plan, because they were impatient to attack King Arthur's men. They were encouraged by the presence there of Lancelot and Bors, who were the most renowned in prowess and chivalry. That night they worked hard at preparing their equipment, being careful to see that there was nothing missing. They kept so quiet that the men in Arthur's army kept talking about it and told the king they were sure there were so few men inside that they would easily be able to take the castle. The king, too, said that he could not believe that there were many men inside.

'On the contrary, my Lord,' said Mador, 'they have many men, I am telling you truthfully, capable of fine chivalry.'

'How do you know?' asked Sir Gawain.

'My Lord, I am quite certain of it,' said Mador, 'and you may cut off my head if you do not see them come out before to-morrow evening.'

In this way the men in the army spoke for a long time that night about the people in the castle, and when it was time to sleep, they had their camp guarded so well and so thoroughly on all sides that no one could have done them much harm.

[112] The next day, as soon as those in the castle were ready and had formed six battalions, they flew the red flag from the highest tower. As soon as this was seen by those lying in wait in the forest, they pointed it out to Bors, who said:

'Now we must be ready to move, because Sir Lancelot has mounted together with his company, and they will be coming out straight away. All we have to do now is to attack the army, so that nothing remains standing in front of us as we come, and everything is struck to the ground.'

And they said that they would all do their best.

Then they left the wood where they had been in hiding and rode on to the plain. They all made their horses move forward as quietly as possible, but they were unable to prevent the men in the army noticing them, since they were able to hear them coming by the sound of their hooves. Those who saw them first shouted:

'Now to arms!'

They shouted so loud that it was quite audible to the men in the castle, who said that Bors' troops had run at the army and that all they had to do was to attack it from another side. This they did; Lancelot commanded that the gate should be opened and that they should make a sortie, keeping their ranks in the correct fashion. They did this at once, because they were very impatient to go out. Meanwhile Bors had left the hiding-place, and as soon as he approached the army, he met King Yon's son, riding a large horse. When they saw each other, they spurred on their horses without delay. King Yon's son broke his lance, and Bors struck him so hard that neither the other man's shield nor his coat of mail could prevent him from putting blade and shaft in his body; and Bors knocked him to the ground ready for death. The other men coming after him began striking down pavilions and tents, killing people and flattening whatever they came across.

Then the hue and cry in the army became so loud that one would not even have heard God thundering. Those without arms ran to fetch them, and when Sir Gawain saw how far things had gone, he ordered his arms to be brought quickly. The man he commanded brought them to him.

The king had himself armed hurriedly, as also did all the barons, prompted by the great noise they heard on all sides. And as soon as the king had mounted, together with those around him, he saw his pavilion fall to the ground, and the dragon surmounting it, and the other pavilions; all this was being done by Bors and Hector who wanted to capture the king.

When Sir Gawain saw the astonishing things they were doing, he pointed them out to the king, saying:

'My Lord, look at Bors and Hector wreaking all that havoc.'

Then Sir Gawain spurred on his horse against Hector; he struck him so hard on his helmet that he quite dazed him, and if Hector had not quickly held on to his horse's neck, he would have fallen to the ground. Sir Gawain hated him mortally, and when he saw him so dazed he did not want to leave him, but, being very experienced in warfare, he struck him another blow, which made him bend forward over his saddle-bow.

When Bors saw that Sir Gawain was pressing Hector so hard

that he had almost struck him to the ground, he could not help going to his aid, because he loved Hector dearly. So he rode up to Sir Gawain, brandishing his sword, and struck him so hard that his sword went two finger-breadths into his helmet. Sir Gawain was so dazed by this that he immediately rode away and left Hector. He rode off from Bors so stunned that he did not know which way his horse was taking him.

[113] Thus the fight began in front of the king's tent; but Bors' men would have been killed if it had not been for Lancelot and the men from the castle who spurred on their horses when they all arrived near the army, and started attacking the others. Then you could have seen blows given and received and men dying in great pain. They fought so much in a short time that they hated one another mortally, because there were so many dead and wounded that day that there is no heart in the world so hard that it would not have taken pity.

But of all those who took part in the battle and bore arms that day, the most outstanding were Sir Gawain and Lancelot. The story tells that Sir Gawain, who still grieved at Gaheriet's death, killed thirty knights that day, and indeed he did not tire from valiant acts before Vespers.

When night had come, King Arthur's knights returned to their tents as soon as they could, because they had fought hard. The others had too, and returned to their castle. When they were back inside they counted how many of their men they had lost, and found that there were at least a hundred knights missing, not to speak of the sergeants who had been killed, about whom the story is silent. In return for all this they had only ten prisoners they had brought back to the castle by force.

[114] When they had disarmed in their lodgings, they all went to dine at court, the wounded and the healthy, just as it had befallen each of them. That night, after supper, they kept talking about Sir Gawain and said that no one had done so well that day except Lancelot and Bors.

When the men from the army were back in their tents and had counted how many of their knights they had lost, they found that there were two hundred missing. They were very angry about this. After they had eaten that evening they began to speak about those in the castle, and said that the castle was certainly not lacking in men and that they were good and valiant knights. The knights they esteemed most that day were Sir Gawain and Lancelot; they said they were the two knights who had been most outstanding in the fighting.

When it was time to sleep, some went to rest, because they were weary and exhausted, while others kept watch all night over the army, since they feared that those from the castle might come to their tents; however, if they did, they would not find them unarmed, but, on the contrary, ready to receive them.

[115] That night after supper Lancelot spoke to his companions and said:

'My Lords, now you have learnt how the men in the army can strike with their swords, because they have put you closely to the test today and so have we them; but they cannot really rejoice at the gains they have made because they have greater numbers than we. We have done well, thanks be to God, since with few men we have held out against their strength. Now decide what we shall do tomorrow and how we shall behave from now on. I would like, if it were possible and God would allow us, to bring this war to such a just conclusion that our honour is as sure as it was at the beginning. Now tell me what you would like me to do, because nothing will be done without your recommendation.'

They said that they wanted to continue fighting the next day.

'My Lords,' said Lancelot, 'since you wish to fight them, decide then who will go out first.'

Bors said that no one would go out before him, because however early day broke he would be ready armed to ride out and attack the men in the army. Hector said he would go out after him with the second battalion. Eliezier, King Pellés' son, a fine bold knight, said he would lead the third battalion and take the men from his country; and another, a knight from Sorelois, the Duke of Aroel, who was a marvellously fine knight, asked to be able to lead the fourth battalion, and this was readily granted him, because he was noble and experienced in warfare.

Afterwards the people in the castle continued until they had established eight battalions, each consisting of a hundred armed knights. In the last, in which they had placed their greatest strength and their greatest confidence, they appointed Lancelot by common agreement.

Thus they arranged all their battalions the night before, and put a good leader at the head of each. That evening they saw to the wounded; when Bors saw that Hector was hurt and knew that Sir Gawain had wounded him, he was not a little angry. He said in front of everyone that he would avenge him, if he had the opportunity. That night the injured men in the castle rested, because they were very weary.

The next day, immediately it was light, before sunrise, they ran to their arms as soon as they were dressed and shod. They left the castle one after the other in very orderly fashion. When the men in the army saw them coming down, they rushed to their arms and ran fully equipped from their tents.

It happened that Sir Gawain led the first battalion, and Bors was at the head of the first on his side. Sir Gawain was not sorry about this, because Bors was the man he most hated in the world with a deadly hatred. When they were close together, they spurred their horses at each other, with their lances at length, and came on as fast as their horses could go. They struck each other so hard that no arms could prevent them from being knocked to the ground with so much steel in them that neither was able to get up. This was not surprising, because the blades had gone right through each of them.

After this blow the two first battalions came together; they spurred their horses at one another and struck one another so amazingly, because they hated one another mortally, that in a very short time you could have seen a good hundred of them fall without being able to get up again, for many lay dead and many wounded; at that moment discomfiture and misfortune were turning the way of those in the army. That was because in the first battalion of men from the castle there was a knight from the Foreign Land who was carrying out such marvellous feats of arms during that attack that King Arthur's men were being defeated by him.

When they had cleared a certain space, the men from the castle ran to where Sir Gawain and Bors lay wounded. They took them and would have carried off Sir Gawain by force, as they found no defence in him, if the men from the army had not come that way to rescue him. Moreover, despite some difficulty they were able to ensure that the men from the castle had to leave him behind, whether they wanted to or not. However, in all their distress and great anguish the men from the castle made such great efforts that they were able to carry Bors back up to the castle on his shield, wounded as he was.

You could never have seen a man or a woman in such great grief as the queen, when she saw him injured and bleeding. The doctors were summoned and drew out of him the fragment of the lance with the whole blade. When they had examined the wound properly, they said it was very difficult to heal; but nevertheless they thought they would be able to make him healthy and well in a short time, with the help of God. They looked after him to the best of their knowledge and ability.

The men assembled in the fields beside the River Humber began the battle at dawn, and it lasted as late as the hour of Vespers in summer. Neither you nor anyone else could ever have seen such a cruel and violent battle as the one that day, since there were many slain on each side. That day King Arthur bore arms, and did it so well that there was no man of his age in the world who could have equalled him; indeed the story affirms that on his side there was no knight, old or young, who bore arms as well as he did. Through the example of his fine chivalry all his men fought so well that the men from the castle would have been conquered if it had not been for Lancelot.

When the king, who recognized Lancelot's arms, saw what he was doing, he said to himself:

'If that man lives much longer, he will put my men to shame.'

Then the king attacked him, brandishing his sword very valiantly. When Lancelot saw him coming, he did not get ready to defend himself, except to cover himself with his shield, because he loved the king too much. The king struck him so hard that he hit his horse in its neck, and knocked Lancelot down. Hector, who was close to Lancelot, saw this blow, and was very angry because he feared Lancelot was wounded; so he galloped up to the king and struck him a great blow on his helmet. As a result, Arthur was so dazed that he did not know whether it was night or day. Hector, well aware that it was the king, struck another blow, and Arthur did not have the strength to remain in his saddle, but crashed to the ground beside Lancelot. Then Hector said to Lancelot:

'My Lord, cut off his head, and our war will be over.'

'Ah, Hector!' said Lancelot, 'What are you saying? Do not say that again, because you would be wasting your time.'

[116] Through saying this Lancelot rescued King Arthur from death, for Hector would have killed him. When Lancelot himself had put King Arthur back on his horse, they left the battle. The king returned to his army and said, in front of all those who were with him:

'Did you see what Lancelot did for me today? He was in a position to kill me but refused to touch me. In faith, today he has surpassed in goodness and courtesy all the knights I have ever seen; now I wish this war had never been begun, because today he has conquered my heart more with his gallantry than the whole world could have done by force.'

This was what the king said in confidence, and it made Sir Gawain, despite his wound, very angry when he heard it.

When Lancelot had returned to the castle, the men who disarmed him found he had many injuries, the smallest of which would have hindered most other knights. When he and Hector were disarmed, they went to see Bors and asked his doctor if he was badly wounded. He replied that his wound was very deep, but that he thought he would soon recover.

[117] Thus the king maintained his siege of the Joyeuse Garde for two months and more. It happened that the men inside often came out and fought against the others; and as a result they lost a great number of their knights, because they did not have as many men as there were in Arthur's army.

During that time the Pope happened to hear that King Arthur had left his wife and promised to kill her if he could catch her. When the Pope heard that she had not been proved guilty of the crime of which she was accused, he ordered the archbishops and bishops of the country to excommunicate and lay under an interdict the whole of the land that Arthur held, unless he took his wife back and lived with her in peace and honour as a king should with his queen.

When the king heard this order he was very angry; and yet he loved the queen so much, although he was sure she had sinned against him, that he was easily persuaded to obey it. However, he said that if she returned, that would not put an end to his war against Lancelot now that he had begun it.

So the Bishop of Rochester went to the queen and said:

'My Lady, you must return to your lord King Arthur, because that is what the Pope has ordered. The king will promise you, in the presence of all his barons, that from now on he will treat you as a king should treat his queen, and that neither he nor any man in his court will take account of anything said about you and Lancelot, wherever you are.'

'My Lord,' she replied, 'I shall take advice and tell you shortly what I have been recommended to do.'

[118] Then the queen summoned Lancelot, Bors, Hector and Lionel to a room, and when they were before her, she said:

'My Lords, you are the men in whom I have the greatest confidence in the world. Now I beg you to advise me on what is best and most honourable for me, depending on what you consider it is my interest to do. I have received a piece of news that ought to please me and you too; the king, the noblest man in the world, as you yourselves say every day, has asked me to return to him, and will hold me just as dear as he ever did in the past. He is paying me a great honour by asking me back and by not paying attention to how I have sinned against him so much. This will be honourable for you too, because I certainly shall never leave here if he does not put aside his ill-feelings towards you, or at least allow you to leave the country and not to suffer the slightest loss while you are still here. Now tell me what you would like; if you would prefer me to stay here with you, I shall stay, and if you prefer me to go, I shall go.'

'My Lady,' said Lancelot. 'if you acted as my heart desired, you would stay; nevertheless, because I want things to work out more to your honour than to my desires, you must return to your lord, King Arthur. Because, if you do not go now, after this offer he has made you, there is no one who would not openly recognize your shame and my great disloyalty. For this reason I want you to send a message to the king saying that you will return tomorrow. I can tell you that when you leave me, you will be so splendidly escorted to the best of our ability that never will a high-born lady have been treated so well. I am not saying this, my Lady, because I love you more than a knight has ever loved a lady during our lifetimes, but for your honour.'

Then the tears came to his eyes, and the queen also began to cry. When Bors heard that Lancelot was allowing the queen to return to King Arthur, he said:

'My Lord, you have agreed this very lightly; may God grant that good may come of it. I certainly think you may never done anything that you will repent so much. You will go to Gaul and my lady the queen will stay in this country, and circumstances will prevent your ever seeing her again at any time. I know your heart so well, and also the great desire you have for her, that I am quite sure that before a month has passed, you would rather have given away the whole world, if it had been yours, instead of granting this. I am afraid you may suffer far more from it than you think.'

When Bors had said this, the other two agreed with him, and began to criticize Lancelot, saying:

'My Lord, what fear do you have of the king that you should return my lady to him?'

But he said that he would send her back, whatever was to come of it, even if he was to die through missing her so much. Thus the conversation ended, when they heard Lancelot say that nothing would prevent him from sending the queen back. She returned to the bishop who was waiting for her in the middle of the hall and said:

'My Lord, now you may go to my lord the king; greet him from me and tell him that I shall never leave here unless he allows Lancelot to depart without suffering the slightest loss either to his possessions or to his retinue.'

When the bishop heard her say this, he thanked God sincerely, because he could see that the war was over. He commended the queen to God, and everyone in the palace as well, and then he went down from the castle and rode right up to the king's tent. He told him the news he had heard in the castle.

Hearing that they were ready to send the queen back, the king said, in front of all those present:

'By God, if it were true about Lancelot and the queen as I was led to understand, he is not in such a bad position in this war that he would give her up for months, if he loved her adulterously. Because he has carried out my wishes so courteously in what I have asked him, I shall do all that the queen has requested. I shall allow him to leave this country and if he comes across anyone who does him the slightest harm, I shall repay him twofold.'

Then he commanded the bishop to go back to the castle and tell the queen in the name of the king that Lancelot might safely leave the country, and because he had so courteously agreed to his request, the king would even lend him part of his own navy to cross over to Gaul.

The bishop mounted straight away, went back to the castle, and told the queen what the king had commanded. Thus the matter was agreed on both sides that the queen would be returned to her lord the next day, and that Lancelot would leave the kingdom of Logres and go with his company to the kingdom of Gaunes, of which they were the lawful lords and inheritors.

That night the men in the army were happy and joyful when they saw the war was over, because most of them feared that they would get the worst of it if it lasted much longer. And if they were much happier and more joyful than they had generally been, the men in the castle were tearful and sad, the poor as well as the rich. Do you know why they were so sad? Because they saw that Bors, Lancelot, Hector and Lionel were grieving as much as if they could see the whole world lying dead before them.

[119] That night there was great sadness at the Joyeuse Garde, and when day broke, Lancelot said to the queen:

'My Lady, today is the day you will leave me, and the day I must leave this country. I do not know if I shall ever see you again. Here is a ring you gave me long ago when I first became acquainted with you, and which I have always kept up till now for love of you. Now I beg you always to wear it for love of me as long as you live; I shall take the one you are wearing on your finger.'

She willingly gave it to him. Thereupon they ended their conversation, and went to prepare themselves as splendidly as they could.

That day the four cousins were richly dressed. When they had mounted with all the other men in the castle, they rode to the army under a safe conduct with more than five hundred horses all covered in silk. They went along jousting and showing the greatest joy that you could ever have seen.

The king came to meet them with a large number of knights, and when the moment came that Lancelot saw the king approaching him, he dismounted and took the queen by the reins of her horse, and said to the king:

'My Lord, here is the queen, whom I am returning to you. She would have died some time ago through the disloyalty of those in your household, if I had not risked my life to save her. I did not do it because of any kindness I have ever had from her, but only because I know her to be the worthiest lady in the world; and it would have been too great a shame and too grievous a loss if the disloyal men in your household who had sentenced her to death had carried out their intentions. It was better for them to die as a result of their disloyalty than that she should be killed.'

Then the king received her, very miserable and pensive after what Lancelot had said to him.

'My Lord,' said Lancelot, 'if I loved the queen adulterously as you have been led to understand, I should not have handed her back to you for months, and you would never have had her through using force.'

'Lancelot,' said the king, 'I am very grateful to you for what you have done; it may stand you in good stead some time in the future.'

Then Sir Gawain came forward and said to Lancelot:

'The king is grateful to you for what you have done. But he requests one more thing of you yet.'

'What, my Lord?' asked Lancelot. 'Tell me and I shall do it, if I can.'

'He requests you,' said Sir Gawain, 'to leave his country and never to set foot here again.'

'My Lord,' said Lancelot to the king, 'is that what you wish me to do?'

'Because that is what Gawain desires,' said the king, 'it is what I want too. Leave my land on this side of the sea and go across to your very beautiful and rich country.'

'My Lord,' said Lancelot, 'when I am in my country, shall I be safe from you? What can I expect from you, peace or war?'

'You can be sure,' said Sir Gawain, 'that you will not be safe from war, because you will have it more violently than you have had it up till now, and it will last until my brother Gaheriet, whom you killed wickedly, is avenged by your own death. Moreover I should not take the whole world in exchange for the chance to cut off your head.'

'Sir Gawain,' said Bors, 'stop threatening now, because I can tell you truly that my lord does not fear you. If you go so far as to come after us to the kingdom of Gaunes or to the kingdom of Banoic, you can be sure of being nearer to losing your head than my lord is. You have said that my lord killed your brother treacherously. If you would like to prove this as an honourable knight, I should defend my lord against you, so that if I were defeated, Sir Lancelot would be dishonoured, while if I could get the better of you, you would be in the bad position of being a false accuser. And the war would thus be ended. Indeed, if you agreed, it would be much better for this quarrel to be settled by you and me than by forty thousand men.'

Sir Gawain threw down his gage and said to the king:

'My Lord, since he has offered to fight, he will not be able to retract, because I am ready to prove against him that Lancelot killed my brother Gaheriet treacherously.'

Bors jumped up and said he was ready to defend himself; and the battle would have been sworn if the king had wanted it, because Sir Gawain desired nothing else, and Bors wished to fight in single combat against him. But the king refused gages from both of them and said he would not allow the battle; however, he said that when they had gone their ways each would have to look after himself, and Lancelot could be sure that as soon as he was back in his country he would find himself in a greater war than he could imagine.

'Indeed, my Lord,' said Lancelot, 'you would not be in such a favourable position to continue the war as you are now, if I had done as much to harm you as I did to help you the day that Galeholt, the Lord of the Distant Isles, became your liege man at the very moment when he had the power to strip you of lands and honour, and when you were very close to receiving the humiliation of losing your crown and being deprived of your birthright. If you remembered that day as you should, you certainly would not be involved in waging this war against me. I am not saying this, my Lord, because I fear you, but because of the love you ought to feel for me if you were as grateful for good deeds done for you as a king should be. Indeed, as soon as we are back in our own country with our liege men, and we have summoned our forces and our friends and provisioned our castles and fortresses, I assure you that if you come and we do all we can to harm you, you will never have done anything that you repent as much as this, because I can tell you it will never bring you any honour. You, Sir Gawain, who are so cruelly causing bitterness between us and the king, you certainly should not be doing that, because if you remembered that I once freed you from the Dolorous Tower on the day I killed Caradoc the Great, and released you from his prison where he had left you as if to die, you would not feel any hatred for me.'

'Lancelot,' replied Sir Gawain, 'there is nothing you have done for me that recently you have not made me pay for very dearly; because you have so grievously taken away from me those I loved most, that our lineage has been quite abased, and I am shamed. For this reason there cannot be peace between us, and there never will be for as long as I live.'

Then Lancelot said to the king:

'My Lord, I shall leave your territory tomorrow and for all the services I have rendered you since I first became a knight, I shall take away nothing in reward.'

[120] Thereupon the conversation ended, and the king went back to his tents and took the queen with him. Then there was as much joy among them as if God himself had descended there. But unlike the men in the army, who were joyful and happy, the men in the castle were miserable, because they were distressed at seeing their lord more pensive than he usually was.

When Lancelot had dismounted, he commanded all his retinue to prepare their equipment, because he was planning to leave for the coast the next day, and to cross the sea to Gaunes. The same day, he called a squire named Kanahin and said to him:

'Take my shield from that room and go straight to Camelot; carry it to St Stephen's Cathedral and leave it in a place where it can remain and be seen, so that everyone who sees it in the future will remember my adventures in this country. Do you know why I am paying that place such an honour? It is because I first received the order of chivalry there, and I love that city more than any other; and also because I want my shield to be there to compensate for my absence, as I do not know if it will ever happen that I shall return there, once I have left this country.'

[121] The boy took the shield and together with it Lancelot gave four pack-horses loaded with riches, so that the church-men could always pray for him, and improve the building. When the people carrying these gifts arrived in Camelot, they were welcomed with great joy. The church-people were no less glad at receiving Lancelot's shield than his other gifts; they immediately had it hung up in the middle of the cathedral on a silver chain, and honoured it as if it had been a holy relic. When the local people heard about it, they came to see it in

great numbers. Many cried when they saw the shield, because of Lancelot's departure.

But now the story stops telling of them and returns to Lancelot and his company.

*

[122] In this part the story tells that after the queen had been returned to the king, Lancelot left the Joyeuse Garde; in fact he gave it, with the king's permission, to one of his knights who had long served him, so that wherever the knight might be he would receive the income from the castle during his lifetime.

When Lancelot had left with all his company, they saw they were about four hundred knights, not counting the squires and the others who followed the procession on foot or on horseback. After Lancelot had arrived at the coast and boarded the ship, he looked at the land and the country where he had had such great fortune and which had honoured him so much. He began to go pale and sigh from the bottom of his heart, and his eyes began to water profusely.

After he had been like that for some time, he spoke under his breath. No one on board heard him except Bors.

[123] 'Ah! sweet land, full of all happiness, and in whom my spirit and my life will remain, I bless you in the name of Jesus Christ; blessed be all those who remain in you, whether my friends or my enemies. May they have peace! May they find rest! May God give them greater joy than I now have! May God give them victory and honour against all those who wish to do you any harm! Indeed, they will have it, because no one could come from such a gentle land as this without being happier than anyone else. I can say that I have put that to the test, because as long as I lived there my happiness was more complete than it would have beeen, had I been in any other land.'

[124] That was how Lancelot spoke when he left the kingdom of Logres; as long as he could see the country he kept his eyes on it, and when it was out of sight he went to lie down on a bed. He began to lament so very deeply that no one who saw him could have failed to take pity on him. This grief continued until they came to the other shore.

When they had disembarked, he mounted on horseback together with his company and they rode until they came to a wood. Lancelot dismounted here and ordered his tents to be put up, because that was where he wished to stay the night. Those whose job it was to see to his needs carried out his instructions immediately.

That night Lancelot slept there; and the next day he left and rode until he arrived in his country. When the local people heard that he was coming, they went to meet him, and welcomed him with great joy because he was their lord.

[125] The day after his arrival, when he had heard mass, he went up to Bors and Lionel, and said:

'Grant me a favour, I beg you.'

'My Lord,' they said, 'it is not for you to beg us but to command us; we shall not fail, even at the cost of life or limb, to carry out your orders straight away.'

'Bors, I want you to be Lord of Banoic, and you, Lionel, will be Lord of Gaunes as your father was. I shall not speak of the Lordship of Gaul, because King Arthur gave it to me; even if he had given me the whole world, I should return it to him at this moment.'

They said that, as it was his wish, they would accept. Lancelot told them he wanted them to be crowned on All Saints' Day.

[126] So they both knelt before him and received their titles from him; and the day he installed them was only a month and two days before All Saints. When the people knew that the two brothers were to be crowned on that day and invested in their lands, one in the kingdom of Banoic and the other in the kingdom of Gaunes, then you could have seen great delight through the whole land, and ordinary people unusually joyful. Everyone could well say that the most pensive and miserable of them all was Lancelot, because he was able to put on a happy look only with great difficulty; in fact he pretended to be far more joyful and light-hearted than he really was.

[127] When the feast of All Saints came, all the high-ranking barons of the country had assembled at Banoic. On the very day that the two brothers were crowned, Lancelot heard that

King Arthur wished to attack him, and would do so without fail once winter had passed. He had already prepared some of his equipment, and the whole thing was due to the incitement of Sir Gawain. When Lancelot heard the news, he replied to the men who brought it to him:

'Let the king come, then; he will be welcome! We shall certainly receive him well, if it pleases God, because our castles are strong in their walls and in other parts, and our land is well provided with food and chivalry. The king may come safely, because he need not fear death in any place where I am present, so long as I can recognize him. But I can tell you that if Sir Gawain comes here, because he is so hostile to us without reason and is doing so much to harm us, he will never leave healthy and well if I have my will. He will never have become involved in any war in all his life that he will repent as much as this, if he comes here.'

Thus Lancelot spoke to the man who brought him the news; he assured him that King Arthur would be better received than he expected.

The other man replied that the king would never have become involved if Sir Gawain had not compelled him to.

But now the story stops speaking about Lancelot and returns to King Arthur and Sir Gawain.

*

[128] Now the story tells that all that winter King Arthur remained in the kingdom of Logres. He was as satisfied as he could be, because there was nothing to displease him. While he went riding through his towns and staying from day to day in his most comfortable castles, Sir Gawain exhorted him so much to reopen hostilities against Lancelot, that he promised as a king that as soon as Easter was past he would march on Lancelot with a drafted army and would strive very hard, even if it caused his death, to destroy the fortresses of Banoic and Gaunes so that not one stone would be left standing on another. This was the promise made to Sir Gawain, and it was a promise he could not keep.

[129] In the spring, after Easter, when the cold weather had

more or less passed, the king summoned all his barons and equipped his ships to cross the sea. They assembled in the city of London.

When they were about to leave, Sir Gawain asked his uncle:

'My Lord, in whose guard are you leaving my lady the queen?'

The king began to think about the person to whom he could entrust her. Then Mordred jumped forward and said to him:

'My Lord, if you like, I shall stay to look after her. With me she would be safer, and you could be surer of her, than if she were in anyone else's keeping.'

The king told Mordred he would be pleased if he stayed and looked after her as he would after himself.

'My Lord,' said Mordred, 'I promise you that I will.'

The king took her by the hand and gave her to Mordred, telling him to care for her as loyally as a liege man should care for his lord's wife. In that way Mordred received her. The queen was very angry that she had been given over to his charge because she knew such wickedness and disloyalty in him that she was sure that suffering and ill would come of it. In fact they were even greater than she could have imagined.

The king gave Mordred the keys of all his treasures, in case he should be in need of gold or silver when he was in the kingdom of Gaunes, so that Mordred could send him some if he called for it. The king commanded the people to do exactly as Mordred wished, and he made them swear on the saints that they would not fail to carry out anything he ordered. This was the oath that the king later repented so grievously, because as a result of it he was to be defeated in the field on Salisbury Plain where the battle was a mortal one, as this very story will describe in detail.

[130] Then King Arthur straight away set out from the city of London together with a great company of good knights, and rode until he arrived at the coast. The queen accompanied him there, whether he wanted to or not.

When the king was about to board his ship, the queen was very sad and said to him in tears, when he kissed her:

'My Lord, may God take you where you have to go and

bring you back safe and sound. I can tell you I have never feared so much for you as I do now. However you may return, my heart tells me I shall never see you again, nor will you see me.'

'My Lady,' said the king, 'you will, if it pleases God; and do not be frightened or apprehensive for me, because fear can do you no good.'

Thereupon the king boarded his ship, and the sails were raised to catch the wind. The master mariners were well equipped to carry out their duties, and it was not long before the wind had taken them so far out from the shore that they could see they were on the open sea. The wind was good, and they soon arrived in Gaul; for this they thanked Our Lord.

When they had disembarked, the king ordered all the equipment to be unloaded from the ships, and for their tents to be set up on the shore, because he wished to rest. His men did exactly as he had commanded. That night the king slept in a meadow close to the shore.

In the morning, as he was leaving there, he counted how many men he had; they found they were more than forty thousand. So they journeyed until they arrived in the kingdom of Banoic. When they were there, they did not find the castles unprepared, because there was not one that Lancelot had not had improved or rebuilt.

After they arrived, the king asked his men which way they should go.

'My Lord,' said Sir Gawain, 'we will go straight to the city of Gaunes, where King Bors, King Lionel and Hector are, with all their forces. If by any chance we can manage to capture them, we shall easily be able to bring our war to an end.'

'By God,' said Sir Yvain, 'it is madness to go straight to that city, because all the strength of this country is there. For that reason it would be much better for us first to destroy the castles and towns around the city of Gaunes, so that we shall not be in danger of attack when we have besieged those inside.'

'Ah!' said Sir Gawain. 'Do not dismay – there will be no one so bold as to dare to leave a castle once they know we are in the country.'

'Gawain,' said the king, 'let us then go and besiege Gaunes, because that is what you want.'

Then King Arthur went straight to Gaunes with his company. When he was not far away, he met a very old woman, richly dressed and riding a white palfrey. When she recognized King Arthur, she said:

[131] 'King Arthur, there is the city that you have come to attack. I can tell you truly that it is great madness and that you are ill-advised, because no honour will come to you from this war you have undertaken. You will never take that city, but will leave without having achieved anything. That is the honour you will have. And you, Sir Gawain, who have recommended the king to do this and have persuaded him to begin this war, be certain that you are so resolutely pursuing your own destruction that you will never again in good health see the kingdom of Logres. Now you can truly say that the time has come that was promised long ago as you left the castle of the Rich Fisher King, where you were dishonoured and disgraced.'

[132] When she had said this, she turned away very quickly without wishing to hear anything that Sir Gawain or King Arthur might say in reply. She rode straight to the city of Gaunes, entered, and went to the main palace, where she found Lancelot and the two kings, who had a great company of knights with them. When she had gone up to the main palace, she came before the two kings and told them that King Arthur was half a league from the city and that already more than ten thousand of his men could be seen. They replied that they were not concerned, because they did not fear them.

Then they asked Lancelot:

'My Lord, what shall we do? King Arthur is encamping his men out there. We ought to attack them before their camp is finished.'

Lancelot said that they would attack them the next day.

King Bors and all the others agreed with this. Lancelot had it announced through the city that his men should be mounted the next morning before Prime; most of them were pleased and happy about this, because they preferred war to peace. That night the men in the army were comfortable and those in the city were left in peace.

In the morning, as soon as it was light, the men in the city arose and took their arms as quickly as they could, because they were waiting impatiently for the hour when they were to attack those outside. When they were ready, they came before the palace and all stopped in the street, on horseback, until it was time to leave.

That day Lancelot and Hector constituted their battalions and appointed a good leader for each. The men in the army also formed twenty battalions. Sir Gawain and Sir Yvain were in the first battalion, because they had heard that Lancelot and Bors were in the first battalion on the other side.

When these two battalions came together, Gawain and Lancelot fought together, and also Yvain and Bors. All four of them knocked each other to the ground, and Yvain almost broke his arm. Then the battalions advanced on both sides, and such a great and violent battle began that you could have seen many knights fall. But Lancelot had remounted his horse, and put his hand to his sword, and was striking great blows around him. Moreover, King Arthur's men had helped Sir Gawain back on to his horse, whether the men from the city wanted that or not.

So all the battalions entered the fight before Terce had passed, and joined the battle in which many good men and many fine knights died. But when King Lionel took part in the battle, you could have seen King Arthur's men very dismayed at the great feats of arms he was carrying out. Moreover they would have lost many men that day if it had not been for King Arthur who acted very valiantly in the battle. He himself wounded King Lionel in the head, and the men from the city were so afraid when they saw him badly injured that the battle ended before Vespers and they returned home.

[133] In that way the men in the army fought against the men from the city four times in a week, and there were many knights killed on both sides. However, the men outside lost more than those inside, because Lancelot and Bors, who were ready for all eventualities and were always well prepared to

harm their enemies, did it very successfully. The men in the city were considerably reassured by the three cousins, because it seemed to them that these three were the only ones of whom the men in the army were really frightened.

But now the story stops talking about all of them and returns to Mordred.

*

[134] Now the story tells that after King Arthur had handed the queen over to Mordred's safe-keeping and had left the kingdom of Logres to march against Lancelot, as has already been related, Mordred, who had been entrusted with all the king's lands, summoned all the high-ranking barons of the country to him, and began to hold great courts and to make many gifts. Eventually he won over the hearts of all the nobles who had remained on King Arthur's territory, to such an extent that there was nothing he could command in the country that was not immediately carried out as if the king had been there.

Mordred was so often with the queen that he fell in love with her and did not see how he could fail to die of love, if his desires were not satisfied. However, he did not dare to admit it, but loved her as deeply as it was possible to love without dying.

Then Mordred planned a great act of treason which has been spoken about ever since. He had a letter written and sealed with a forgery of King Arthur's seal; this was then taken to the queen and read before the barons by an Irish bishop. This is what the letter said:

[135] 'I greet you as one who has been mortally wounded at Lancelot's hand; all my men have been killed and slaughtered. I feel more pity for you than for any other people, because of the great loyalty I have found in you. For the sake of peace I beg you to appoint Mordred king of the land of Logres. (I have always treated him as my nephew, but he is not.) You will certainly never see me again, because Lancelot has mortally wounded me and killed Gawain. Moreover, I request you on the oath you swore to me that you marry the queen to

Mordred. If you did not do this you might suffer as a result, because if Lancelot knew she was not married, he would attack you and take her as his wife. That is the thing my soul would most regret.'

[136] All this was written in the false letter and read out word for word before the queen. When Mordred, who had carried out this act of treason without anyone knowing about it apart from himself and the boy who had brought the letter, had heard the contents read out, he pretended that he was very distressed, and fell down among the barons as if in a swoon. However, the queen was quite convinced that the news was true, and one can really say that she was so grieved that no one could have seen her without feeling pity for her.

In all parts of the palace people began to lament so loudly that one could not have heard God thundering. When the news had spread round the city and it was known that King Arthur had been slain together with all those who had gone with him, poor and rich lamented greatly for the king, because he was the most loved of all the princes in the world and had always been kind and courteous to them. The grief caused by this news lasted so intensely for a whole week that no one was able to sleep a great deal.

When they were beginning to feel a little better, Mordred went to the most powerful of the barons and asked them what they were going to do about the king's orders. They said that they would discuss the matter together.

At their meeting they decided to make Mordred king, marry the queen to him, and become his liege men. This was right for two reasons, they said: first, King Arthur had asked them to do this, and secondly they did not see among them another man so worthy of such an honour as Mordred was.

[137] So they told Mordred that they would do exactly what the king had requested, and he thanked them.

'Since you agree that the king's request should be carried out,' he said, 'it only remains to summon the queen. This archbishop will perform the marriage ceremony.'

They said they would fetch her, and went to find her in a room where she was, and said:

'My Lady, the high-ranking barons of your land are waiting for you in the palace and beg you to come to them, and you will hear what they have to say. If you do not wish to come, they will come before you.'

She said she would go, because they had asked her. She got up and went into the hall, and when the barons saw her coming they stood up and received her with great honour. One of them, the best speaker among them, made the following speech :

[138] 'My Lady, we have asked you to come for one reason, and may God grant that it turns out for the best, for you and for us. Indeed, that is what we wish, and we shall tell you what it is.

'We all know that your lord, King Arthur, is dead. He was a very noble man and kept us in peace for a long time; we are very sad that he has passed out of this world. Since this kingdom, in which great power is spread over many lands, is now without a governor, it is necessary for us to decide on a man worthy of ruling an empire as rich as this, and to whom you can be given in marriage, because the man to whom God gives the honour of this kingdom must certainly marry you. We have seen to the matter, since it was necessary, by choosing for you a good man and a fine knight who will be able to rule the kingdom well. Also, we have decided among ourselves that he will marry you, and we shall pay him homage. My Lady, what do you say?'

[139] The queen was grieved by this, and, in tears, told the man who had spoken to her that she had no wish to take a husband.

'My Lady,' he said, 'that cannot be. No one can defend this point of view of yours, because in no circumstances can we leave this kingdom without a ruler. If we did, we should not fail to suffer from it if we were involved in a war somewhere. Therefore you must, whether you like it or not, carry out our wishes in this matter.'

She replied that she would rather leave the country as an exile than ever take a husband.

'And do you know,' she asked, 'why I am saying this? Because I could never have such a noble husband as I have had, and therefore I beg you not to discuss the matter any further, because I refuse what you ask, and I should hold it against you.'

Then the others attacked her, saying:

'My Lady, your refusal means nothing, because you must do what you are obliged to do.'

When she heard them, she was infinitely more dismayed than before, and asked those who were pressing her:

'Tell me, then, whom you want to give me as a husband.'

They replied, 'Mordred; we do not know any knight among us who is as worthy of ruling an empire or a kingdom as he is, because he is a fine, noble and valiant knight.'

[140] When the queen heard this, she thought her heart would leave her body, but she did not reveal her emotion, so that those with her should not notice. She intended to escape from their plans in quite a different way from what they might have expected.

After she had spent some time reflecting on what they had said, she replied:

'Indeed, I do not say that Mordred is not a fine and noble knight, and I am not against doing as you say, although I am not promising yet. But give me time to make up my mind and I will give my answer tomorrow at Prime.'

Mordred jumped forward and said:

'My Lady, you may have much more time than you have asked for; they will give you a week's grace, provided you promise me that after that time you will do what they request.'

She promised readily, wishing only to be rid of them.

[141] That was the end of the conversation, and the queen went off to her room and shut herself up almost alone except for the company of a girl. When she tried to reflect on what they had said, she began to lament as much as if she could see the whole world dead before her. She called herself wretched and miserable and beat her face and twisted her hands.

After she had grieved in that way for some time, she said to the girl with her:

'Go and look for Labor and tell him to come and speak to me.'

The girl said she would willingly do that. Labor was a splendid knight of great prowess, and a cousin of the queen. He was the man in whom the queen first confided in time of need, after Lancelot. When he arrived, she told the girl to leave, and she did. The queen herself locked the door on the two of them.

When she saw herself alone with the man in whom she had so much confidence, she began to be very miserable, and said to the knight, in tears:

'Cousin, for God's sake, advise me.'

When Labor saw her crying so bitterly, he was very distressed and said:

'My Lady, why are you tormenting yourself in this way? Tell me what is wrong. If I can help you in your sadness by anything I can do, I shall free you from it – I promise you that as a loyal knight.'

Then the queen said, in tears:

'Cousin, I am suffering as much as a woman can suffer, because the men of this kingdom want to marry me to that traitor, that perjurer, who is, I tell you truthfully, my lord King Arthur's son. Even if he were not his son, he is so disloyal that I would not accept him for anything; I would rather they burnt me. But I will tell you what I have thought of doing – advise me what you think. I want to fortify the tower of this city with sergeants and bowmen and provision it with food, and I want you to find the sergeants and make each of them swear individually on the saints that he will not reveal to anyone why he has been installed there. If they ask me why I am equipping the tower, during the time before I am due to give them my reply, I shall answer that it is in preparation for my wedding celebrations.'

'My Lady,' said Labor, 'there is nothing I would not do for your safety; I shall find you knights and sergeants to guard the tower, and in the meantime you will have it provisioned. When you have fully equipped it, if you take my advice, you will send a message to Lancelot, asking him to rescue you. I can tell you that when he knows your need, nothing will prevent him from coming to help you with enough men to be able to free you easily from the situation in which you find yourself, despite everyone in this country. Even Mordred, I am quite sure, would not be bold enough to wait for him on the battle-field. Moreover, if my lord the king were still alive – for I do not think he is dead – and the messenger could by chance find him in Gaul, he would return to this country with all the men he took with him as soon as he heard the news. In that way you could be rid of Mordred.'

[142] When the queen heard this advice, she said that she quite agreed, because in that way she expected to be fully released from the danger in which Mordred's men had put her.

So they ended their conversation, and Labor obtained knights and sergeants among those in whom he had the greatest trust, until, before a week had passed, he had assembled two hundred sergeants or knights who had all sworn to him on the saints that they would go into the Tower of London and defend the queen against Mordred, as long as they could hold out, and until death. All this was arranged so secretly that no one knew about it except those involved; and during this time the queen had had the tower provisioned with everything that was help-ful or useful to a man and which could be found in the country.

On the day when the queen had promised to give her reply, all the high-ranking barons of the kingdom, who had been summoned to attend, arrived and assembled in the hall. The queen had not forgotten the date, and had commanded all the men who were to protect her to enter the tower. They were all as well equipped with arms as they possibly could be. When they were all inside, the queen joined them, and straight away had the drawbridge raised. She went up to the battlements and spoke to Mordred, who was down below and realized that he had failed to capture the queen.

'Mordred, Mordred,' she said, 'you have forgotten that my lord was your lord, when you tried to marry me whether I agreed or not. You will certainly regret having formed that plan, and I want you to know it will be the cause of your death.'

Then she climbed down from the battlements and went into a

room inside the tower and asked those with her what she could do.

'My Lady,' they said, 'do not dismay; you can be sure that we shall successfully defend this tower against Mordred if he intends to attack it. We fear his strength very little, and in any case neither he nor any of his company will be able to enter here for so long as we have food.'

The queen was very reassured by these words, and when Mordred, who was outside with his men, realized how he had been tricked by the queen and had lost her, he asked the barons what he could do about it.

'For the tower is strong and easily defended, and remarkably well supplied with food, and those inside are very noble and bold. My Lords,' he said, 'what do you recommend?'

'My Lord,' they replied, 'the only thing is for the tower to be attacked frequently from all sides. We can tell you it is not strong enough to hold out against us for very long, because they cannot receive help except from the outside.'

'In faith,' said Mordred, 'I would not be in a mind to besiege it unless I were surer of you than I am at present.'

They told him they would give him all the assurances he might ask from them.

'Then I beg you,' he said, 'that you all affirm faithfully and swear on the saints that you will help me against my mortal enemies until death, even against King Arthur, if he should ever chance to come here.'

'We will very willingly do that,' they said.

Then they knelt before him and all became his liege men, swearing to him on the saints that they would help him against all men until death. When they had made this oath, he said to them:

'My Lords, thank you! You have done me a great service by electing me lord above you all and paying me homage. Indeed I am now so sure of you that there is no man in the world so valiant that I would not dare to meet him in battle, because I should have your strength on my side. Now there only remains for you to recognize me as lord of your castles and fortresses.'

They all straight away gave him their gages as a sign that the lordship passed to him, and he received them from each of them.

Then he ordered the tower to be besieged straight away from all sides, his men to arm themselves, and siege-engines and ladders to be brought up on which to climb to the battlements.

However, the men inside the tower ran to their arms and you could have seen a great and vigorous assault there because those outside, being very numerous, wanted to climb up, while those inside would not allow this but killed them and knocked them down into the ditch. They defended themselves so well that before the assault was over you could have seen more than two hundred men lying in the ditch.

When those outside saw that their enemies were doing them so much harm, they withdrew and ordered the assault to stop. The assailants did just as they were commanded, because they were very downhearted by the fact that those inside were defending themselves so well.

In that way the queen was repeatedly besieged and attacked in the Tower of London, but nevertheless it happened that she had men with her capable of defending her at all times.

One day the queen called a boy, a messenger of hers in whom she had great confidence, and said to him:

'Go to Gaul, to find out the news about my lord the king, whether he is dead or alive. If he is alive, tell him the situation in which I find myself and beg him for God's sake not to fail to come and rescue me as soon as he possibly can. Otherwise I should be dishonoured, because this tower cannot hold out against Mordred and those on his side for ever. If it is true that my lord is dead and you can find out the truth about him and Sir Gawain, go straight to Gaunes or Banoic, where you will find Lancelot. When you have found him, tell him I send him friendly greetings and ask him not to fail for any reason to come and rescue me with all the forces he has in Gaunes and Banoic. You can tell him that if he does not rescue me, I shall be shamed and dishonoured, for I shall not be able to hold out against Mordred for long, as he has all the men of this country on his side.'

'My Lady,' said the boy, 'I shall certainly do all that, if God grants that I may arrive safe and sound in the land of Gaunes; but I am very worried that I might not be able to leave this tower as I wish, because it is so surrounded on all sides by our enemies that I do not know what to do.'

'You must escape somehow,' she said, 'and deliver the message I have given you, because otherwise I shall never be freed from these traitors.'

[143]   In the evening, when it was dark, the boy took leave of his lady, went to the gate, and managed to get away between Mordred's men. As it happened, he was not stopped on either side, because everyone who saw him thought that he belonged to his party. As soon as he was away from them, he went to look for lodgings in the town and managed to obtain a good strong horse. He straight away started out, rode to the coast, and crossed the sea. Then he heard the news that King Arthur was not dead, but had besieged the city of Gaunes; and the boy was extremely pleased to hear this piece of news.

But now the story stops telling of the messenger and returns to King Arthur and his companions.

*

[144]   Now the story tells that when King Arthur had been besieging the city of Gaunes for about two months, he realized that there would never be an honourable outcome for him, because those inside were defending themselves remarkably well and were managing to inflict losses on Arthur's men all the time.

One day King Arthur said to Sir Gawain, in confidence:

'Gawain, you have made me undertake something which will never turn to our honour – I mean the war you have begun against King Ban's kinsmen, because they are so noble at arms that they have no equals anywhere. Now decide what we can do; I am telling you that we risk losing more than we gain here, since they are on their own land and among their friends and have great numbers of knights. You can be sure, Gawain, that if they hated us as much as we hate them, we should have lost everything, because they have great power and strength. Now you must determine what we shall do next.'

'My Lord,' replied Sir Gawain, 'I shall give thought to the matter, and let you know my reply tonight or tomorrow morning.'

That day Gawain was unusually deep in thought, and when he had considered the matter to his satisfaction, he called one of his boys and said:

'Go out to the city of Gaunes and tell Lancelot del Lac that if he is bold enough to dare to defend the accusation that he killed my brother treacherously, I am ready to prove in single combat that he is guilty. If he can conquer me and disprove my accusation, my uncle will return to the kingdom of Logres with his whole army, and will never call the men of Banoic to account for any differences there may be between us; however, if I can overcome him on the battle-field, I shall ask no more, and the war will end straight away if the two kings agree to hold their land from King Arthur; and if they refuse, we shall never leave here until they are dishonoured and slain.'

When the boy heard him say this, he began to cry tenderly, and said to Sir Gawain:

'My Lord, what are you trying to do? Are you so determined to bring on your own shame and death? Sir Lancelot is a very fine and hardened knight, and if you were killed fighting him, we should all be humiliated and dishonoured, because you are the finest knight in this army and the noblest man. May it please God, I will not carry that message, in which I see your death so clearly, because I would be too wicked and disloyal if such a noble man as you went to his death through anything I did or said.'

'Everything you are saying is nonsense,' said Sir Gawain; 'you must take that message, because otherwise this war will never be ended, and it is right for it to be ended by Lancelot and me. He started it, and then I joined in; after the first part had finished, I made my uncle King Arthur recommence it – so it is right I should be the first to receive joy or suffering from it. I can tell you that if it were not obvious to me that I was on the side of justice, I should not now fight with him for the finest city in the world, because I well know and realize that he is the finest knight that I have ever met. But everyone knows that wrong and treachery would make the world's finest knight a coward, and that justice and loyalty make the worst a solid and noble knight. That is the reason why I fear Lancelot less, since I know he is guilty and I am on the side of justice. Therefore neither you nor anyone else ought to worry about me, because Our Lord always protects the innocent – that is my faith and belief.'

Sir Gawain spoke to the boy until he promised to go to the city of Gaunes and tell Lancelot the message with which he had been entrusted.

'Be sure,' said Sir Gawain, 'that you go before Prime tomorrow.'

The boy said that he certainly would.

[145] That night they spoke no more about the matter. They had made a truce eight days before, and it was to expire in three days' time. The next day, before Prime, the boy went to the city of Gaunes and waited until Lancelot and the two kings had risen and heard mass. When they had come to the palace and sat in the high seats, the boy went up to Lancelot and said:

'My Lord, I have been sent by my lord Sir Gawain; he sends a message through me to say that if your men and ours continue to fight together as they have begun, it can only cause grievous harm to both sides. But do what is best – Sir Gawain says that if you dare to accept his challenge, he is ready to prove before all the people of this country that you killed his brothers treacherously. If he can show you to be guilty of that accusation, you will not escape with your life, because he certainly would not accept the whole world as a ransom for your head. However, if you are able to defend yourself and force him to surrender, his uncle the king will return to the kingdom of Logres and will remain at peace with you all the days of his life, and will never speak again of this matter. If you refuse because you do not dare to meet him, the whole world ought to reproach you for it, since it could easily see and recognize that you were guilty of that of which he accuses you. Now decide what you will do, because he sends you this message through me.'

When Lancelot heard what the messenger said, he was very

angry at the news, because he certainly did not wish to fight with Sir Gawain. He replied:

'My friend, I am really angered and annoyed by that message, because I should never wish in all my life to fight against Sir Gawain for anything in the world because of his nobility and the companionship he has given me since I was first made a knight. However, his accusation, which refers to treason, would be so humiliating for me if I did not defend myself, that I should lose all my honour, because a man is more debased and shamed by an accusation of treachery than by any other thing, if he does not defend himself. Therefore tell him from me that, if he will give a pledge to keep this agreement, he will find me armed and on the battle-field at any time he wishes. Now you can go. Tell him just what I have told you, not because I am frightened of him, but because I love him so much that I should never wish to fight with him in single combat.'

The boy said he would deliver the message, and he left straight away.

King Bors said to Sir Lancelot:

'It is true that no man as sensible as Sir Gawain has ever become involved in such an unreasonable accusation, because everyone knows that you never killed his brothers treacherously, but quite openly, in a place where there were more than a hundred knights.'

'I can tell you,' said King Lionel, 'why he is pressing it in this way; he is grieving so much for his dead brothers that he would rather die than live. He would rather take his revenge on Sir Lancelot than on anyone else, and for that reason he has so wickedly accused him, because it is the same to him whether he lives or dies.'

'I think,' said Lancelot, 'that the battle will take place fairly soon, and I do not know what the outcome will be, but I do know that if I were the winner and ought to cut off his head, I should not kill him for all the world, because I think he is too noble. Moreover, he is the man, out of all those in the world that have meant anything to me, that I have most loved, and still do, excepting only the king.'

171

'It is certainly remarkable of you,' said King Bors, 'to love him so deeply when he hates you mortally.'

'Find it remarkable if you wish,' replied Lancelot, 'but he will never be able to hate me so much that I stop loving him. I would not have said this so openly, but my life is in the balance, because I am forced to undertake battle against him.' [146] That was how Lancelot spoke about Sir Gawain, and all those who heard him were highly surprised and held him in higher esteem than they had done before.

The boy who had been sent by Sir Gawain had heard Lancelot's reply, and left the city of Gaunes and rode until he came back to his lord. He told him straight away everything he had heard there, and also said:

'My Lord, you will certainly have your battle, if you give pledges to Sir Lancelot that the king will return to his country if he can conquer you on the field.'

'In faith,' said Sir Gawain, 'if I do not manage to make the king agree to that, I shall not want to bear arms. Now be quiet, and say no more about the matter, because I think I can arrange it all.'

Then Sir Gawain went to the king, knelt before him, and said:

'My Lord, I beg and request you to grant me a gift.'

The king courteously granted it, not knowing what Sir Gawain wanted, and, taking him by the hand, made him stand up. Then Sir Gawain thanked him and said:

'My Lord, do you know what gift you have granted me? You have promised to pledge to Lancelot that if he can conquer me on the battle-field, you will abandon the siege, return to the kingdom of Logres, and never as long as you live restart the war against them.'

When the king heard what he said, he was astounded and said to Sir Gawain:

'Have you then arranged a battle with Lancelot? What made you do that?'

'My Lord,' replied Sir Gawain, 'here is the reason; the war cannot end until one of us lies dead or defeated.'

'I am very saddened by what you have undertaken, Gawain,'

said the king; 'in fact it is a long time since I have been as annoyed by anything that happened to me as I am by this. I do not know any knight in the world against whom I would not prefer you to fight, because we recognize him as the noblest and most experienced in the world, and the most outstanding that one could find. I am so worried for you that I can tell you I would rather have lost the best city I possess than that you should have ever spoken of the matter.'

'My Lord,' said Sir Gawain, 'the matter has gone so far now that it cannot be stopped; and even if it could be, I should not avoid a battle for any reason, because I hate him so mortally that I would rather die than fail to risk my life attempting to kill him. If God were so courteous as to permit me to put him to death and avenge my brothers, I should never be saddened by anything that might happen to me. If he should manage to kill me, at least that would be the end of the grief that afflicts me night and day, because I can tell you that I have undertaken this battle in order to be at peace in some way, either dead or alive.'

'Gawain,' said the king, 'may God help you, because you have certainly never undertaken anything that dismays me as much as this, and rightly so, because Lancelot is a very fine and hardened knight, and you have experienced that for yourself, as you yourself have told me.'

Then Sir Gawain said to the boy who had acted as messenger:

'Go and tell Lancelot to come and speak to my uncle the king and me between the army and the city. He should come unarmed, because my lord and all the men with him will also be without arms.'

The boy left his lord, went to the city, and found Lancelot, Bors and his brother having a private conversation at a window and still talking about the message Sir Gawain had sent. Lancelot was saying that he much regretted the battle and that there were not two knights in the army against whom he would not more willingly fight than against Sir Gawain because of the love he had for him. The messenger went straight to where he saw Lancelot, knelt before him and said:

'My Lord, I have been sent by the king and Sir Gawain, who ask you to go and speak to them out there, unarmed, with your two companions, because they will all come unarmed too. There the battle will be sworn on both sides so that no one can withdraw from the agreement.'

Lancelot said that he would willingly go and would take King Bors and his brother Hector with him. The messenger left immediately, returned to the tents, and told the king and Sir Gawain what had happened.

[147] King Arthur mounted straight away and commanded King Caradoc to go with him; the third person was Sir Gawain. They mounted their horses and went unarmed towards the city gate. They were wearing clothes made of taffeta, because of the great heat. When they had arrived near the city, they saw King Bors, Lancelot and Hector come out.

As they were coming close enough together to talk to one another, Lancelot said to Bors:

'Let us dismount to meet my lord the king as he comes, because he is the noblest man alive.'

They said they would not dismount to meet their mortal enemy, if it pleased God.

Lancelot said that however much he might be his enemy, he would dismount for love of him. Straight away he got off his horse and his companions did the same.

The king said to those accompanying him:

'By God, there is much in those three men that everyone ought to admire; they are more polite and courteous than any other people, and they are so gifted in chivalry that their equals are not to be found in the whole world. Would to God there were now as much love between us as I have ever seen in the past; may God help me, I would be happier than if I were given the finest city in the world.'

Then he dismounted, and so did his companions; and Lancelot, as soon as he was close to him, greeted him with great shame and embarrassment. However, the king did not return his greeting because he saw that would annoy Sir Gawain too much.

Lancelot said to him:

'My Lord, you have asked me to come and speak to you and I have come to hear what you have to say.'

Sir Gawain jumped forward and answered for the king.

'Lancelot,' said Sir Gawain, 'my lord the king has come here to do what you have asked me; you know that together we have undertaken a battle as great as mortal treason demands, in respect of the deaths of my brothers whom you killed treacherously and disloyally, as we all know. I am the plaintiff and you are the defendant. But because you do not want another battle to be begun after this one, am I right in thinking that you want the king to promise that, if you win this battle and overcome me, neither he nor his men will harm you as long as he lives, but will abandon the siege and return home?'

'Sir Gawain,' said Lancelot, 'if you would allow it, I should like to forget about this battle, even though I could not abandon it now without the dishonour being mine and without people accusing me of cowardice; but you have done so much for me, you and my lord the king who is here, that I could scarcely wish to bear arms against you, especially in mortal combat. I beg you to realize that I am not saying this out of cowardice or because I fear you, but only out of kindness, because as soon as I am armed and on my horse, I could well, if it pleases God, defend myself against you. Moreover I am not saying it to boast or to deny you are the finest knight in the world, but because, if you agreed, I should very much like there to be peace between us. In order to obtain peace I should straight away do whatever you cared to command, such as to become your liege man together with my brother Hector, and all my kinsmen would pay you homage, except the two kings, because I should not like them to be subservient to anyone. I will do all this – and still more, because I will immediately swear on the saints, if you wish, that I will leave Gaunes tomorrow before Prime and go into exile, barefoot and dressed as a penitent, without any companions, for a period of ten years. If I die within that time, I forgive you my death and acquit you of blame from all my kinsmen; and if I return at the end of ten years and you are still alive then, and also my lord the king here, I wish to enjoy the company of you both just as I always did. I will also make you another oath that you will not expect, so that there may be no occasion for violence between myself and you. I will swear on the saints that I never killed Gaheriet knowingly, and that I greatly regretted his death. I shall do all this not because I fear you more than I reasonably should, but because I think it would be a great pity if one of us were to kill the other.'

[148] When the king heard Lancelot's great proposal for peace, he was quite astounded, because he could never have imagined that Lancelot would make such an offer.

He said to Sir Gawain, with tears in his eyes:

'Gawain, for God's sake do what Lancelot is asking you, because he is certainly offering you all the amends that one knight can make another for having killed a kinsman. No man of his nobility has ever said as much as he has said to you.'

'It is useless to ask me,' replied Sir Gawain; 'I would rather be struck through the chest with a lance and have my heart cut from my body than fail to do to you what I have promised, whether I live or die as a result.'

Then he held out his gage and said to the king:

'My Lord, here I am, ready to prove that Lancelot killed my brother treacherously, and may the battle be arranged for any day that pleases you.'

Lancelot came forward and said to the king, in tears:

'My Lord, since I see that the battle cannot be avoided, I should not be considered a true knight if I did not defend myself. Here is my gage to make my defence. I am very sorry I have to fight, and I should like the battle to be tomorrow, if Sir Gawain will allow.'

He agreed at once, and the king accepted the gages of both of them.

Then Lancelot said to the king:

'My Lord, I beg you to promise me as a king that if God allows me to win this battle, you will abandon the siege of this city and return to the kingdom of Logres with all your men; and so long as you live neither you nor any of your kinsmen will do us any harm unless we harm you first.'

176

He promised as befitted a king. Then they parted, but as they were about to leave, Hector said to Sir Gawain:

'Sir Gawain, you have refused the finest offer and the greatest compensation that so noble a man as Lancelot ever offered to any knight. As far as I am concerned, I should like things to turn out badly for you, and I think they will.'

Then Lancelot told Hector to be quiet because he had already said enough. Hector obeyed. Straight away they ended their meeting, went to their horses and mounted, and went back respectively to the city and to their tents.

But you could never have seen such great lamentation and grief as Sir Yvain began to show when he knew for certain that the battle had been arranged on both sides between Sir Gawain and Lancelot, and that it was now unavoidable. He went to Sir Gawain and began to reproach him bitterly, saying:

'My Lord, why have you done this? Do you hate your life so much, to have undertaken a battle against the finest knight in the world, against whom no man could ever hold out on the battle-field without eventually being dishonoured? My Lord, why have you undertaken this battle, and wrongly too, because he will defend himself with justice on his side? You have certainly never done anything so foolhardy.'

'Do not worry, Sir Yvain,' said Sir Gawain. 'I know quite certainly that right is on my side and wrong on his, and for that reason I should fight against him with even greater confidence if he were twice as fine a knight as he is.'

'I can tell you, Yvain,' said King Arthur, 'that I would rather have lost half my kingdom than that this thing should have come to pass. However, since it cannot be avoided, we shall see what happens and await the mercies of Our Lord. Lancelot did something very remarkable, because in order to obtain peace he offered to become Gawain's liege man together with all his companions except only the two kings, and if this was not enough, he would go into exile for ten years, and when he came back he would ask for no more than to be in our company.'

'He made such a great offer there,' said Sir Yvain, 'that I can only see unreason on our side in Gawain's refusal. May God grant that things do not turn out too badly for us, because I have certainly never feared disaster as much as I do now; I see right on their side and wrong on ours.'

[149] There was great sadness in the army and among King Arthur's men that Sir Gawain had undertaken to fight against Lancelot. Even the boldest wept, and they lamented so much that their tongues did not dare to express what they felt in their hearts. However, the people in the city were not unduly sorry, because when they heard details of what Lancelot had proposed to Sir Gawain, they said that God should bring him dishonour because he had been too haughty and presumptuous.

That night Lancelot kept vigil in the main church of the city together with a great company of men, and he also confessed to an archbishop all the sins about which he felt most guilty before Our Lord. He was very worried that things might turn out badly for him against Sir Gawain, because of Gawain's brothers that he had killed.

When day broke he slept till Prime, and so did all the others who had kept vigil with him. When Prime came, Lancelot, who was very apprehensive about what he had to do, arose and dressed and saw the barons who were waiting for him. He asked for his arms straight away, and they were brought to him, fine, strong, tenacious and light. His friends armed him to the best of their ability; you could have seen a great number of barons there, each striving hard to serve him and make sure he lacked nothing.

After they had equipped him as well as they were able, they went down from the palace into the courtyard. Lancelot mounted a strong, swift horse which was covered in steel down to its hooves. When he had mounted, the others did too, to accompany him. As he left the city, you could have seen ten thousand men in his retinue, of whom there was not one who would not have given up his life out of love for him, if it had been necessary.

[150] They rode until they came to a meadow outside the walls, where the battle was to take place. None of them was armed except Lancelot, and none of them entered the battle-

field; instead, they grouped themselves around it on the side of the city.

When the men in the army saw that the others had left the city, they took Sir Gawain his horse – his barons had armed him some time before. They went to the field just as the men from the city had done. The king took Sir Gawain by the right hand and led him on to the field, but he was crying bitterly as if he could see everyone in the world dead before him.

Bors took his lord by the right hand and led him on to the field, saying:

'My Lord, go forward, and may God grant you victory in this battle!'

Lancelot made the sign of the cross as he entered the field, and commended himself entirely to Our Lord.

[151] The day was fine and bright; the sun was up and was beginning to reflect on their arms. Noble and confident, the knights spurred on their horses, which were worthy and reliable, against each other and struck each other so violently on their bodies and shields that they were both knocked to the ground. They were so dazed by this that neither knew what to do, as if they were dead.

The horses, feeling themselves disburdened of their masters, fled, one this way, and one that, but there was no one to catch hold of them, for all had their minds on something else. When the two knights had fallen, you could have seen many noble men dismayed and in tears; however, after a time Lancelot was the first to get up and put his hand to his sword, but he was quite stunned by his fall. Sir Gawain was no slower than Lancelot, but ran to his shield that had flown from his neck, and put his hand to Excalibur, King Arthur's good sword. Then he ran to attack Lancelot and gave him such a great blow on his helmet that he dented and twisted it. Lancelot, who had given and received many blows, did not spare him in any way, but struck him so violently on his helmet that Gawain had great difficulty in withstanding it.

Then a great battle began between the two of them, the most violent combat that had ever been seen between two knights; whoever could have seen the blows given and received would have realized that the two men were of great nobility. The fight continued in that way for some time, and eventually they took to their sharp swords, with which they struck each other so often that their coats of mail split on their arms and hips. Their shields were so damaged and torn at top and bottom that you could have put your fist through the middle of them. Their helmets, which had been held in place by strong straps, were now almost useless because they were so damaged by blows from their swords that they were half lying on their shoulders.

If they still possessed as much strength as they had had at the beginning, they could not have stayed alive for long, but they were now so exhausted and weary that it often happened that their swords turned in their hands when they went to strike each other. Both of them had many wounds, the least of which could have killed another man, and yet despite their exhaustion, caused by the blood they had lost, they continued the fight until nearly Terce. Then they had to rest, because they could not endure it any longer. First, Sir Gawain drew back and leant on his shield to regain his breath; then Lancelot did the same.

[152] When Bors saw that Lancelot had drawn back after the first part of the battle, he said to Hector:

'Now I am worried about my lord for the first time, since he has had to rest before being able to overcome a knight, and he is now regaining his breath in the middle of the battle; that is certainly something that I find dismaying.'

'My Lord,' said Hector, 'you can be sure that he would not have done it but for his love for Sir Gawain, because he did not really need to.'

'I do not know what he means to do,' said King Bors, 'but, as for me, I should have given all that he possesses, if it had been mine; in order to continue fighting against Sir Gawain, because the story would certainly have ended already.'

[153] Thus the two knights fought together, and one was gaining the upper hand over the other, but when it happened that Sir Gawain saw clearly that it was noon, he called Lancelot to battle as fresh as if he had not struck a single blow all

day, and attacked him so splendidly that Lancelot was quite taken aback.

'In faith,' he said to himself, 'I should not be surprised if this man was not a demon or a phantom, because I thought just now, when I let him rest, that he was conquered; now he is just as fresh as if he had not yet struck a blow in this battle.'

This is what Lancelot said about Sir Gawain, who had regained his strength and swiftness of movement around noon. He was right, and it had not begun there, because in every place where he had fought people had seen that his strength increased around noon, and in case anyone considers this a fable, I will explain to you how it came about.

[154] It is true that it was in the Orkneys that Sir Gawain was born, in a city called Nordelone. After his birth, King Lot, his father, who was overjoyed, had him taken into a forest nearby to see a hermit who lived there. This good man led such a holy life that Our Lord carried out miracles for him every day such as righting wrongs, giving sight to the blind, and many other things for love of him. The king sent his son to him because he did not want him to receive baptism from any other hand than his.

When the hermit saw the child and knew who his father was, he was happy to baptize him, and called him Gawain, because that was his own name. The child was baptized at about noon. After the ceremony, one of the knights who had brought the child said to the hermit:

'My Lord, will you ensure that the kingdom will benefit from you and that the child, through your prayers, will be more endowed with grace than anyone else, when he reaches the age to bear arms?'

'Grace does not come from me, my Lord,' said the hermit, 'but from Jesus Christ; without him there is no grace of any worth. However, if through my prayers this child can be more endowed with grace than any other knight, he will be. Stay here tonight and tomorrow I shall be able to tell you what kind of a man he will be and how fine a knight.'

That night the king's messenger stayed there; and in the

morning, when the hermit had sung mass, he came to them and said:

'My Lords, I can tell you quite certainly about this child that he will be esteemed for his prowess above his companions, and so long as he lives he will never be defeated around noon, because he has been so endowed by my prayers that every day, at midday, at the same time that he was baptized, his strength and valour will increase wherever he is, and despite all the pain or weariness he may have had up till then, he will feel quite fresh and full of energy from that moment on.'

It happened exactly as the hermit had said, because his strength and valour always increased around midday wherever he was. In that way, since he had started bearing arms, he killed many noble knights and won many battles. When he happened to be fighting against a knight of great strength, he would attack him and harass him as much as he could until noon, by which time the other man would be so weary that he could not continue; when his opponent hoped to rest, Gawain would attack him as vigorously as he could, because that was the hour when he was swiftest and most valiant, until he had driven him to surrender. For that reason, many knights feared to fight against him unless it was in the afternoon.

[155] The grace and valour he had received through the hermit's prayers were well evident on the day that he was fighting against the son of King Ban of Banoic, because everyone saw that until then Gawain had been near defeat and surrender, and had been forced to rest; but when his strength had returned, as it normally did, he attacked Lancelot so swiftly that no one who saw him would not have said that he looked as if he had not struck a single blow that day, so rapid and energetic was he.

Then he harassed Lancelot so vigorously that he made the blood flow from his body in numerous places. Sir Gawain made a great effort because he expected to bring him to defeat, and was well aware that if he failed to overcome him around noon, he would never be able to. Therefore he struck and beat Lancelot with his sharp sword, making him quite dazed and yet causing him to suffer.

When King Bors saw that Lancelot was in such a bad position that all he could do was suffer, he said, loud enough for many to hear:

'Ah, God! What do I see? Ah, prowess, what has become of you? Ah, my Lord, have you been enchanted, that you are beginning to be defeated by a single knight? I have always seen you perform alone more feats of arms than two of the best knights in the world could do, and now you are being so hard pressed by the prowess of a single knight!'

[156] So the battle continued until after noon, and Lancelot could do no more than suffer Sir Gawain's force and cover himself; but by doing this he had rested a little and had regained his strength and his breath. He attacked Sir Gawain very rapidly and gave him such a great blow that he made him stagger. Sir Gawain was so affected by the blow that he had to use all his strength to right himself. Then Lancelot began to strike him and and give him great blows with his sharp sword, and to gain ground on him.

Sir Gawain, who now had the greatest fear that he could ever have, and who saw he risked being completely dishonoured if he was unable to defend himself, strove under fear of death and made use of all his prowess. He defended himself with such great difficulty that in his exertion the blood burst from his nose and his mouth, not to mention the other wounds he had, which were bleeding more than was good for him.

In that way the battle between the two knights lasted until None; by then they were both in such a bad state that each of them could not help suffering, and the battle-field was quite strewn with links from their coats of mail and fragments of their shields. But Sir Gawain was so affected by the wounds he had received that he was sure he would die from them, and Lancelot, because of his injuries, really needed to rest more than to fight, because Sir Gawain had pressed him very hard and the blood was flowing from his body in more than thirteen places. If they had been other knights, they would long before have died of the exhaustion they had suffered, but they were so great-hearted that they felt they would have done little if they did not hold out until death or surrender, so that the winner could be recognized.

[157] In that way the fighting continued till Vespers, and then Sir Gawain was so exhausted that he could hardly hold his sword. Lancelot, not yet too weary and still able to fight, rained blows on him and drove him now forward and now back. However, he held out and endured it, and covered himself with as much of his sword as he had left. When Lancelot realized that he had got the better of him and that all the spectators could clearly see this because there was no fight left in him of any consequence, he drew a little nearer Sir Gawain and said:

'Ah! Sir Gawain, it would be very reasonable for me to be acquitted of the accusation you laid on me, because I have defended myself well against you until Vespers, and a man who accuses another of treason must have proved his point and won his battle before then, or by rights he loses his case. Sir Gawain, I am telling you this so that you can have mercy on yourself, because if you continue this battle, one of us will have to die basely, and this will be held against our families. So, in order to make it possible for you to ask me, I beg you that we should end this battle.'

Sir Gawain answered that he would never willingly agree to that, may God help him, but said to Lancelot:

'Be sure that it must necessarily happen that one of us dies on this battle-field.'

Lancelot was very saddened by this, because he had no wish for Sir Gawain to die through him. He had put him severely to the test, and in the morning he had not thought there would be such great prowess in him as he had in fact found; and the man who in all the world most loved fine knights was Lancelot.

Then he went over to where he saw the king, and said:

'My Lord, I begged Sir Gawain to abandon this battle, because if we continue, one of us two must suffer for it.'

When the king, who was well aware that Sir Gawain was on the point of defeat, heard Lancelot's courtesy, he replied:

'Lancelot, Gawain will never abandon the battle if he does not wish to, but you may leave it if you wish, because the time-limit is past, and you have done what is necessary.'

'My Lord,' said Lancelot, 'if I did not think you would consider it cowardly on my part, I should go away and leave Sir Gawain on the field.'

'Indeed,' said the king, 'you would never have done anything for which I should be as grateful to you as that.'

'Then with your leave I shall go,' replied Lancelot.

'Be commended to God,' said the king, 'and may He lead you to safety as the finest and most courteous knight that I have ever seen.'

[158] Then Lancelot went back to his men, and when Hector saw him coming, he said to him:

'My Lord, what have you done? You were on the point of defeating your mortal enemy, and did not avenge yourself, but let him escape after he had accused you of treason. Go back, my Lord, and cut off his head – then your war will be over.'

'Ah, my brother!' said Lancelot, 'what are you saying? May God help me, I would rather be struck through the body with a lance than kill such a noble man.'

'He would have killed you if he could,' said Hector. 'Why did you not do the same to him?'

'I could not do it,' said Lancelot, 'because my heart, which directs me, would not allow it for anything.'

'I certainly regret it,' said King Bors, 'and I think it is something you will repent yet.'

Then Lancelot mounted a horse prepared for him and went back into the city. When he had arrived in the great courtyard and was disarmed, the doctors saw that he was so seriously wounded and had lost so much blood that another man would have died of it. Hector was very dismayed when he saw his wounds, and after the doctors had examined them, he asked them if Lancelot would recover.

'Yes, indeed,' they said, 'he is in no danger of death; however, he has lost so much blood and his wounds are so deep that we are very concerned. But we know he will recover.'

Then they saw to Lancelot's wounds and treated them with what they thought best. When they had attended to him to the best of their knowledge, they asked him how he felt.

'Very well,' said Lancelot.

Then he said to King Lionel and King Bors who had come to see him:

'My Lords, I can tell you that since I first bore arms I have never been afraid of any single knight except today, and I was certainly more frightened today than I had ever been, because when noon came and I had harassed Sir Gawain to the point where he was almost defeated and could hardly defend himself, I suddenly found him so keen and swift that I should not have escaped with my life if he had continued that prowess for long. I am amazed how that could have happened, because before then I knew he was near defeat and surrender, and in a very short time he regained so much strength that he was swifter and more valiant than he had been at the beginning.'

'Indeed,' said Bors, 'you are quite right. At that time I feared more for you than I ever have, and if he had maintained what he began then, you would not have escaped with your life, because he would not have been so courteous to you as you were to him. After seeing you both I know you are the two finest knights in the world.'

In that way the people of Gaunes talked about the battle and marvelled how Sir Gawain had been able to hold out against Lancelot for so long, because they all knew Lancelot was the finest knight in the world and younger than Sir Gawain by about twenty-one years. At that time Sir Gawain must have been seventy-six years old and King Arthur ninety-two.

[159] When the men in the army saw that Lancelot had returned to the city, they went over to Sir Gawain who was leaning on his shield, so ill that he could not hold himself up. They put him on a horse and led him straight before the king. Then they disarmed him and found him so ill that he swooned in their hands. The doctor was sent for; when he had examined the wounds, he said he would bring him back to complete health within a short time, except for a deep wound he had in his head.

The king said to Sir Gawain:

'Nephew, your folly has killed you, and that is a pity, because never again will your family produce such a fine knight as you are and always have been.'

Sir Gawain had not the strength to reply to anything the king said, because he was so sick that he did not expect to see another day.

Everyone there, high and low, wept when they saw Sir Gawain so ill. Rich and poor, all cried, because they all loved him dearly. They all came before him to see what his condition was, because they thought he might die in their hands at any time. All night Sir Gawain did not open his eyes or say anything or do any more than if he were dead, except that after a long time he groaned bitterly.

Before it was light, the king commanded his tents and pavilions to be taken down, because he did not want to remain there any longer, but would go and stay in Gaul and not move from there until he knew whether Sir Gawain would recover or not.

In the morning, as soon as day broke, the king keft Gaunes in great sadness, and had Sir Gawain carried in a litter, so ill that even the doctors expected him to die.

[160] The king went to stay in a city called Meaux and remained there until Sir Gawain was on the way to recovery. After the king had stayed in that city for some time, he said that he would shortly return to the kingdom of Logres.

Then a piece of news arrived that displeased him greatly, because a boy said to him one morning when he had just arisen:

'My Lord, I bring you very unpleasant news.'

'What is it?' asked the king. 'Tell me.'

'My Lord, the Romans have entered your territory. They have burnt and destroyed the whole of Burgundy, and wounded and killed the people, and pillaged the land. I know for sure that they will attack you this week with an army, and will wish to fight a battle against you, but you have never seen as many men as they possess.'

When King Arthur heard this news, he told the boy to be quiet, because if his men heard him telling it in that way, some might well be more dismayed than they should be. The boy said that he would not repeat it.

The king went to Sir Gawain, who had more or less recovered

except for the head-wound that was certain to cause his death. He asked him how he felt.

'Well, my Lord, thanks to God,' replied Sir Gawain. 'I am now quite well enough to bear arms.'

'You will need to be,' said the king, 'because very bad news has arrived today.'

'What is it?' asked Sir Gawain. 'Please tell me.'

'In faith,' he replied, 'a boy has told me that the Roman army has entered this land and that it is to attack us this week and fight a battle against us. Now tell me what we can do.'

'The best thing I can see,' said Sir Gawain, 'is for us to march against it tomorrow and to fight a battle against it. I think the Romans are so weak-hearted and lacking in vigour that they will not hold out against us for long.'

The king said he would do that. Then he again asked Sir Gawain how he felt, and he replied that he was as energetic as he had ever been and equally strong, except for his head-wound, 'which has not healed as I would have wished; however, I will not let it prevent me from bearing arms as soon as it is necessary.'

The next day the king left the castle at which he had stayed, and rode with his men until, between Champagne and Burgundy, he met the Roman Emperor, who had a large army with him; but they were not such fine knights as those of Great Britain.

Before they came together, King Arthur sent some of his knights to the Roman army to ask the emperor for what reason he had entered his territory without his leave. In reply, the emperor said:

'I have not entered his territory, but ours, because there is no land he ought not to hold from us; and I have come here to avenge one of our princes, Frollo of Germany, whom Arthur killed with his own hand some time ago; for this act of treachery he will never have peace from us, until he has paid us homage and agreed to recognize us as his overlords. He must pay us tribute every year, and so must those who come after him.'

The king's messengers replied:

'My Lord, because we cannot obtain any other reply from you, we challenge you on behalf of King Arthur. You should know that you have come for the battle in which you will be dishonoured and all your men slain.'

'I do not know what will happen,' said the emperor, 'but we have come here for the battle, and in battle we shall keep or lose this territory.'

Thereupon the messengers left the emperor, and when they had returned to the king, they told him what had been said.

'In that case, all we can do is to fight them,' said the king, 'because I would rather die than have the Romans as my over-lords.'

[161] In the morning the men of Logres armed themselves, and the king set up his battalions. When they had been formed, the first went and struck the Romans so splendidly that they were all taken aback. Then one could have seen knights fall on both sides in the battle, until the whole ground was covered with them. The Romans were not so well trained and experienced at bearing arms as the men from Logres, and for that reason you could have seen them fall like wild animals. When King Arthur, at the head of the last battalion, had joined the battle, then you could have seen him killing Romans and accomplishing marvellous feats of chivalry; at that time there was no man of his age who could have done so much.

Sir Gawain, who was at the other end with Kay the sene-schal and Girflet, began to fight so well that no one could have blamed him. As he was making his way through the battle, which was a huge one, he happened to meet the emperor and one of his nephews. These two had been causing great harm to the men of Logres, because they had been killing and striking whomever they came against. Seeing the amazing things they were doing, Sir Gawain said to himself:

'If those two live much longer, it could cause us a lot of trouble, because they are fine knights.'

So he spurred on his horse at the emperor's nephew and gave him such a great blow with his sword that he struck off his left shoulder. Mortally wounded, he fell to the ground. At that moment the Romans assembled there and attacked Sir Gawain on all sides. They struck him all over with their swords and lances and wounded him seriously. However, nothing hurt him as much as the blows they gave him on the head, because his wound there re-opened, and it was to cause his death.

When the emperor saw his nephew so badly wounded, he attacked Kay the seneschal and hit him so violently that his lance went through his body. He struck him down so badly wounded that he lived only for three days. The emperor drew his sword, went over to Girflet, and gave him such a blow on his helmet that he was quite dazed; he was unable to remain in the saddle and fell to the ground.

King Arthur saw these two blows and was well aware that it was the emperor; so he spurred on his horse towards him and with his bright and keenly sharp sword he struck the emperor on his helmet with all his strength. Nothing could prevent him from feeling the blade as far down as his teeth. Arthur wrenched out his sword and the emperor fell to the ground dead. This was a great shame, because he was a very fine knight and only a young man.

[162] When the Romans saw their lord dead, they all straight away lost heart and fled wherever they could. Arthur's men pursued them, killing them and cutting them down so violently that only a hundred survived, whom they captured and led before King Arthur. He said to them:

'You will die if you do not swear to carry out my wishes.'

They swore to this.

Then Arthur had the emperor's body taken and put in a bier, and said to the Romans:

'You will carry your emperor to Rome, and tell everyone you meet that instead of the tribute for which they asked I am sending them the body of their emperor; that is the only tribute that King Arthur will ever send them.'

They said they would bear this message, and left the king. He remained at the spot where the battle had taken place, because he did not want to travel at night.

Now the story stops telling of them, and returns to the boy that Queen Guinevere had sent to King Arthur to tell him of

Mordred's act of treason and how he had besieged her in the Tower of London.

*

[163] Now the story tells that on the very day the Romans were defeated, as has already been described, the boy whom Queen Guinevere sent to Gaunes from the kingdom of Logres, with the news about Mordred, arrived before King Arthur, who was happy and delighted at the splendid outcome that God had allowed him, except for Sir Gawain who was so badly wounded that it was quite obvious that he would not recover.

Sir Gawain never complained of any wound he had received as much as of the head-wound that Lancelot had given him, and the Romans had made it as painful as ever by the great blows they had given him on his helmet. He bled so profusely because he had done extremely well in the battle that day; if he had not been so full of chivalry the Romans would not have been defeated, however many men there had been against them.

Then the queen's messenger came before the king and said:

'My Lord, your wife Queen Guinevere has sent me to you to say that you have betrayed and deceived her, and have not prevented her from being dishonoured, together with all her kinsmen.'

Then he related how Mordred had erred, how he had been crowned King of Logres, and how all the high-ranking barons holding fiefs from Arthur had paid Mordred homage, with the result that if King Arthur returned he would not be received as their lord but as their mortal enemy. He also told how Mordred had besieged the queen in the Tower of London, which he attacked every day.

'And because my lady is frightened that he may kill her, she asks you for the sake of God to rescue her as quickly as you can; because it is quite certain that if you delay she will soon be captured. Mordred hates her so mortally that he will defile her body and you will be dishonoured.'

[164] When the king heard what he said, he was at first so unhappy that he could not say a word. Then he told the boy that he would certainly help her, if God permitted. He began to cry very bitterly, and when he spoke after some time, he said:

'Ah! Mordred, now you make me realize that you are the serpent I once saw issuing from my stomach, which burnt my lands and attacked me. But never will a father have done to a son what I shall do to you, because I shall kill you with my two hands. May the whole world know this; God forbid that you die at anyone else's hands but mine.'

Many barons heard what he said, and they were astounded, because they learnt from the king's outburst that Mordred was his son. And many of them were quite amazed.

The king commanded all those around him to instruct the whole army that night to be ready to leave the next morning, because he was going to the coast to cross over to the kingdom of Logres. When the men in the army had heard this, then you could have seen tents and pavilions taken down on all sides; and the king ordered a horse-drawn bier to be made in which Sir Gawain could be carried. This was because Arthur did not wish to leave Gawain far from him, because he was dying, and Arthur wished to see him die. He would be happier if he could be present at his death.

Arthur's men did exactly as he had ordered.

[165] In the morning, as soon as it was light, the army set out; and when they were on their way, they rode until they arrived at the coast. Then Sir Gawain spoke gently to the men around him, and asked:

'Ah! God, where am I?'

'My Lord,' said one of the knights, 'we are on the sea-shore.'

'And where do you want to go?' he asked.

'My Lord, we want to cross over to the kingdom of Logres.'

'Ah! God,' said Sir Gawain, 'blessed be you for enabling me to die in my own land, as I have so greatly desired.'

'My Lord,' said the knight who was speaking to him, 'do you then expect to die?'

'Yes indeed,' he said. 'I am quite sure that I shall not last a fortnight; and I am sadder at not being able to see Lancelot before I die than I am about the thought of dying. If I could only see the man I know to be the finest and most courteous knight in the world and beg his forgiveness for having been so uncourtly to him recently, I feel my soul would be more at rest after my death.'

The king arrived at this moment and heard what Sir Gawain was saying.

'Nephew,' said King Arthur, 'your wickedness has done me great harm because it has robbed me of you, whom I loved above all men, and also Lancelot, who was so feared that if Mordred had known that he was on as good terms with me as formerly, he would never have been so bold as to attempt the kind of disloyalty that he has undertaken. Now I think that I shall be lacking in good men, since I shall not have you or those I most trusted in times of need; the traitor has assembled all the forces of my land against me. Ah! God, if I now had in my company the men that I used to have, I should not fear the whole world if it were against me.'

[166] That was what King Arthur said to Sir Gawain, who was very distressed, and made a big effort to speak, saying:

'My Lord, if you have lost Lancelot through my madness, recover him through your wisdom; you could easily persuade him to come back to you if you wished, as he is the noblest man that I have ever seen and the most courteous in the world. He loves you so dearly that I know for certain he would come back to you, if you asked him. I think that you undoubtedly need him, and do not fail to ask him because of any hopes you may have in me, because certainly neither you nor anyone else will ever see me bearing arms again.'

When King Arthur heard what Sir Gawain said, that he could not escape with his life, he was so saddened and grief-stricken that there was no man there who did not feel great pity for him.

'Nephew,' said the king, 'is what you say then true, that you are soon leaving us?'

'Yes, my Lord,' he said, 'I know for certain that I shall not see the fourth day from now.'

'I have much cause for regret, then,' said the king, 'because the greatest fault is mine.'

'My Lord,' said Sir Gawain, 'in any case I recommend you to ask Lancelot to come and help you, and I know that he will definitely come as soon as he receives your letter, because he loves you much more dearly than you imagine.'

'I have certainly hurt him so much,' replied the king, 'that I do not think my requesting him would be of any use; so I shall not ask him.'

[167]   Thereupon the sailors went up to the king and said:

'My Lord, when you like, you can board your ship, because we have done everything necessary to equip it. A fine, strong wind has risen in the right direction, so it would be unwise for you to delay any longer.'

Then the king ordered his men to take Sir Gawain and carry him aboard ship; he was made as comfortable as those looking after him were able to make him. Then the richest barons went abroad, taking with them their arms and their horses. The other barons boarded their ships with their men.

So King Arthur was angry about the great disloyalty that Mordred had shown towards him, but he was even more regretful about Sir Gawain who was visibly sinking further and getting nearer to his death every day. That was the grief that touched his heart more than any other; that was the grief that did not allow him to rest day or night; that was the grief that did not let him eat or drink.

But now the story stops telling of him and returns to Mordred.

*

[168]   Now the story relates that Mordred had maintained the siege of the Tower of London for so long that it was damaged and weakened, because he had often brought up catapults and made vigorous attacks on it. The people inside would not have been able to hold out for as long as they did if they had not defended themselves so remarkably.

While the siege of the tower lasted, Mordred never stopped summoning the barons of Ireland and Scotland and the foreign countries that held lands from him. When they arrived he gave them such fine gifts that they were astonished, and he so cleverly won them over in that way that they promised themselves completely to him, and all said that nothing would prevent them from helping him against all men, even against King Arthur, if he happened to enter Mordred's land. In that way Mordred won over all the high-ranking men who had held fiefs from Arthur, and kept them in his retinue for a long time. He was able to do this because, before leaving, Arthur had left him all his treasure everywhere, and because everyone brought him gifts. People thought it worth while because of his great generosity.

One day when he had attacked the tower, it happened that one of his messengers came to him and said to him secretly, a short distance from the others:

'My Lord, I have important news for you; King Arthur has arrived in this country with all his forces and he is marching on you with a great number of men. If you wish to wait for him here, you will see him in two days, and you cannot escape a battle, because he is not coming against you for any other reason. Now decide what you will do, because if you do not make good plans, you may lose everything.'

When Mordred heard this piece of news he was quite dumbfounded and helpless, because he was very frightened of King Arthur and his forces, especially because of his treachery, which he feared might rebound on him and harm him more than anyone else. Then he took advice from the men in whom he most confided, and he asked them what he could do.

They said:

'My Lord, we cannot give you any other advice than that you should assemble your men and march against him, demanding him to leave your land, with which the barons have invested you. If he refuses to leave, you have more men than he has, and they love you greatly, so that you can fight with confidence. You can be quite sure that his men will not be able to hold out against you, because they are weary and weak and we are fresh and well rested. We have not borne arms for some time. Before you leave here, ask your barons if they agree with the idea of a battle; we are sure that they will not have any other suggestions than what we have said.'

Mordred said that he would do that. He summoned to him all his barons and all the high-ranking men of the country who were in the city. They came to him, and when they had arrived he told them that King Arthur was marching on them with all his forces and that he would be in London by the day after next. Those who were present said to Mordred:

'My Lord, why should you be worried by his arrival? You have more men than he has and can march against him with confidence, because we will risk death to defend the land you have given us, and we will not fail you as long as we are able to bear arms.'

When Mordred heard that they were exhorting one another to fight, he was extremely pleased. He thanked them all and told them to take their arms, because there was no reason for delay. He wanted to meet King Arthur before he had done the country any damage.

Thus the news was made known through the whole country that they were going to set out the next morning to march against King Arthur. That night they all strove hard to equip themselves. The next day, as soon as it was light, they left London and calculated that they were more than ten thousand in number.

Now the story stops speaking of them and returns to Queen Guinevere, King Arthur's wife.

*

[169] Now the story tells that when Mordred had left London with his men, the people in the tower had heard the news that King Arthur was coming and that the others were marching against him. They told the queen, who was both glad and sorry: glad because she would be free, and sorry because she feared that King Arthur might die in the battle. Then she began to think, and was so miserable that she did not know what to do.

While she was deep in thought, it happened that her cousin

came to her, and when he saw her crying, he was very distressed, and said:

'Ah! my Lady, what is wrong? For God's sake, tell me, and I shall give you the best advice that I can.'

'Then I shall tell you,' replied the queen. 'Two things made me so pensive. The first is that I see that my lord the king is going to fight in this battle, and if Mordred wins he will kill me; on the other hand, if my lord has the honour of the battle, nothing will prevent him from thinking that Mordred has slept with me, because of the great force he has used to try to capture me. I am sure that the king will kill me as soon as he can get his hands on me. For these two reasons you see quite obviously that I cannot escape from death on one side or the other. Now tell me if it is possible for me to be much at ease.'

He could not advise her what to do, because he saw her death threatening her on all sides.

'My Lady,' he said, 'if it pleases God, my lord the king will be more merciful with you than you think; do not be so utterly dismayed, but pray to God, Our Lord Jesus Christ, that the king may have victory and honour in the battle, and that he may forgive you for causing his anger, if he is really angry with you.'

That night the queen was able to sleep little through being so distressed and frightened, because she could not see any way of escape.

[170] The next day, as soon as it was light, she woke two of her maids-in-waiting, in whom she had the greatest confidence. When they were dressed and ready she had each of them mount a palfrey, took two squires with her, and ordered two pack-horses laden with gold and silver to be led out of the tower. In that way the queen left London; she went to a forest nearby where there was an abbey of nuns which her ancestors had founded. When she arrived, she was received as honourably as such a lady should be. She ordered all the treasure she had brought with her to be unloaded there, and then she said to the girls who had accompanied her:

'If you wish you may go, and if you wish you may stay here,

because as for myself I can tell you that I am staying here and joining the nuns; my mother, the Queen of Tarmelide, who was considered a good woman, came to spend the end of her life here.'

When the girls heard what the queen said, they cried bitterly and said:

'My Lady, you will never receive that honour without us.'

The queen said that she would be delighted with their company.

The the abbess came forward; as soon as she saw the queen, she was very joyful. The queen asked to be allowed to join the order there.

'My Lady,' said the abbess, 'my Lady, if my lord the king had passed on from this world, we should have been delighted to make you a lady and companion of our order, but as he is still alive, we dare not receive you, because he would certainly kill us as soon as he discovered it. There is another difficulty too, my Lady; if we admitted you today, you would not be able to comply with our order, because it is extremely difficult, especially for you when you have had all the comfort in the world.'

'My Lady,' said the queen, 'if you do not admit me, it will turn out badly for both of us; because if I go from here and anything unfortunate befalls me, I shall suffer and the king will take his revenge on you, you can be sure of that, because it will have befallen me through your fault.'

The queen kept speaking to the abbess until she did not know what to reply; she drew the abbess to one side and told her how suffering and fear had made her want to join the order.

'My Lady,' said the abbess, 'I will tell you what to do. Stay here, and if it happens through misfortune that Mordred overcomes King Arthur and wins the battle, then at the right moment you can take on our dress and enter the order completely; while if the God of Glory allowed your lord to win this battle and return here safe and sound, I should make peace between you and you would be on better terms with him than ever in the past.'

The queen replied to the abbess:

'My Lady, I think that that is a good and faithful piece of advice, and I shall do exactly what you have suggested.'

So the queen stayed there with the nuns because she was frightened of King Arthur and Mordred.

But now the story stops telling of her and returns to King Arthur.

*

[171] Here the story relates that, when King Arthur had set sail for the kingdom of Logres in order to destroy and dishonour Mordred, they had a good strong wind that soon carried him across with all his men, and they arrived beneath Dover Castle. When they had reached the shore and disembarked their arms, the king instructed the people of Dover to open the gate and receive him. They did this with great joy, and told him they had thought he was dead.

'I can tell you that Mordred was the author of that treachery,' said King Arthur, 'and he will die for it, if I have any power in the matter, as a traitor and a perjurer before God and his liege lord.'

[172] That day at about Vespers Sir Gawain said to those around him : 'Go and tell my lord uncle to come and speak to me.'

One of the knights went to the king and told him that Sir Gawain was asking for him. When the king had come, he found Sir Gawain so ill that no one could get a word out of him. Then the king began to cry bitterly and to lament greatly.

When Sir Gawain heard his uncle lamenting over him, he recognized him. He opened his eyes and spoke as best he could, saying :

'My Lord, I am dying. For God's sake, if you can avoid fighting against Mordred, do so, because I tell you truthfully that if you die at the hands of any man you will die at his. Greet my lady the queen for me. And you, my Lords, if there is anyone among you who, with God's help, will see Lancelot, tell him that I greet him above all the men I have ever seen and that I beg his forgiveness. I pray to God to keep him as well as when I left him. I beg him not to fail for any reason to come and see my tomb as soon as he hears of my death, if he feels any pity for me.'

Then he said to the king:

'My Lord, I beg you to have me buried at Camelot with my brothers, and I want to be placed in the very same tomb that received the body of Gaheriet, because he was the man I loved most in all the world. Have an inscription put on the tomb saying: "HERE LIE GAHERIET AND GAWAIN WHOM LANCELOT KILLED THROUGH GAWAIN'S FOOLISHNESS". I want this inscription to be placed there, so that I may be blamed for my own death as I deserve.'

When the king, who was lamenting greatly, heard what Sir Gawain said, he asked him:

'What, nephew, is Lancelot then the cause of your death?'

'Yes, my Lord, by the wound he gave me in my head; I should have recovered completely from it, but the Romans opened it again in the battle.'

After he had said this, no one heard him say a word, except that he said:

'Jesus Christ, Father, do not judge me by my sins.'

Then he passed away from this world, with his hands crossed on his chest.

The king wept, and grieved greatly and swooned over him many times; he called himself wretched and miserable and unhappy, and said:

'Ah! Fortune, contrary and changeable, the most faithless thing in the world, why were you ever so courteous or so kind to me if you were to make me pay so dearly for it in the end? You used to be my mother; now you have become my stepmother, and to make me die of grief you have brought Death with you, in order to dishonour me in two ways at once, through my friends and through my land. Ah! base Death, you should not have attacked a man such as my nephew, who surpassed the whole world in goodness.'

[173] King Arthur was greatly angered by his death, and he felt such deep grief that he did not know what to say. He swooned so many times that the barons feared he might die in their hands. They carried him into another room where he

could not see the body, because he would never stop lamenting as long as it was before him.

All day the grief in the castle was so great that one could not have heard God thundering, and each of them cried as much as if Sir Gawain had been his own cousin. This was not surprising, because of all the knights in the world, Sir Gawain had been the one most loved by different kinds of people. They paid his body all possible honours and laid it in silk cloths worked with gold and precious stones. That night the lights were so intense that you would have thought that the castle was on fire.

In the morning, as soon as it was light, King Arthur, who felt that everything was burdening him, chose a hundred knights and had them arm themselves. He ordered them to take a horse-drawn bier and to place Sir Gawain's body on it. He said to them:

'You will take my nephew to Camelot, and you will have him buried exactly as he requested and placed in Gaheriet's tomb.'

While he was saying this, he was crying so bitterly that those present were no less affected by his grief than he was by Sir Gawain's death. Then the knights mounted, and there were more than a thousand others accompanying them, who all went weeping and wailing after the body, saying:

'Ah! good and reliable, courteous and generous knight, cursed be Death which has robbed us of your company!'

In that way everyone was crying before Sir Gawain's body.

When they had accompanied the body for some distance, the king stopped and said to those who were to take it:

'I cannot go any further; go to Camelot and do what I have told you.'

Then the king turned back as sadly as could be and said to his men:

'Ah! my Lords, we shall see how well you do from now on, because you have lost the man who was your father and shield in all times of need. Ah! God, now I feel that before long we shall miss him very much.'

So spoke the king as he rode along.

[174] The men taking the body rode the whole day, until

chance led them to a castle called Beloé, of which the lord was a knight who had never liked Sir Gawain. He had in fact hated him out of envy, because Sir Gawain was a better knight than he was.

The men carrying the body dismounted before the main palace, and there was none of them who did not feel great grief in his heart. At that moment the lady of the castle arrived, and asked who the knight was; they told her it was Sir Gawain, King Arthur's nephew.

When she heard them say this, she ran, as if out of her mind, to where she saw the body, and swooned on it. When she had come round, she said:

'Ah! Sir Gawain, your death is such a great loss, especially for ladies and girls! I have lost more than any other woman, because he was the man I most loved in all the world; may everyone here know that I have never loved any man but him, and shall never love anyone else so long as I live.'

As she was saying this the lord of the castle came out, and was very angry when he saw her lamenting Sir Gawain. He ran into a room, and took his sword. Then he went towards the bier and struck his wife, who was standing above it, so violently that he cut off her shoulder and the blade went several inches into her body.

The lady cried:

'Ah! Sir Gawain, now I am dying for you! For God's sake, my Lords,' she said, 'I beg you to carry my body where you are taking his, so that everyone who sees our tombs will know that I have died for him.'

The knights did not really listen to what she was saying, because they were very sad that she had died through such great misfortune. They ran to the knight, and took his sword, and one of them said to him in anger:

'My Lord, you have certainly done us a great dishonour in killing this lady before us, and for no reason; however, may God help me, I think that you will never strike a lady without having something by which to remember it.'

Then he took the sword and struck the lord of the castle so violently that he received a mortal injury. Feeling wounded to death, he tried to turn and flee, but the knight did not let him, since he gave him another blow and struck him dead in the middle of the palace.

Then a knight who was present shouted:

'Ah! that wretched knight has killed my lord.'

He spread the news around the whole town: the inhabitants ran to their arms and said that the knights would regret having come, and would pay dearly for the death of their lord. Then they came to the palace and attacked them; but Arthur's men defended themselves well, because they were fine knights and good friends, with the result that the townsmen thought they had been foolish to attack them, and were driven back from the palace in a short time.

[175] So Arthur's men spent the night there and ate and drank what they could find. In the morning they made a bier, and carried away the lady of the castle with them, riding until they arrived at Camelot.

When the inhabitants knew it was Sir Gawain's body that was being brought, they were very sad and miserable at his death, and said they were completely overcome. They accompanied the body to the cathedral and placed it in the middle of it. When the ordinary city-people heard that Sir Gawain's body had been brought, so many came that no one could have counted them.

After the body had lain, as was correct, until Terce, they put it in the tomb with his brother Gaheriet, and put an inscription on the outside saying:

'HERE LIE THE TWO BROTHERS, SIR GAWAIN AND GAHERIET, WHOM LANCELOT DEL LAC KILLED THROUGH SIR GAWAIN'S FOOLISHNESS'.

So Sir Gawain was buried with his brother Gaheriet, and those present greatly lamented his death.

But now the story stops telling of Sir Gawain and the lady of Beloé, and returns to King Arthur and his company.

*

[176] Now the story tells that, when King Arthur had left the body of Sir Gawain, which he had sent to Camelot, he

returned to Dover Castle and spent the whole day there. The next day he left; he set out to march against Mordred and rode out with all his army. That night he slept at the edge of a forest. In the evening, when he had gone to bed and fallen asleep, he dreamt that Sir Gawain came before him, more handsome than he had ever seen him, and a crowd of poor people followed him, saying:

'King Arthur, we have secured the admission of your nephew Sir Gawain to the house of God because of his great generosity and charity towards us. If you follow his example you will be acting very wisely.'

The king said that he was delighted; then he ran to his nephew and embraced him. Sir Gawain said to him, in tears:

'My Lord, avoid fighting against Mordred; if you fight against him you will die or be mortally wounded.'

'I shall quite certainly fight him,' said the king, 'even if I have to die as a result, because I should be a coward if I did not defend my land against a traitor.'

At that moment Sir Gawain started to leave, with the greatest grief in the world, saying to his uncle the king:

'Ah! my Lord, what sadness and what a loss, when you hasten your own death in this way!'

Then he returned to the king and said:

'My Lord, send for Lancelot, because you can be sure that if you have him on your side Mordred will never be able to hold out against you. If you do not send for him at this time of need, you will never escape with your life.'

The king replied that even so he would not send for him, because he had done him so much harm that he thought he would not come if requested. Then Sir Gawain turned away in tears and said:

'My Lord, I can tell you that all noble men will suffer as a result.'

This is what King Arthur dreamt. In the morning, when he awoke, he made the sign of the cross on his face and said:

'Ah! dear Lord God Jesus Christ, who have given me so many honours since I first wore a crown and began to possess land, dear God, through your mercy, do not allow me to be defeated in this battle, but grant me victory over my enemies who are perjurers and traitors towards me.'

When the king had said this, he got up and went to hear mass of the Holy Spirit, and when he had heard it through he ordered all his army to eat a little breakfast, because they did not know at what time they would meet Mordred's men. After they had eaten, they continued on their way and rode gently and leisurely all day so that their horses would not be too weary, at whatever time the battle started. That night they stayed in the meadow at Lovedon and were very comfortable. The king slept quite alone in his tent except for his chamberlains.

When Arthur had fallen asleep, he dreamt that a lady came before him, the most beautiful he had ever seen in the world, who lifted him up from the ground and took him up into the highest mountain he had ever seen. There she placed him on a wheel, on which there were seats, some rising and some falling. The king looked to see at which part of the wheel he was sitting, and saw he was at the highest point.

The lady asked him :

'Arthur, where are you?'

'My Lady,' he replied, 'I am on a high wheel, but I do not know what kind of a wheel it is.'

'It is the wheel of Fortune,' she replied. Then she asked him, 'Arthur, what can you see?'

'My Lady, I think I can see the whole world.'

'That is true,' she said, 'you can see it, and there is very little of which you have not been lord up till now. Of all the circle you can see you have been the most powerful king there ever was. But such is earthly pride that no one is seated so high that he can avoid having to fall from power in the world.'

Then she took him and pushed him to the ground so roughly that King Arthur felt that he had broken all his bones in the fall and had lost the use of his body and his limbs.

[177] In that way King Arthur saw the misfortunes that were to befall him. In the morning, when he had got up, he heard mass before he put on his arms, and he confessed to an archbishop, as well as he could, all the sins of which he felt guilty

before his creator. After he had confessed and had begged for forgiveness, he told him about the two dreams he had had during the two previous nights. When the good man heard them, he said to the king:

'Ah! my Lord, for the safety of your soul and your body and your kingdom turn back to Dover with all your men and ask Lancelot to come and help you – he will very willingly come. Otherwise, if you fight Mordred now, you will be mortally wounded or killed, and as a result we shall suffer as long as the world lasts. King Arthur, this will happen to you if you fight Mordred.'

'My Lord,' said the king, 'you are being unreasonable in forbidding me to do something from which I cannot turn back.'

'You must turn back,' said the good man, 'if you do not wish to be dishonoured.'

That was how the archbishop spoke to King Arthur, thinking he would be able to restrain him from carrying out what he planned to do; but he was unsuccessful, because the king swore by the soul of his father Utherpendragon that he would never turn back, but would fight Mordred.

'My Lord,' said the archbishop, 'it is a pity that I cannot dissuade you from your plans.'

And the king told him to be quiet, because he would not fail to carry out his plans for all the honour in the world.

[178] That day the king rode towards Salisbury Plain by the most direct route possible, well aware that it was on that plain that the great mortal battle would take place, of which Merlin and the other diviners had much spoken. When King Arthur arrived on the plain, he told his men to encamp there, because that was where they would wait for Mordred. They did just as he ordered; they set up the camp in a short time and got ready as best they could.

That evening after supper King Arthur went for a ride on the plain with the archbishop, and they came to a high and solid rock. The king looked up at the rock and saw there was an inscription cut into it. Then he turned to the archbishop and said:

'My Lord, you can see something remarkable; there is an

inscription which was carved into this rock long ago. Tell me what it says.'

He looked at the inscription, which read:

'ON THIS PLAIN WILL TAKE PLACE THE MORTAL BATTLE WHICH WILL ORPHAN THE KINGDOM OF LOGRES'.

'My Lord,' he said to the king, 'I can tell you what it means. If you fight Mordred, your kingdom will be orphaned because you will die or will be mortally wounded. No other outcome is possible, and so that you believe me when I say that there is only truth in that inscription, I can tell you that Merlin himself wrote it, and there was never anything but truth in whatever he said, because he was certain about things which happen in the future.'

'My Lord,' said King Arthur, 'now I see so much that if I had not come so far I should turn back, whatever my plans had been up till now. But may Jesus Christ help us now, because I shall never leave until Our Lord has granted victory to me or to Mordred. If it turns out badly for me, that will be a result of my sin and my folly, because I have a greater number of good knights than Mordred.'

King Arthur said this in an unusually diffident and worried way, because he had seen so many pointers to his own death. The archbishop was in tears because he could not make him turn back.

The king returned to his tent, and when he was there a boy went up to him and said:

'King Arthur, I shall not greet you, because my lord is a mortal enemy of yours, Mordred, the King of Logres. He tells you through me that you have unwisely entered his territory; but if you will promise as a king that you will leave tomorrow with all the men who have come with you, he will be satisfied and will not do you any harm. If you refuse to do that, he summons you to battle tomorrow. He asks you therefore what you intend to do, because he does not want to destroy you if you will leave his land.'

[179] The king, when he had heard this message, said to the boy:

'Go and tell your lord that I refuse to leave this land for him, because it is mine by inheritance. In fact, I have come to my land in order to defend it and to expel him as a perjurer. May Mordred the perjurer know that he will die by my hands; inform him of this from me. I prefer fighting him to leaving my land, even if he is to kill me.'

After he had said this the boy did not delay, but departed without taking leave. He rode until he came to Mordred, and told him the king's message word for word, He said:

'My Lord, I can tell you that you will certainly have your battle tomorrow, if you dare to wait for it.'

'I shall wait for it without fail,' said Mordred, 'because there is nothing I desire as much as a pitched battle against him.'

[180] Thus the battle was decided in which many noble men died without deserving it. That night King Arthur's men were very frightened, because they knew they had considerably fewer men than Mordred had on his side. For this reason they were very apprehensive about fighting against them. Moreover, Mordred had persuaded the Saxons to come to his aid. They were a great strong race, but they were not so experienced in war as King Arthur's men; however, they hated the king mortally. The highest barons of Saxony had turned towards Mordred and paid him homage, because they saw the opportunity for taking revenge on King Arthur for all the great harm he had done them in the past. Thus there was a large army assembled on each side.

As soon as it was light, King Arthur got up and heard mass; then he armed himself and commanded his men to take up their arms. The king formed his battalions. Sir Yvain led the first, King Yon the second, King Caradoc the third, King Kaberentin the fourth, King Aguisant the fifth, Girflet the sixth, Lucan the Butler the seventh, Sagremor the Foolish the eighth, Guivret the ninth, and King Arthur the tenth, in which they put their greatest strength. Those in the front put their hopes in the last battalion too, because there were so many fine knights in it that could not easily be defeated unless they were attacked by too many men.

[181] When the king had arranged and formed his battalions in that way he begged each baron to strive to do his best,

because if they were able to win the battle, there would never be any other people who would dare to show themselves against him.

In that way the king ordered his battalions, and Mordred did the same, but because he had more men than King Arthur he formed twenty battalions, and put in each as many men as he needed, with good knights to lead them. He put his greatest strength in the last one and assembled there the knights in whom he had the greatest confidence. He led it himself, and said he would fight against Arthur with this battalion, because his spies had told him that the king would be leading the last of his. In his first two battalions Mordred had no knight who was not from Saxony, and in the next two were the Scots. Next came the Welsh, and their men made up two battalions, and then the men from North Wales in the next three. In that way Mordred had chosen the knights of ten kingdoms, and they rode in ranks until they came to the great plain of Salisbury and saw King Arthur's battalions, and his banners fluttering in the wind.

King Arthur's army waited, all on horseback, until Mordred's men arrived. When they were so close that there was nothing to do but strike, then you could have seen lances lowered. At the head of all the others on the Saxon side came Arcan, their king's brother, and he came fully armed on a war-horse. When Sir Yvain, who was at the head of his companions and was waiting for the first joust, saw Arcan coming, he spurred on his horse at him with his lance lowered. Arcan struck Sir Yvain and broke his lance; Sir Yvain struck him so violently that he pierced his shield and transfixed his body with the blade of his lance. He gave it a good thrust and knocked him from his horse to the ground. As he fell the lance broke, and he lay stretched out on the ground mortally wounded. Then one of Sir Yvain's kinsmen said, loud enough for many to hear:

'Saxony is deprived of its finest heir!'

Then the battalions rushed to attack, the first on Arthur's side against the two of Saxons, and in the fight you could have seen many splendid blows with the lance, many fine knights knocked to the ground, and many good horses running about the field riderless, with no one to catch them. In a short time you could have seen the ground covered with knights, some dead and some wounded.

Thus the battle began on Salisbury Plain; it was to lead to the destruction of the kingdom of Logres and also of many others, because afterwards there were fewer noble men than there had been before. Moreover, after their deaths, lands remained devastated and waste, through lack of good lords, because they were all killed in great pain and slaughter.

[182] The first part of the battle was vigorous and forceful; when the men in front had broken their lances they put their hands to their swords and gave such great blows that they sank them right through helmets down into men's brains. Sir Yvain fought well that day and did the Saxons great damage; when the king of the Saxons had watched him for some time, he said to himself:

'If that man lives much longer, we shall be defeated.'

He rushed through the fighting towards Sir Yvain as fast as he could drive his horse, and as he came he struck him so violently with all his strength that Sir Yvain's shield could not protect him from having the Saxon's lance thrust into his left side, but he was not mortally wounded. As he went past, Sir Yvain struck him so hard with his keen-edged sword that his head flew off and his body fell to the ground.

Seeing their lord struck down, the Saxons began to lament greatly, but when the men of Logres saw their grief they were not concerned, but attacked them, brandishing their swords. They killed and destroyed so many of them that before long they were obliged to flee, because there was not a single one of them without some wound, great or small, and they were overcome more through the death of their lord than for any other reason.

When the Saxons had been repelled and had turned to flight, the men of Logres pursued them until they joined the Irishmen. These latter spurred on their horses to help them and attacked Sir Yvain's men; since they were fresh and rested, they struck them so hard that there were a great many killed. Sir Yvain's men, being bold and preferring to die rather than retreat, received them as well as they could, although they were weary and exhausted. It was then that Sir Yvain was struck down and wounded by two lances; he would have been killed then and all his companions slaughtered, had it not been for King Yon, leading the second battalion, who went to their rescue as soon as he could with all the men he could muster.

Then they struck out so mortally that they transfixed one another with their lances. They knocked one another off their horses, some on this side and some on that, and in a short time one could have seen the plain covered with dead or wounded men. When the Irish and King Yon's men met in battle, you could have seen blows given and received. and knights struck to the ground. King Yon, who was making a tour of the ranks, came to the place where Sir Yvain was on foot among his enemies, attempting unsuccessfully to remount because the others were pressing him too hard.

When the king saw this, he spurred on his horse against those who were trying their hardest to kill Sir Yvain, and gave them violent blows where he could reach them. He separated and scattered them whether they wished or not. and made them draw back until Sir Yvain had remounted his horse, which the king himself had given him.

[183] When Sir Yvain had remounted, he rejoined the fighting, since he was of great valour; and King Yon said to him:

'My Lord, be as careful as you possibly can, if you do not wish to die.'

Sir Yvain replied that he had never feared dying before that day, 'and', he continued, 'I am amazed how that can be, because the risk of death was never able to affect me in the past.'

Then they joined the battle and started again to strike great blows, but so energetically that it seemed as if they had not yet struck a single one that day. They acted with such great prowess that the Irish were defeated and were taking to flight when an Irish knight spurred on his horse, brandishing a keen-edged lance, and struck King Yon so violently that no armour could prevent him from being transfixed with blade and shaft, with the result that much of the blade came out of the other side of him. The Irishman gave King Yon a great thrust and knocked him to the ground so badly wounded that a doctor would have been no use to him.

When Sir Yvain saw this, he was as saddened as could be, and said:

'Ah! God, what a loss there is in the death of that good man. Ah! Round Table, now your nobility will be badly abased, because I think that today you will be robbed of your members, who have maintained your great renown until now.'

That was what Sir Yvain said when he saw King Yon lying on the ground; he spurred on his horse towards the man who had killed him and gave him such a violent blow that he split his head down to his teeth and struck him to the ground dead, saying:

'Now this man is dead, and yet it does not bring that noble knight back to life.'

[184] When King Yon's knights saw their lord dead, they called themselves miserable and wretched, and because of their grief they stopped pursuing their enemies. When those at the front of the fleeing Irish saw that the others had remained by the body, they knew that the man for whom they were lamenting had been some high-ranking person. Because of that they regained their courage, and turned and attacked those who were grieving. They struck them great blows to such mortal effect that they killed many of them, and indeed they would have killed them all, had it not been for the third battalion which came to their aid as soon as its men saw they were being slaughtered in such a fashion.

As soon as King Caradoc, the leader of the third battalion, knew that their grief was for King Yon, whom the enemy had killed, he said to his men:

'My Lords, we shall join this battle, but I do not know what will become of me. If it happens that I am killed, I beg you for God's sake not to show any grief, because your enemy could take courage and boldness from that.'

That was what King Caradoc said when he entered the battle, and when he was among his enemies no one who saw him could have taken him for a coward. Because of the prowess in him the Irishmen all turned their backs and fled, since they saw only their own deaths. King Caradoc's men killed so many of them before they received help, that you could have seen the whole place covered with them. When the high-ranking barons from Scotland saw their comrades so badly harassed, they could stand it no longer, but spurred on their horses against King Caradoc's men; and Heliades, who had been appointed by Mordred to be Lord of Scotland, galloped to attack King Caradoc, who had a finer and richer mount than any of his men. Being bold enough to meet the finest knight in the world, King Caradoc did not refuse to fight; they struck each other so vigorously with their lances that they pierced each other's shields. Then they came together so violently that they transfixed each other's body with their sharp lances, so that the blades passed right through them. They knocked each other to the ground with so much steel in them that neither of them could mock the other, as they were both badly wounded.

To rescue these two, men rushed up from both sides to help their leader and attack his adversary. King Caradoc's men managed by force to capture Heliades, but they found his soul had left his body, as a result of his being transfixed by the lance. Their comrades disarmed King Caradoc and asked him how he was. He said:

'I ask you only to avenge my death, because I am quite sure that I shall not see None; but for God's sake do not make it obvious, because our men could be quite disheartened, and our loss would be all the greater. However, manage to take off my coat of mail and carry me on my shield over to that hillock, and in that way I shall be able to die in greater comfort than I could here.'

And they did exactly as he commanded; they carried him over to the hill very sadly, because they loved their lord greatly. When they had placed him under a tree, he said to them:

'Go back to the battle and leave me here under the guard of four squires. Avenge my death as soon as you are able; and if it happens that any of you escape from here, I beg you to carry my body to Camelot to the cathedral where Sir Gawain lies buried.'

They said they would willingly do that. Then they asked him:

'My Lord, do you think we shall be as defeated in this battle as you say?'

'I can tell you,' he said, 'that since Christianity came to the land of Logres, there has never been a battle in which as many noble men died as will die in this one; it is the last battle there will be in King Arthur's time.'

When they heard him say this, they left him and returned to the battle. King Caradoc's and King Yon's men did so well that the Scots, Irish and Saxons were defeated. King Arthur's men, in three battalions, were pressed so hard that more than half of them lay dead on the ground, because they had borne the great burden of destroying Mordred's six battalions, and had been so successful that they went on to attack the battalions which had come from Wales.

There were many noble men in these two battalions who were very impatient to join the battle, and who regretted that they had been inactive for so long. They received King Arthur's men so valiantly that few of the latter remained in the saddle; this was because they had done nothing all day, while King Arthur's men were weary and exhausted through giving and receiving blows. During this encounter Sir Yvain was struck down, and was so weary and exhausted that he lay unconscious for some time. Now it was King Arthur's men who were pursued, and in the rush more than five hundred knights passed over Sir Yvain, wounding him so badly that if he had not already felt much pain that day, he certainly felt it then. This was what most weakened him and drained his strength and vigour.

Thus all King Arthur's men turned to flight. When King Kaberentin of Cornwall saw that they were at a disadvantage, he said to his men:

'Let us go to help them! Our side is being hard pressed.'

Then King Arthur's fourth battalion broke its ranks, and as they came you could have heard battle-cries from various men, and you could have seen knights knocked to the ground and falling, some dead and others wounded. You would never have seen such a grievous encounter as this, because they hated one another mortally. When they had broken their lances, they put their hands to their swords and gave one another great blows, crushing their helmets and splitting their shields. They knocked one another from their horses to the ground, and each did his best to hasten the death of his opponent.

It was not long before Mordred sent two squadrons to help his men. When King Aguisant, at the head of the fifth battalion, saw them rapidly crossing the battle-field, he said to the men who were with him:

'Now let us go that way, so that we can fight the men who have just left their companions. Make sure you do not touch any of the others until you have reached them; when you arrive there go and strike them so that they lose courage.'

They did exactly as he had commanded, passing all those he had pointed out and going to attack the battalions which had left Mordred. As their lances met you would have heard such a great noise that one could not have heard God thundering; you would have seen more than five hundred men on the ground in that battle, and those on Mordred's side suffered heavy losses straight away. Thus in two places the battle was begun more cruelly than necessary.

[186] When Aguisant's men had split their lances, they put their hands to their swords and attacked their enemies, striking them wherever they could catch them. The others defended themselves well and killed great numbers; and as King Aguisant was making a tour of the ranks, brandishing his sword, he looked in front of him and saw Sir Yvain. Badly wounded, he was trying to mount a horse, but his enemies had knocked him down two or three times. When the king saw Sir Yvain, he spurred on his horse towards him as fast as it would go. There were four men who were trying to kill Sir Yvain; the king galloped towards them, and struck one so hard that his helmet could not protect him from tasting the steel in his brain. He rushed among them, and they were all amazed at where such prowess could come from. King Aguisant was so valiant that he managed to rescue Sir Yvain from all the men who had set on him; he gave him a horse and helped him to mount. When he

had remounted, and as weary as he was, he rejoined the battle and achieved so much, considering what he had already done, that everyone was astounded.

Thus all the battalions fought together before Terce, except the last two, King Arthur's and the one led by Mordred. The king had commanded a boy to climb a hill in order to see how many men there could be in Mordred's battalion, the last one. When the boy had been up the hill and had seen what the king had commanded, he went back to him and told him in confidence:

'My Lord, he has at least twice as many men in his battalion as you have in yours.'

'That is certainly a great blow!' said the king. 'Now may God come to our aid, because otherwise we shall be dead and buried.'

Then he thought regretfully of his nephew Sir Gawain and said:

'Ah! nephew, now I need you and Lancelot; if only God would permit you both to be armed and standing next to me! We should certainly win this battle with the help of God and the prowess I know to be in you. But, dear nephew, I am afraid I was foolish not to believe you when you told me to ask Lancelot to come and help me against Mordred, because I am sure that if I had asked him he would have come willingly and courteously.'

[187] King Arthur said this in great despair, and his heart foretold accurately a part of the ills that were to befall him and his company. He was well and very richly armed; then he went to the knights of the Round Table, of which there were about seventy-two around him.

'My Lords,' he said, 'this battle is the most fearful that I have ever seen. For God's sake, you who are brothers and companions of the Round Table, keep together, all of you, because if you do that you cannot easily be defeated. There are two of them against one of us, and they are very experienced at fighting; that is why we should fear them all the more.'

'My Lord,' they replied, 'do not despair, but ride ahead confidently, because you can already see Mordred galloping to-

216

wards you at great speed. Do not fear, because no good can come either to us or to you from too much fear.'

Then the king's standard was brought forward, and more than a hundred knights were set to guard it. Mordred, who had selected four hundred of the boldest knights in his company, said to them:

'Leave us and go straight to that hill. When you have arrived there, return as quietly as you can along that valley. Then direct yourselves towards the standard and gallop so hard that no one is left standing. If you can manage to do that, I can tell you truthfully that the king's men will be so disheartened that they will not hold out, but will turn to flight, because they have nowhere to turn back to.'

They said they would do that willingly, because he had commanded them.

[188] Then they spurred on their horses to where they saw the king's battalion, and they struck among them with their lances lowered. As they went, you would have thought that the whole earth was about to collapse, because the noise of the striking-down of knights was great enough to be heard two leagues away. King Arthur, recognizing Mordred, galloped towards him, and Mordred rushed forward too; they struck each other nobly and valiantly. Mordred struck the king first, and pierced his shield, but his coat of mail was strong and its links could not be broken. His lance flew into pieces with the thrust he made, but the king did not falter; instead, being strong and tough and accustomed to giving blows with the lance, he struck him with such violence that he knocked him and his horse to the ground in one heap. However, he did not cause him any injury, because Mordred was too well armed.

Then King Arthur's men broke their ranks and tried to capture Mordred, but you could have seen two thousand men coming to his rescue, dressed in steel, every single one prepared to risk his life out of love for him. You could have seen many blows given and received over him, and too many knights killed. Around him there was in fact such a great conflict that in a short time you would have seen more than a hundred men lying on the ground, of which there was not one who was not dead or mortally wounded. However, because the strength of Mordred's side kept increasing, Mordred was put back on his horse despite all his enemies, but before this he had received three great blows at the hand of the king himself, the least of which would have overcome any other knight.

Nevertheless, Mordred was a fine, bold knight; he spurred on his horse at King Arthur to avenge himself, because he was very much ashamed at having been struck down in that way among his men. The king did not refuse battle, but turned the head of his horse towards him. They gave each other such great blows with their keen-edged swords that they were dazed and could hardly remain in their saddles; if they had not both held on to the necks of their horses, they would have fallen to the ground, but the horses were strong and carried them away from each other till there was more than an acre of land between them.

[189] Thereupon the battle began again, vigorously and impressively. Galegantin the Welshman, who was a bold and noble knight, spurred on his horse against Mordred. The latter, who was very angry, hit him with all his strength and struck his head off. This was a great pity, because he was loyal towards King Arthur. When Arthur saw Galegantin on the ground, he was unhappy and said that he would avenge him if he could Then he rushed towards Mordred again, and as he was going to strike him, a knight from Northumberland caught him sideways; he struck the king in his left side, which was uncovered, and he could have wounded him very seriously if his coat of mail had not been so strong, but it held firm and no links were broken. The knight gave a great thrust, and knocked Arthur under the belly of his horse.

When Sir Yvain, who was close by, saw this blow, he said:

'Ah! God, how sad it is when such a noble man is knocked to the ground so basely!'

Then he spurred on his horse against the knight from Northumberland and struck him so violently with a short thick lance that no armour could prevent him from thrusting it through his body, blade and shaft. As he fell the lance broke. Then Sir Yvain went back to the king and helped him to mount despite all his enemies. Mordred, who was so annoyed by the fact that the king had remounted that he almost went out of his mind, turned to Sir Yvain and held his sword with both hands. The blow was weighty and came from high up; it cleft Sir Yvain's helmet and his steel cap down to his teeth, and struck him to the ground dead. This was a grievous shame, because at that time Sir Yvain was considered to be one of the finest knights in the world, and also one of the noblest.

[190]   When King Arthur saw the blow, he said:

'Ah! God, why did you allow me to see the worst traitor in the world kill one of the noblest men?'

And Sagremor the Foolish replied:

'My Lord, such are the tricks of Fortune; now you can see that she is making you pay very dearly for the great prosperity and honour that you used to have, when she robs you of your best friends. God grant that things do not become worse!'

While they were speaking about Sir Yvain, they heard a great outcry behind them, because Mordred's four hundred knights were shouting just as they approached the standard, and King Arthur's men were shouting too. In that encounter you could have seen lances broken and knights falling, but King Arthur's men, who were good hardened knights, received them so well that they struck down more than a hundred of them as they came. They drew their swords on both sides, struck one another with all their strength, and killed as many of their opponents as they could. King Arthur's men who were guarding the standard fought off that attack so well that out of Mordred's four hundred knights, there were only twenty who by None had not been killed or wounded where they fought. If you had been in the battle-field at that time, you could have seen the whole place strewn with the dead and a good many wounded men too.

A little after None the battle was drawing to a close, as out of all those who had assembled on the plain, more than a hundred thousand in number, there were now fewer than three hundred who had not been killed. It had happened that out of all the companions of the Round Table only four remained; they had fought with greater abandon because of the great need they saw. Out of the four that remained one was King Arthur, another Lucan the Butler, the third Girflet, and the fourth Sagremor the Foolish. However, Sagremor had received such a serious body-wound that he could hardly hold himself in the saddle.

They reassembled their men and said that they would rather die than leave the battle without a definite outcome. Mordred spurred on his horse against Sagremor and struck him so violently before the king that his head flew off into the air. When the king saw this blow, he said, in great sadness:

'Ah! God, why do you let me be so abased in earthly prowess? For the sake of that blow I vow to God that either Mordred or I must die here.'

He was holding a thick strong lance, and he spurred on his horse as fast as it would gallop. Mordred, realizing that the king's only intention was to kill him, did not refuse battle but turned his horse's head towards him; and the king, who was coming with all his strength, struck him so violently that he broke the links on his coat of mail and put the blade of his lance through his body. The story tells that when Arthur wrenched out the lance, a ray of sunlight passed through the wound so clearly that Girflet saw it. The local people said that this had been a sign of Our Lord's anger. When Mordred saw he was so badly injured, he was sure his wound was mortal; and he struck King Arthur so violently on the helmet that nothing could save him from feeling the sword in his skull. In fact he lost a piece of his skull, and King Arthur was so dazed by the blow that he fell from his horse to the ground. Mordred did the same, and they were both in such a state that they were unable to get up, but lay beside one another.

[191] In that way the father killed the son, and the son gave his father a mortal wound. When Arthur's men saw the king on the ground, they were so grief-stricken that a human heart cannot imagine the suffering they felt.

They said:

'Ah! God, why are you allowing this battle?'

They they attacked Mordred's men and were attacked in return, and the mortal battle began again with the result that before Vespers all had been killed except Lucan the Butler and Girflet. When those who were left saw what the outcome of the battle had been, they began to cry bitterly and said:

'Ah! God, has any mortal man ever seen such great suffering? Ah! battle, how many orphans and widows you have made in this country and others. Ah! day, why did you ever dawn if you were to reduce the kingdom of Great Britain to such great poverty when its heirs, who are lying here dead and destroyed in such suffering, were so renowned for prowess? Ah! God, what more can you take away from us? We can see all our friends dead before us.'

After they had lamented in this way for some time, they went up to where King Arthur was lying and asked him:

'My Lord, how do you feel?'

He replied:

'All we can do is to mount and leave this place, because I know my end is approaching and I do not wish to die among my enemies.'

Then he climbed on to a horse quite easily. All three of them left the battle-field and rose straight towards the sea, until they came to a chapel called the Black Chapel. Mass was sung there every day by a hermit who had his hut quite close by in a copse. The king dismounted, and the others too, and they took the reins and saddles off their horses.

Arthur went in and knelt before the altar, and began to say his prayers as he had learnt them. He stayed there till the morning without moving, and without ceasing to pray to Our Lord to have mercy on his men who had been killed that day; as he was thus praying, he cried so bitterly that those with him could hear he was crying.

[192] King Arthur spent the whole night in prayer. The next day it happened that Lucan the Butler was behind him, watching him and noticing that he did not move. Then he said in tears:

'Ah! King Arthur, how great is your grief!'

When the king heard him say this, he stood up with difficulty because of the weight of his arms; he took Lucan, who was unarmed, and embraced him, holding him so tightly that he burst his heart inside him. Lucan was unable to say a word before his soul left his body. When the king had been in that position for some time, he released his hold, because he did not realize he was dead. Girflet looked at Lucan for a long time and, seeing that he did not move, he knew that he was dead and that the king had killed him. Then he began grieving once again and said:

'Ah! my Lord, what a bad thing you have done in killing Lucan!'

When the king heard this, he gave a start, looked round him and saw his butler lying dead on the ground. Then his grief became even greater and he replied to Girflet, obviously in great anger:

'Girflet, Fortune, who has been my mother until now, but has become my step-mother, is making me devote the remainder of my life to grief and anger and sadness.'

Then he told Girflet to put the reins and saddles on their horses. This he did. The king mounted and rode towards the sea until he arrived there at noon. He dismounted on the shore, ungirded the sword he was wearing, and drew it from its scabbard. After he had looked at it for some time, he said:

'Ah! Excalibur, you fine rich sword, the best in the world except the one with the Strange Belt, now you will lose your master. Where will you find a man who will put you to such great use as I have, unless you come into Lancelot's hands? Ah! Lancelot, the noblest man in the world and the finest knight, would to Jesus Christ that you could hold it and that I would know! My soul would certainly be at greater ease evermore.'

Then the king called Girflet and said:

'Go up that hill, where you will find a lake, and throw my sword into it, because I do not want it to remain in this kingdom, in case our wicked successors gain possession of it.'

'My Lord,' he said, 'I shall carry out your commandment, but I would rather, if you please, that you gave it to me.'

'I shall not,' replied the king, 'because it would not be put to good use in you.'

So Girflet climbed the hill, and when he came to the lake, he drew the sword from the scabbard and began to look at it. It seemed so fine and beautiful that he thought it would be a great pity to throw it into the lake as the king had commanded, because it would be lost. It would be better for him to throw in his own and tell the king he had thrown it. So he ungirded his sword and threw it into the lake, and laid the other one in the grass. Then he went back to the king and said:

'My Lord, I have carried out your commandment and thrown your sword into the lake.'

'And what did you see?' asked the king.

'Nothing, my Lord,' he replied, 'except good.'

'Ah!' said the king, 'you are trying me. Go back and throw it in, because you have not done it yet.'

So he returned to the lake and drew the sword from its scabbard; he began to have great regrets about it and said that it would be a great shame if it were lost in that way. Then he thought he would throw in the scabbard and keep the sword, because he or someone else might have need for it. He took the scabbard therefore, and straight away threw it into the lake. He then took the sword, put it down under a tree, and went back to the king, saying:

'My Lord, now I have carried out your commandment.'

'And what did you see?' asked the king.

'My Lord, I saw nothing that I should not have seen.'

'Ah!' said the king, 'you have not thrown it in yet. Why are you annoying me so? Go and throw it in, and you will see what happens, because it will not be lost without a great marvel.'

When Girflet saw that he had to do it, he went back to where the sword was. He picked it up and began to gaze at it and to have regrets about it, saying:

'You splendid and beautiful sword, what a great pity it is for you that you will not fall into the hands of some noble man!'

Then he hurled it into the lake as deep and as far from him as he could, and as it fell near the water, he saw a hand come out of the lake which revealed itself up to the elbow, but he saw nothing of the body to which it belonged. The hand seized the sword by the hilt and brandished it in the air three or four times.

[193] When Girflet had clearly seen this, the hand disappeared back into the water together with the sword. He waited there for some time to see if it would show itself again, but when he saw he was wasting his time he left the lake and returned to the king. He said he had thrown the sword into the lake, and told him what he had seen.

'By God,' said the king, 'I thought indeed that my end was very near.'

Then he began to think, and as he thought the tears came to his eyes. After he had been deep in thought for some time, he said to Girflet:

'You must go from here and leave me; from now on you will never see me again as long as you live.'

'If that is the case,' said Girflet, 'I shall not leave you for anything.'

'You will,' said the king, 'or else I shall hate you mortally.'

'My Lord,' said Girflet, 'how could I possibly leave you here alone and go away, especially when you tell me I shall never see you again?'

'You must do what I say,' said the king. 'Go quickly, because you must not delay. I am asking you to go, by the love there has been between us.'

Hearing that the king was asking him to go so tenderly, Girflet replied:

'My Lord, I shall do what you command, as sadly as can be; but please tell me if you think I shall ever see you again.'

'No,' said the king, 'you can be sure of that.'

'Where do you expect to go, my dear Lord?'

'I cannot tell you,' said the king.

When Girflet saw that he would learn no more, he mounted and left the king, and as soon as he had left him, very heavy rain began to fall, and continued until he reached a hill a good half-league away from the king. When he had reached the hill, he waited under a tree for the rain to stop. He looked back to where he had left the king, and saw a ship entirely occupied by women coming across the sea. When the ship had come to the shore opposite where Arthur was, they came to the side, and their lady, who was holding King Arthur's sister Morgan by the hand, called to Arthur to come aboard. As soon as Arthur saw his sister Morgan, he arose from the ground where he was sitting, and went aboard ship, taking his horse and his arms with him.

When Girflet had seen all this from the hill he turned back as fast as his horse would carry him until he reached the shore. When he arrived he saw King Arthur among the ladies, and recognized Morgan the Fay, because he had seen her many times. In a short time the ship had travelled from the shore more than eight times the distance one can shoot from a crossbow; and when Girflet saw that he had thus lost the king, he dismounted on to the shore and suffered the greatest grief in the world. He remained there all day and all night without eating or drinking anything; neither had he eaten or drunk the day before.

[194] In the morning when day appeared and the sun had risen, and the birds had begun singing, Girflet was as grief-stricken and miserable as could be; and, sad as he was, he mounted his horse and left there, riding until he came to a copse near by. In that copse lived a hermit he knew well; he went to him and stayed with him for two days, because he felt rather unwell from all the great grief he had suffered. He told the hermit what had happened to King Arthur.

On the third day he departed and decided to go to the Black Chapel to see if Lucan the Butler had been buried yet. When he arrived there at about noon, he dismounted at the entrance, tied his horse to a tree, and went in. Before the altar he found two rich and beautiful tombs, but one of them was far richer and more beautiful than the other. On the less beautiful one there was an inscription saying: 'HERE LIES LUCAN THE BUTLER, WHOM KING ARTHUR CRUSHED TO DEATH'. On the very splendid and rich tomb there was written: 'HERE LIES KING ARTHUR WHO THROUGH HIS VALOUR CONQUERED TWELVE KINGDOMS'.

Seeing this, he swooned on the tomb, and after he had regained consciousness he kissed it very tenderly, in great grief. He remained there until the evening, until the arrival of the hermit who served the altar. When the hermit had come, Girflet asked him straight away:

'My Lord, is it true that King Arthur lies here?'

'Yes, my friend, he truly lies there; he was brought here by some ladies whom I did not know.'

Girflet immediately thought that they were the ladies who had taken him aboard ship. He said that as his lord had left this world, he would not stay in it any longer. So he begged the hermit to receive him as a companion.

[195] So Girflet became a hermit and served in the Black Chapel, but it was not for long because after King Arthur's death he lived only eighteen days.

While Girflet was living in the hermitage, Mordred's two sons came forward. They had stayed at Winchester to guard the town, if it should be necessary, and Mordred had left them there.

These two were good hardened knights, and as soon as they heard of the death of their father and King Arthur and the other noble men who had taken part in the battle, they took all the men in Winchester and went occupying the country around, in all directions. They were able to do this because they found no one to challenge them, since all the good men and fine knights of the region had died in the battle.

When the queen heard of the death of King Arthur and had been told that Mordred's sons were seizing the country, she was frightened they might kill her if they could catch her; so she straight away took nuns' habits.

[196] While this was happening, a messenger came from the kingdom of Logres to Lancelot, where he was in the city of Gaunes, and told him the whole truth about King Arthur, how he had been killed in the battle and how Mordred's two sons had seized the land after his death. When Lancelot heard this news he was overcome, as he had loved King Arthur dearly; all the other fine knights of Gaunes were also grief-stricken. Lancelot discussed with the two kings what he could do, because he hated nothing as much as he hated Mordred and his sons.

'My Lord,' said Bors, 'I shall tell you what to do: we shall summon our men far and near, and when they have assembled here we shall leave the kingdom of Gaunes and cross over to Great Britain. After we have arrived, if Mordred's sons do not take to flight, they can be sure of being killed.'

'Do you want us to do that?' asked Lancelot.

'My Lord,' said Bors, 'we do not see at all how we could take our revenge in any other way.'

Then they summoned their men near and far from the kingdoms of Banoic and Gaunes, with the result that within a fortnight more than twenty thousand had assembled, both on foot and on horseback. They met in the city of Gaunes, and the knights and noble men of the country came there. Then King Bors, King Lionel, Lancelot, Hector, and all their companions left the kingdom of Gaunes and they rode day after day until they came to the sea. They found their ships ready, went aboard, and had such a good wind that they arrived in Britain the same day. When they had landed in good health they were delighted, and they encamped on the shore with great joy.

The next day the news was brought to Mordred's two sons that Lancelot had landed with a great number of men. When they heard this news they were very dismayed because there was no man they feared so much as Lancelot. They discussed among themselves what they should do, and decided to take up their arms and go to fight against Lancelot in a pitched battle. Whomever God allowed to win, let him win, because they would rather die than go fleeing through the country.

They did exactly as they planned, because they straight away summoned their men and assembled them at Winchester; and they had made so much progress in a short time that all the noble men in the kingdom had paid them homage. When they had assembled their men, as I have said, they set out from Winchester one Tuesday morning. They were immediately told by a messenger that Lancelot was marching against them with an army and was already only five English leagues away; they could be certain of having a battle before Terce.

[197] When they heard this news, they said they would fight

227

there and wait for Lancelot and his men, because there could be no other outcome than a battle; they straight away dismounted from their horses to let them rest. Thus the men of Winchester stopped there, while Lancelot rode on with his company.

However, Lancelot was as sad and grief-stricken as could be, because that same day on which the battle was to be fought he heard the news that his lady the queen had died and passed out of this world three days previously. This had in fact happened just as he was told, because the queen had just died, but never had a high-born lady had a finer and more repentant end to her life, or more tenderly begged Our Lord for forgiveness. Lancelot was very grieved and saddened by her death, when he heard the truth about it.

Then he rode to Winchester in great anger, and when those awaiting him saw him coming, they mounted their horses and fought a great battle against his men. In that encounter you could have seen many knights unhorsed and killed, and many horses, dead and straying, whose masters lay on the ground with their souls departed from their bodies. The battle lasted until None, because there were many men on both sides.

At about None it happened that the elder of Mordred's two sons, whose name was Melehan, took a short thick lance with a newly sharpened blade, and spurred on his horse as fast as it would go to attack King Lionel. He struck him so violently with all his strength that neither his shield nor his coat of mail could prevent him from sticking his lance through his body. He thrust the king so hard with all his strength that he struck him to the ground; as he fell, the lance broke, and the blade as well as a large piece of the shaft remained in his body.

King Bors saw this blow and was well aware that his brother was mortally wounded; he was so saddened that he thought he would die of grief. Then he attacked Melehan, brandishing his sword, and struck him on his helmet with all the experience of the many great blows he had given. As a result he cut open his helmet and his steel cap and split his head down to his teeth. He wrenched away his sword and Melehan fell to the ground, dead. When Bors saw him down, he looked at him and said:

'Treacherous and faithless man, your death is poor compensation for all the harm that you have done me! You have certainly put so much grief in my heart that it will never be free of it.'

Then he attacked the others where he saw the greatest number of them, and began to strike down and kill everyone he saw in front of him in such a way that everyone thought it remarkable. When the knights of Gaunes saw King Lionel fall, they dismounted by him, took him, and carried him out of the battle underneath an elm. Seeing him so seriously wounded, they were all extremely saddened, but they did not dare to show their grief openly in case their enemies should notice.

[198] So the murderous and painful battle continued till None, so evenly that one could scarcely see who was at an advantage. After None it happened that Lancelot joined the battle. He met Mordred's younger son and recognized him by his arms, because he wore the same ones as his father had formerly done. As he hated him mortally, Lancelot attacked him, brandishing his sword. The other man did not refuse battle, but covered himself with his shield as he saw him coming. Lancelot struck him with all his strength, so that he split his shield down to the boss and also cut off the hand with which he was holding it. Feeling himself disabled, he turned to flight, but Lancelot pressed him so hard that he did not have either the opportunity or the ability to defend himself. Lancelot dealt him a great blow that struck off his head together with his helmet more than half a lance-length from his body.

When the others saw this man dead after his brothers, they did not know how they could recover; they turned to flight to save their lives as best they could, and rode to a forest close by at less than two English leagues' distance. Their opponents pursued them and killed as many as they could, because they hated them mortally; they slew them in fact as though they were wild animals. Lancelot went on striking them down and killing them in such numbers that behind him you could have seen the line of those he had knocked to the ground.

Eventually he met the Earl of Gorre, whom he knew to be a treacherous and faithless man who had caused harm to many high-born men. As soon as he saw him, he shouted:

'Ah! traitor, now you are definitely finished and dead, because nothing can save you.'

He looked round straight away, and when he saw it was Lancelot who was threatening him and following him, brandishing his sword, he realized he was finished if Lancelot could catch him; so he spurred on his horse and fled as quickly as he could. He was well mounted, and so was Lancelot; in that way the chase began that was to take them at least half a league deep into the forest. Then the Earl's horse broke its heart and fell dead beneath him.

Lancelot, who was not far behind him, saw him on the ground. He attacked him, armed as he was, and struck him so violently that his sword sank down to his teeth. The Earl fell to the ground, tormented by death. Lancelot did not once look at him, but went on at a great speed; however, when he hoped to return to his men, he got further and further away in the depth of the forest.

[199] He rode up and down in the forest, quite lost, just as adventure took him, until after Vespers he came to a heath, and then he saw a foot-messenger going towards Winchester. He asked him where he had come from. When the boy saw him he thought he was from the kingdom of Logres and had fled from the battle. He said:

'My Lord, I have come from the battle, where it has turned out a mournful day for our men, because so far as I know not even a single one of them has escaped. Nevertheless, the men on the other side are very grief-stricken at the death of King Lionel.'

'What?' said Lancelot. 'Is he dead, then?'

'Yes, my Lord,' said the boy, 'I saw him dead.'

'That is a pity,' said Lancelot. 'He was a kind man and a fine knight.'

Then he began to cry bitterly, and tears ran down his face beneath his helmet.

The boy said:

'My Lord, it is late now, and you are a long way from people and from anywhere to stay; where do you expect to spend the night?'

'I do not know,' he said, 'I do not care where I sleep.'

When the boy realized he would not obtain any other reply from him, he left him straight away. Lancelot went on riding through the forest, suffering the greatest grief in the world. He said that he no longer had anything left, now that he had lost his lady and his cousin.

[200] Angry and grieving, he rode on all night where adventure carried and took him, for he never rode along any straight path. In the morning it happened that he came upon a mountain covered in rocks where there was a hermitage quite unknown to most people. He turned his reins that way and thought he would go to see the place, to find out who lived there. He went up a path until he came to the hermitage, which was very poor. There was a small and ancient chapel there. He dismounted at the door, took off his helmet, and went in. Before the altar he found two hermits dressed in white robes, who seemed to be priests, and so they were. He greeted them, and when they had heard him speak, they returned his greeting. When they had looked at him they ran to him with arms outstretched and kissed him and welcomed him with great joy. Lancelot asked them who they were, and they replied:

'Do you not recognize us?'

He looked at them and realized that one of them was the Archbishop of Canterbury, the man who had striven for a long time to bring peace between King Arthur and the queen; the other man was Bleobleeris, Lancelot's cousin. Lancelot was very pleased, and said:

'My fine Lords, when did you come here? I am delighted to have found you.'

They said they had been there since the grievous day, the very day of the battle on Salisbury Plain.

'We can tell you that to our knowledge none of our companions survived except King Arthur, Girflet and Lucan the Butler, but we do not know what became of them. Adventure brought us here; we found a hermit here who welcomed us to stay with him, but he has since died and we have stayed on after him. If it pleases God, we shall spend the rest of our days in the service of Our Lord Jesus Christ, and we pray to him to forgive us our sins. You, my Lord, who until now have been the finest knight in the world, what will you do?'

'I shall tell you what I shall do,' he said. 'You have been my companions in the delights of the world; now I shall keep you company in this life and in this place, and I shall never move from here for as long as I live. If you do not receive me here, I shall look elsewhere.'

When they heard him, they were extremely happy; they thanked God sincerely and stretched out their hands to heaven. In that way Lancelot remained with the hermits.

But now the story stops telling of him and returns to his cousins.

*

[201] Now the story tells that when the battle of Winchester was over and Mordred's sons' men had fled, those who were able to, and the rest had been killed, King Bors entered Winchester with all the force he had, whether those inside wanted him to or not. When he knew truly that his brother Lionel was dead, he suffered such great grief that I could scarcely describe it. He had the body buried in the city of Winchester in a way befitting a king. After the burial, he sent men to look for Lancelot far and near and in all directions, but no one could find him. When Bors saw he could not be found, he said to Hector:

'Hector, dear cousin, since my lord is lost and cannot be found, I wish to return to our country. You will come with me, and when we have arrived there, take which of the two kingdoms you prefer, because you may freely have the one you want.'

He replied that he had no desire to leave the kingdom of Logres then, but would stay there a little while longer, 'and when I leave I shall come straight to you, because you are the man I most love in the world, as I should by rights.'

Thus Bors left the kingdom of Logres and returned to his country with his men, while Hector rode up and down the land until by chance he came to the hermitage where Lancelot was living. The archbishop had already taken him so far that he had been ordained a priest; he sang mass every day and led a life of such great abstinence that he ate and drank only bread and water and roots he collected in the bushes.

When the two brothers saw each other, there were many tears shed on both sides, because they loved each other deeply. Hector said to Lancelot:

'My Lord, since I have found you here in such high service as the service of Jesus Christ, and I see that you enjoy living here. I shall never leave here so long as I live, but shall keep you company for all the days of my life.'

When the others heard this, they were very joyful that such a fine knight had offered himself to Our Lord's service; they received him as their companion. Thus the two brothers lived at the hermitage together and occupied themselves daily with the service of Jesus Christ.

Lancelot spent four years there, and no man alive could have suffered pain and discomfort as he suffered: fasts, vigils, prayers and early rising. In the fourth year Hector died and passed away from this life. He was buried inside the hermitage. [202] On the fifteenth day before May Lancelot fell ill. When he felt that he was going to die, he asked the archbishop and Bleobleeris that, as soon as he was dead, they should carry his body to the Joyeuse Garde and place it in the tomb where the body of Galeholt, the Lord of the Distant Isles, lay. They promised him as brothers that they would do it.

Lancelot lived four days after making this request and passed away from this world on the fifth day. At the moment that his soul left his body neither the archbishop nor Bleobleeris were with him, but both were asleep outside, beneath a tree. It happened then that Bleobeeris awoke first and saw the archbishop sleeping beside him; he was having a dream which was giving him the greatest joy in the world, and said:

'Ah! God, be blessed. Now I see all I wanted to see.'

When Bleobleeris saw he was sleeping and laughing and talking, he was greatly surprised, and was afraid that the Enemy might have entered his body. He woke him gently, and when he opened his eyes and saw Bleobleeris, he said:

'Ah! brother, why have you taken me from the great joy that I was experiencing?'

The other man asked him what joy it was.

'I was having such great delight,' he said, 'and was in such a great company of angels that I have never seen so many people in any place in which I have been; they were carrying to heaven the soul of our brother Lancelot. Let us go and see if he is dead.'

'Let us go,' said Bleobleeris.

They straight away went to where Lancelot was and found that his soul had left him.

'Ah! God,' said the archbishop, 'be blessed! Now I know for certain that the angels were giving this man's soul as great a welcome as I witnessed; now I know that penitence is more valuable than any other thing. I shall never leave penitence for as long as I live. Now we must carry his body to the Joyeuse Garde, because we promised him that while he was alive.'

'That is true,' said Bleobleeris.

Then they prepared a bier, and when it was ready they placed Lancelot's body in it. They each took one end of it and carried it day after day with great pain and difficulty until they arrived at the Joyeuse Garde. When the people of the Joyeuse Garde knew that it was Lancelot's body, they went to meet it and received it tearfully. You could have heard such great lamentation and noise around the body that one could scarcely have heard God thundering. They went down to the main church of the castle and treated the body with as much honour as they could, and as was fitting for such a noble man as he had been.

[203] On the very same day that the body was brought there, King Bors arrived at the castle accompanied only by a single knight and a squire. When he heard that the body was in the church, he went there, had it uncovered, and looked at it until he recognized that it was his lord's. When he was sure, he straight away swooned on the body and began to suffer the greatest grief that people had ever seen, and to lament bitterly.

That day there was great sadness in the castle, and that night they had Galeholt's tomb opened, which was as rich as could

234

be. The next day they placed Lancelot's body inside; afterwards they had an inscription put on the tomb, saying: 'HERE LIES THE BODY OF GALEHOLT, THE LORD OF THE DISTANT ISLES, AND WITH HIM RESTS LANCELOT DEL LAC, WHO WAS THE FINEST KNIGHT THAT EVER ENTERED THE KINGDOM OF LOGRES, EXCEPT FOR HIS SON GALAHAD'. After the body had been buried, you could have seen the people of the castle kissing the tomb. Then they asked King Bors how he had arrived just at the right moment for Lancelot's funeral.

'In fact,' said King Bors, 'a hermit monk who lives in the kingdom of Gaunes told me that if I were in this castle today I should find Lancelot either alive or dead. It happened to me exactly as he said. But, for God's sake, if you know where he has lived since I last saw him, please tell me.'

The archbishop immediately told him about Lancelot's life and also his death, and when King Bors had listened to this, he replied:

'My Lord, because you were with him until he died, I shall keep you company in place of him for as long as I live. I shall go with you and spend the rest of my life in the hermitage.'

The archbishop tenderly thanked Our Lord.

[204] On the next day King Bors left the Joyeuse Garde, sent away his knight and his squire, and ordered his men to choose whomever they liked as king, as he would never return. Then he left with the archbishop and Bleobleeris and spent the rest of his life with them out of love for Our Lord.

At this point Master Walter Map will end the *Story of Lancelot*, because he has brought everything to a proper conclusion according to the way it happened; and he finishes his book here so completely that no one can afterwards add anything to the story that is not complete falsehood.

Appendix

1. (p. 46). In the *Lancelot* we are told how King Pellés' daughter falls in love with Lancelot providentially. Her governess, Brisane, tricks Lancelot into believing that Guinevere is at a nearby castle, and he sleeps with the girl without being aware of the deception. On awakening, he is very angry at having involuntarily deceived the queen. The son born of this union, Galahad, was of course destined to accomplish the Grail quest.

2. (p. 53). The opening pages of the *Lancelot* recount the birth and youth of Lancelot, son of King Ban of Banoic, and of Lancelot's cousins Lionel and Bors, sons of King Bors of Gaunes. Banoic and Gaunes are imaginary places situated somewhere in the West of Gaul.

3. (p. 66). The full story is related in the *Lancelot*.

4. (p. 70). This is a reference to Lancelot's first rendez-vous with the queen, arranged by Galeholt, Lord of the Distant Isles. Galeholt's friendship with Lancelot, and his machinations to bring about a meeting between him and Guinevere, are related in detail in the *Lancelot*.

5. p. 71). Lancelot's conquering of the castle of the Douloureuse Garde is his first great exploit after being dubbed a knight at the age of eighteen. The story is recounted in the first section of the *Lancelot*.

6. (p. 134). The Perilous Seat is the seat at the Round Table reserved for Galahad. Many knights had died through being so bold as to sit in it. At the beginning of *The Quest of the Holy Grail*, Galahad enters Arthur's court in a scene of great nobility, and occupies the seat.

7. (p. 137). This is a reference to an episode in the *Lancelot*. In the Grail castle at Corbenic, Gawain sees a battle between a serpent and a leopard. This is later explained to him by a hermit as symbolizing a war which is to take place between Arthur and one of his knights, and in which Gawain himself will die.

FOR THE BEST IN PAPERBACKS, LOOK FOR THE (🐧)

In every corner of the world, on every subject under the sun, Penguin represents quality and variety – the very best in publishing today.

For complete information about books available from Penguin – including Puffins, Penguin Classics and Arkana – and how to order them, write to us at the appropriate address below. Please note that for copyright reasons the selection of books varies from country to country.

In the United Kingdom: Please write to *Dept E.P., Penguin Books Ltd, Harmondsworth, Middlesex, UB7 0DA.*

If you have any difficulty in obtaining a title, please send your order with the correct money, plus ten per cent for postage and packaging, to *PO Box No 11, West Drayton, Middlesex*

In the United States: Please write to *Dept BA, Penguin, 299 Murray Hill Parkway, East Rutherford, New Jersey 07073*

In Canada: Please write to *Penguin Books Canada Ltd, 2801 John Street, Markham, Ontario L3R 1B4*

In Australia: Please write to the *Marketing Department, Penguin Books Australia Ltd, P.O. Box 257, Ringwood, Victoria 3134*

In New Zealand: Please write to the *Marketing Department, Penguin Books (NZ) Ltd, Private Bag, Takapuna, Auckland 9*

In India: Please write to *Penguin Overseas Ltd, 706 Eros Apartments, 56 Nehru Place, New Delhi, 110019*

In the Netherlands: Please write to *Penguin Books Netherlands B.V., Postbus 195, NL-1380AD Weesp*

In West Germany: Please write to *Penguin Books Ltd, Friedrichstrasse 10–12, D–6000 Frankfurt/Main 1*

In Spain: Please write to *Alhambra Longman S.A., Fernandez de la Hoz 9, E–28010 Madrid*

In Italy: Please write to *Penguin Italia s.r.l., Via Como 4, I-20096 Pioltello (Milano)*

In France: Please write to *Penguin Books Ltd, 39 Rue de Montmorency, F-75003 Paris*

In Japan: Please write to *Longman Penguin Japan Co Ltd, Yamaguchi Building, 2–12–9 Kanda Jimbocho, Chiyoda-Ku, Tokyo 101*